W9-BGU-419

The Chink in the Armor

Other books by Marie Belloc Lowndes:

The Chink in the Armor
The End of Her Honeymoon
From Out the Vasty Deep
Jane Oglander
The Lodger
Mary Pechell
Studies in Love and Terror
The Uttermost Farthing

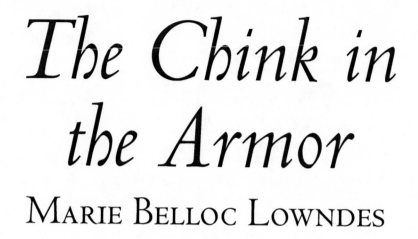

The Chink in the Armor

Marie Belloc Lowndes

ÆGYPAN PRESS

1912

The Chink in the Armor
A publication of
ÆGYPAN PRESS

www.aegypan.com

"*But there is one chink in the chain armor of civilized communities. Society is conducted on the assumption that murder will not be committed.*"

— THE SPECTATOR

Chapter I

A small, shiny, pink card lay on the round table in Sylvia Bailey's sitting room at the Hôtel de l'Horloge in Paris.

She had become quite accustomed to finding one or more cards — cards from dressmakers, cards from corset-makers, cards from hairdressers — lying on her sitting room table, but there had never been a card quite like this card.

Although it was pink, it looked more like a visiting-card than a tradesman's advertisement, and she took it up with some curiosity. It was inscribed "Madame Cagliostra," and underneath the name were written the words *"Diseuse de la Bonne Aventure,"* and then, in a corner, in very small black letters, the address, "5, Rue Jolie, Montmartre."

A fortune-teller's card? What an extraordinary thing!

Like many pretty, prosperous, idle women, Sylvia was rather superstitious. Not long before this, her first visit to Paris, a London acquaintance had taken her to see a noted palmist named "Pharaoh," in Bond Street. She had paid her guinea willingly enough, but the result had vaguely disappointed her, and she had had the feeling, all the time she was with him, that the man was not really reading her hand.

True, "Pharaoh" had told her she was going abroad, and at that time she had no intention of doing so. The palmist had also told her — and this was really rather curious — that she would meet, when abroad, a foreign woman who would have a considerable influence on her life. Well, in this very Hôtel de l'Horloge Mrs. Bailey had come across a Polish lady, named Anna Wolsky, who was, like Sylvia herself, a young widow, and the two had taken a great fancy to one another.

It was most unlikely that Madame Wolsky would have the slightest influence on her, Sylvia Bailey's, life, but at any rate it was very curious coincidence. "Pharaoh" had proved to be right as to these two things — she had come abroad, and she had formed a friendship with a foreign woman.

Mrs. Bailey was still standing by the table, and still holding the pink card in her hand, when her new friend came into the room.

"Well?" said Anna Wolsky, speaking English with a strong foreign accent, but still speaking it remarkably well, "Have you yet decided, my dear, what we shall do this afternoon? There are a dozen things open to us, and I am absolutely at your service to do any one of them!"

Sylvia Bailey laughingly shook her head.

"I feel lazy," she said. "I've been at the Bon Marché ever since nine o'clock, and I feel more like having a rest than going out again, though it does seem a shame to stay in a day like this!"

The windows were wide open, the June sun was streaming in, and on the light breeze was borne the murmur of the traffic in the Avenue de l'Opéra, within a few yards of the quiet street where the Hôtel de l'Horloge is situated.

The other woman — Anna Wolsky was some years older than Sylvia Bailey — smiled indulgently.

"*Tiens!*" she cried suddenly, "what have you got there?" and she took the pink card out of Sylvia's hand.

"Madame Cagliostra?" she repeated, musingly. "Now where did I hear that name? Yes, of course it was from our chambermaid! Cagliostra is a friend of hers, and, according to her, a marvelous person — one from whom the devil keeps no secrets! She charges only five francs for a consultation, and it appears that all sorts of well-known people go to her, even those whom the Parisians call the *Gratin,* that is, the Upper Crust, from the Champs Elysées and the Faubourg St. Germain!"

"I don't think much of fortune-tellers," said Sylvia, thoughtfully. "I went to one last time I was in London and he really didn't tell me anything of the slightest interest."

Her conscience pricked her a little as she said this, for "Pharaoh" had certainly predicted a journey which she had then no intention of taking, and a meeting with a foreign woman. Yet here she was in Paris, and here was the foreign woman standing close to her!

Nay more, Anna Wolsky had become — it was really rather odd that it should be so — the first intimate friend of her own sex Sylvia had made since she was a grown-up woman.

"I do believe in fortune-tellers," said Madame Wolsky deliberately, "and that being so I shall spend my afternoon in going up to Montmartre, to the Rue Jolie, to hear what this Cagliostra has to say. It will be what you in England call 'a lark'! And I do not see why I should not give myself so cheap a lark as a five-franc lark!"

"Oh, if you really mean to go, I think I will go too!" cried Sylvia, gaily.

She was beginning to feel less tired, and the thought of a long lonely afternoon spent indoors and by herself lacked attraction.

Linking her arm through her friend's, she went downstairs and into the barely furnished dining room, which was so very unlike an English hotel dining room. In this dining room the wallpaper simulated a vine-covered trellis, from out of which peeped blue-plumaged birds, and on each little table, covered by an unbleached tablecloth, stood an oil and vinegar cruet and a half-bottle of wine.

The Hôtel de l'Horloge was a typical French hotel, and foreigners very seldom stayed there. Sylvia had been told of the place by the old French lady who had been her governess, and who had taught her to speak French exceptionally well.

Several quiet Frenchmen, who had offices in the neighborhood, were *"en pension"* at the Hôtel de l'Horloge, and as the two friends came in many were the steady, speculative glances cast in their direction.

To the average Frenchman every woman is interesting; for every Frenchman is in love with love, and in each fair stranger he sees the possible heroine of a romance in which he may play the agreeable part of hero. So it was that Sylvia Bailey and Anna Wolsky both had their silent admirers among those who lunched and dined in the narrow green and white dining room of the Hôtel de l'Horloge.

Only a Frenchman would have given a second look at the Polish lady while Sylvia was by, but a Frenchman, being both a philosopher and a logician by nature, is very apt to content himself with the second-best when he knows the best is not for him.

The two friends were in entire contrast to one another. Madame Wolsky was tall, dark, almost swarthy; there was a look of rather haughty pride and reserve on her strong-featured face. She dressed extremely plainly, the only ornament ever worn by her being a small gold horse-shoe, in the center of which was treasured — so, not long ago, she had confided to Sylvia, who had been at once horrified and thrilled — a piece of the rope with which a man had hanged himself at Monte Carlo two years before! For Madame Wolsky — and she made no secret of the fact to her new friend — was a gambler.

Anna Wolsky was never really happy, she did not feel more than half alive, when away from the green cloth. She had only left Monte Carlo when the heat began to make the place unbearable to one of her northern temperament, and she was soon moving on to one of the French watering-places, where gambling of sorts can be indulged in all the summer through.

Different in looks, in temperament, and in tastes were the two young widows, and this, perhaps, was why they got on so excellently well together.

Sylvia Bailey was the foreign ideal of a beautiful Englishwoman. Her hair was fair, and curled naturally. Her eyes were of that blue which looks violet in the sunlight; and she had a delicate, rose leaf complexion.

Married when only nineteen to a man much older than herself, she was now at twenty-five a widow, and one without any intimate duties or close ties to fill her existence. Though she had mourned George Bailey sincerely, she had soon recovered all her normal interest and pleasure in life.

Mrs. Bailey was fond of dress and able to indulge her taste; but, even so, good feeling and the standard of propriety of the English country town of Market Dalling where she had spent most of her life, perhaps also a subtle instinct that nothing else would ever suit her so well, made her remain rigidly faithful to white and black, pale grey, and lavender. She also wore only one ornament, but it was a very becoming and an exceedingly costly ornament, for it consisted of a string of large and finely-matched pearls.

As the two friends went upstairs after luncheon Madame Wolsky said earnestly, "If I were you, Sylvia, I would certainly leave your pearls in the office this afternoon. Where is the use of wearing them on such an expedition as that to a fortune-teller?"

"But why shouldn't I wear them?" asked Sylvia, rather surprised.

"Well, in your place I should certainly leave anything as valuable as your pearls in safe keeping. After all, we know nothing of this Madame Cagliostra, and Montmartre is what Parisians call an eccentric quarter."

Sylvia Bailey disliked very much taking off her pearls. Though she could not have put the fact into words, this string of pearls was to her a symbol of her freedom, almost of her womanhood.

As a child and young girl she had been under the close guardianship of a stern father, and it was to please him that she had married the rich, middle-aged man at Market Dalling whose adoration she had endured rather than reciprocated. George Bailey also had been a determined man — determined that his young wife should live his way, not hers. During their brief married life he had heaped on her showy, rather than beautiful, jewels; nothing of great value, nothing she could wear when in mourning.

And then, four months after her husband's death, Sylvia's own aunt had died and left her a thousand pounds. It was this legacy — which her trustee, a young solicitor named William Chester, who was also a friend and an admirer of hers, as well as her trustee, had been proposing to invest in what he called "a remarkably good thing" — Mrs. Bailey had insisted on squandering on a string of pearls!

Sylvia had become aware, in the subtle way in which Women become aware of such things, that pearls were the fashion — in fact, in one sense, "the only wear." She had noticed that most of the great ladies of the neighborhood of Market Dalling, those whom she saw on those occasions when town and county meet, each wore a string of pearls. She had also come to know that pearls seem to be the only gems which can be worn with absolute propriety by a widow, and so, suddenly, she had made up her mind to invest — she called it an "investment," while Chester called it an "absurd extravagance" — in a string of pearls.

Bill Chester had done his very best to persuade her to give up her silly notion, but she had held good; she had shown herself, at any rate on this one occasion, and in spite of her kindly, yielding nature, obstinate.

This was why her beautiful pearls had become to Sylvia Bailey a symbol of her freedom. The thousand pounds, invested as Bill Chester had meant to invest it, would have brought her in £55 a year, so he had told her in a grave, disapproving tone.

In return she had told him, the color rushing into her pretty face, that after all she had the right to do what she chose with her legacy, the more so that this thousand pounds was in a peculiar sense her own money, as the woman who had left it her was her mother's sister, having nothing to do either with her father or with the late George Bailey!

And so she had had her way — nay, more; Chester, at the very last, had gone to great trouble in order that she might not be cheated over her purchase. Best of all, Bill — Sylvia always called the serious-minded young lawyer "Bill" — had lived to admit that Mrs. Bailey had made a good investment after all, for her pearls had increased in value in the two years she had had them.

Be that as it may, the young widow often reminded herself that nothing she had ever bought, and nothing that had ever been given her, had caused her such lasting pleasure as her beloved string of pearls!

But on this pleasant June afternoon, in deference to her determined friend's advice, she took off her pearls before starting out for Montmartre, leaving the case in the charge of M. Girard, the genial proprietor of the Hôtel de l'Horloge.

Chapter II

With easy, leisurely steps, constantly stopping to look into the windows of the quaint shops they passed on the way, Sylvia Bailey and Anna Wolsky walked up the steep, the almost mountainous byways and narrow streets which lead to the top of Montmartre.

The whole population seemed to have poured itself out in the open air on this sunny day; even the shopkeepers had brought chairs out of their shops and sat on the pavement, gaily laughing and gossiping together in the eager way Parisians have. As the two foreign ladies, both young, both in their very different fashion good-looking, walked past the sitting groups of neighbors — men, women, and children would stop talking and stare intently at them, as is also a Parisian way.

At first Sylvia had disliked the manner in which she was stared at in Paris, and she had been much embarrassed as well as a little amused by the very frank remarks called forth in omnibuses as well as in the street by the brilliancy of her complexion and the bright beauty of her fair hair. But now she was almost used to this odd form of homage, which came quite as often from women as from men.

"The Rue Jolie?" answered a cheerful-looking man in answer to a question. "Why, it's ever so much further up!" and he vaguely pointed skywards.

And it was much further up, close to the very top of the great hill! In fact, it took the two ladies a long time to find it, for the Rue Jolie was the funniest, tiniest little street, perched high up on what might almost have been a mountain side.

As for No. 5, Rue Jolie, it was a queer miniature house more like a Swiss châlet than anything else, and surrounded by a gay, untidy little garden full of flowers, the kind of half-wild, shy, and yet hardy flowers that come up, year after year, without being tended or watered.

"Surely a fortune-teller can't live here?" exclaimed Sylvia Bailey, remembering the stately, awe-inspiring rooms in which "Pharaoh" received his clients in Bond Street.

"Oh, yes, this is evidently the place!"

Anna Wolsky smiled good-humoredly; she had become extremely fond of the young Englishwoman; she delighted in Sylvia's radiant prettiness, her kindly good-temper, and her eager pleasure in everything.

A large iron gate gave access to the courtyard which was so much larger than the house built round it. But the gate was locked, and a pull at the rusty bell-wire produced no result.

They waited a while. "She must have gone out," said Sylvia, rather disappointed.

But Madame Wolsky, without speaking, again pulled at the rusty wire, and then one of the châlet windows was suddenly flung open from above, and a woman — a dark, middle-aged Frenchwoman — leant out.

"Qui est là?" and then before either of them could answer, the woman had drawn back: a moment later they heard her heavy progress down the creaky stairs of her dwelling.

At last she came out into the courtyard, unlocked the iron gate, and curtly motioned to the two ladies to follow her.

"We have come to see Madame Cagliostra," said Sylvia timidly. She took this stout, untidily-dressed woman for the fortune-teller's servant.

"Madame Cagliostra, at your service!" The woman turned round, her face breaking into a broad smile. She evidently liked the sound of her peculiar name.

They followed her up a dark staircase into a curious little sitting room. It was scrupulously clean, but about it hung the faint odor which the French eloquently describe as "shut in," and even on this beautiful hot day the windows were tightly closed.

On the red walls hung various drawings of hands, of hearts, and of heads, and over the plain mantelpiece was a really fine pastel portrait of a man, in eighteenth century dress and powdered hair.

"My ancestor, Count Cagliostro, ladies!" exclaimed the fat little woman proudly. "As you will soon see, if you have, as I venture to suppose, come to consult me, I have inherited the great gifts which made Count Cagliostro famous." She waited a moment. "What is it you desire of me? Do you wish for the Grand Jeu? Or do you prefer the Crystal?"

Madame Cagliostra gave a shrewd, measuring glance at the two young women standing before her. She was wondering how much they were good for.

"No doubt you have been told," she said suddenly, "that my fee is five francs. But if you require the Grand Jeu it will be ten francs. Come, ladies, make up your minds; I will give you both the Grand Jeu for fifteen francs!"

Sylvia Bailey's lip quivered; she felt a wild wish to burst out laughing. It was all so absurd; this funny queer house; this odd, stuffy, empty-looking room; and this vulgar, common-looking woman asserting that she was descended from the famous Count Cagliostro! And then, to crown everything, the naïve, rather pathetic, attempt to get an extra five francs out of them.

But Sylvia was a very kindly, happy-natured creature, and she would not have hurt the feelings of even a Madame Cagliostra for the world.

She looked at her friend questioningly. Would it not be better just to give the woman five francs and go away? They surely could not expect to hear anything of any value from such a person. She was evidently a fraud!

But Anna Wolsky was staring at Madame Cagliostra with a serious look.

"Very well," she exclaimed, in her rather indifferent French. "Very well! We will both take the Grand Jeu at fifteen francs the two."

She turned and smiled at Sylvia. "It will be," she said, quaintly, and in English, "my 'treat,' dear friend." And then, as Sylvia shook her head decidedly — there were often these little contests of generosity between the two women — she added rather sharply,

"Yes, yes! It shall be so. I insist! I see you do not believe in our hostess's gift. There are, however, one or two questions I must ask, and to which I fancy she can give me an answer. I am anxious, too, to hear what she will say about *you.*"

Sylvia smiled, and gave way.

Like most prosperous people who have not made the money they are able to spend, Mrs. Bailey did not attach any undue importance to wealth. But she knew that her friend was not as well off as herself, and therefore she was always trying to pay a little more of her share than was fair. Thanks to Madame Wolsky's stronger will, she very seldom succeeded in doing so.

"We might at least ask her to open the window," she said rather plaintively. It really was dreadfully stuffy!

Madame Cagliostra had gone to a sideboard from which she was taking two packs of exceedingly dirty, queer-looking cards. They were the famous Taro cards, but Sylvia did not know that.

When the fortune-teller was asked to open the window, she shook her head decidedly.

"No, no!" she said. "It would dissipate the influences. I cannot do that! On the contrary, the curtains should be drawn close, and if the ladies will permit of it I will light my lamp."

Even as she spoke she was jerking the thick curtains closely together; she even pinned them across so that no ray of the bright sunlight outside could penetrate into the room.

For a few moments they were in complete darkness, and Sylvia felt a queer, eerie sensation of fear, but this soon passed away as the lamp — the *"Suspension,"* as Madame Cagliostra proudly called it — was lit.

When her lamp was well alight, the soothsayer drew three chairs up to the round table, and motioned the two strangers to sit down.

"You will take my friend first," said Anna Wolsky, imperiously; and then, to Sylvia, she said, in English, "Would you rather I went away, dear? I could wait on the staircase till you were ready for me to come back. It is not very pleasant to have one's fortune told when one is as young and as pretty as you are, before other people."

"Of course I don't mind your being here!" cried Sylvia Bailey, laughing — then, looking doubtfully at Madame Cagliostra, though it was obvious the Frenchwoman did not understand English, "The truth is that I should feel rather frightened if you were to leave me here all by myself. So please stay."

Madame Cagliostra began dealing out the cards on the table. First slowly, then quickly, she laid them out in a queer pattern; and as she did so she muttered and murmured to herself. Then a frown came over her face; she began to look disturbed, anxious, almost angry.

Sylvia, in spite of herself, grew interested and excited. She was sorry she had not taken off her wedding-ring. In England the wise woman always takes off her wedding-ring on going to see a fortune-teller. She was also rather glad that she had left her pearls in the safe custody of M. Girard. This little house in the Rue Jolie was a strange, lonely place.

Suddenly Madame Cagliostra began to speak in a quick, clear, monotonous voice.

Keeping her eyes fixed on the cards, which now and again she touched with a fat finger, and without looking at Sylvia, she said:

"Madame has led a very placid, quiet life. Her existence has been a boat that has always lain in harbor —" She suddenly looked up: "I spent my childhood at Dieppe, and that often suggests images to me," she observed complacently, and then she went on in quite another tone of voice: —

"To return to Madame and her fate! The boat has always been in harbor, but now it is about to put out to sea. It will meet there another craft. This other craft is, to Madame, a foreign craft, and I grieve to say it, rather battered. But its timbers are sound, and that is well, for it looks to me as if the sails of Madame's boat would mingle, at any rate for a time with this battered craft."

"I don't understand what she means," said Sylvia, in a whisper. "Do ask her to explain, Anna!"

"My friend asks you to drop metaphor," said the older woman, dryly.

The soothsayer fixed her bright, beady little eyes on Sylvia's flushed face.

"Well," she said deliberately, "I see you falling in love, and I also see that falling in love is quite a new experience. It burns, it scorches you, does love, Madame. And for awhile you do not know what it means, for love has never yet touched you with his red-hot finger."

"How absurd!" thought Sylvia to herself. "She actually takes me for a young girl! What ridiculous mistakes fortune-tellers do make, to be sure!"

"— But you cannot escape love," went on Madame Cagliostra, eagerly. "Your fate is a fair man, which is strange considering that you also are a fair woman; and I see that there is already a dark man in your life."

Sylvia blushed. Bill Chester, just now the only man in her life, was a very dark man.

"But this fair man knows all the arts of love." Madame Cagliostra sighed, her voice softened, it became strangely low and sweet. "He will love you tenderly as well as passionately. And as for you, Madame — but no, for me to tell you what you will feel *and what you will do* would not be delicate on my part!"

Sylvia grew redder and redder. She tried to laugh, but failed. She felt angry, and not a little disgusted.

"You are a foreigner," went on Madame Cagliostra. Her voice had grown hard and expressionless again.

Sylvia smiled a little satiric smile.

"But though you are a foreigner," cried the fortune-teller with sudden energy, "it is quite possible that you will never go back to your own country! Stop — or, perhaps, I shall say too much! Still if you ever do go back, it will be as a stranger. That I say with certainty. And I add that I hope with all my heart that you will live to go back to your own country, Madame!"

Sylvia felt a vague, uneasy feeling of oppression, almost of fear, steal over her. It seemed to her that Madame Cagliostra was looking at her with puzzled, pitying eyes.

The soothsayer again put a fat and not too clean finger down on the upturned face of a card.

"There is something here I do not understand; something which I miss when I look at you as I am now looking at you. It is something you always wear —"

She gazed searchingly at Sylvia, and her eyes traveled over Mrs. Bailey's neck and bosom.

"I see them and yet they are not there! They appear like little balls of light. Surely it is a necklace?"

Sylvia looked extremely surprised. Now, at last, Madame Cagliostra was justifying her claim to a supernatural gift!

"These balls of light are also your Fate!" exclaimed the woman impetuously. "If you had them here — I care not what they be — I should entreat you to give them to me to throw away."

Madame Wolsky began to laugh. "I don't think you would do that," she observed dryly.

But Madame Cagliostra did not seem to hear the interruption.

"Have you heard of a mascot?" she said abruptly. "Of a mascot which brings good fortune to its wearer?"

Sylvia bent her head. Of course she had heard of mascots.

"Well, if so, you have, of course, heard of objects which bring misfortune to their wearers — which are, so to speak, unlucky mascots?"

And this time it was Anna Wolsky who, leaning forward, nodded gravely. She attributed a run of bad luck she had had the year before to a trifling gift, twin cherries made of enamel, which a friend had given her, in her old home, on her birthday. Till she had thrown that little brooch into the sea, she had been persistently unlucky at play.

"Your friend," murmured Madame Cagliostra, now addressing herself to Anna and not to Sylvia, "should dispossess herself as quickly as possible of her necklace, of these round balls. They have already brought her ill-fortune in the past, they have lowered her in the estimation of an estimable person — in fact, if she is not very careful, indeed, even if she be very careful — it looks to me, Madame, as if they would end by strangling her!"

Sylvia became very uncomfortable. "Of course she means my pearls," she whispered. "But how absurd to say they could ever do me harm."

"Look here," said Anna Wolsky earnestly, "you are quite right, Madame; my friend has a necklace which has already played a certain part in her life. But is it not just because of this fact that you feel the influence of this necklace so strongly? I entreat you to speak frankly. You are really distressing me very much!"

Madame Cagliostra looked very seriously at the speaker.

"Well, perhaps it is so," she said at last. "Of course, we are sometimes wrong in our premonitions. And I confess that I feel puzzled — exceedingly puzzled — today. I do not know that I have ever had so strange a case as that of this English lady before me! I see so many roads stretching before her — I also see her going along more than one road. As a rule, one does not see this in the cards."

She looked really harassed, really distressed, and was still conning her cards anxiously.

"And yet after all," she cried suddenly, "I may be wrong! Perhaps the necklace has less to do with it than I thought! I do not know whether the necklace would make any real difference! If she takes one of the roads open to her, then I see no danger at all attaching to the preservation of this necklace. But the other road leads straight to the House of Peril."

"The House of Peril?" echoed Sylvia Bailey.

"Yes, Madame. Do you not know that all men and women have their House of Peril — the house whose threshold they should never cross — behind whose door lies misery, sometimes dishonor?"

"Yes," said Anna Wolsky, "that is true, quite true! There has been, alas! more than one House of Peril in my life." She added, "But what kind of place is my friend's House of Peril?"

"It is not a large house," said the fortune-teller, staring down at the shining surface of her table. "It is a gay, delightful little place, ladies — quite my idea of a pretty dwelling. But it is filled with horror unutterable to Madame. Ah! I entreat you" — she stared sadly at Sylvia — "to beware of unknown buildings, especially if you persist in keeping and in wearing your necklace."

"Do tell us, Madame, something more about my friend's necklace. Is it, for instance, of great value, and is it its value that makes it a source of danger?"

Anna Wolsky wondered very much what would be the answer to this question. She had had her doubts as to the genuineness of the pearls her friend wore. Pearls are so exquisitely imitated nowadays, and these pearls, if genuine, were of such great value!

At first she had not believed them to be real, then gradually she had become convinced of Sylvia's good faith. If the pearls were false, Sylvia did not know it.

But Madame Cagliostra's answer was disappointing — or prudent.

"I cannot tell you that," she said. "I cannot even tell you of what the necklace is composed. It may be of gold, of silver, of diamonds, of pearls — it may be, I'm inclined to think it is, composed of Egyptian scarabei. They, as you know, often bring terrible ill-fortune in their train, especially when they have been taken from the bodies of mummies. But the necklace has already caused this lady to quarrel with a very good and sure friend of hers — of that I am sure. And, as I tell you, I see in the future that this necklace may cause her very serious trouble — indeed, I see it wound like a serpent round her neck, pressing ever tighter and tighter —"

She suddenly began shuffling the cards. "And now," she said in a tone of relief, "I will deal with you, Madame," and she turned to Anna with a smile.

Sylvia drew her chair a little away from the table.

She felt depressed and uncomfortable. What an odd queer kind of fortune had been told her! And then it had all been so muddled. She could scarcely remember what it was that *had* been told her.

Two things, however, remained very clear in her mind: The one was the absurd prediction that she might never go back to her own country; the second was all that extraordinary talk about her pearls. As to the promised lover, the memory of the soothsayer's words made her feel very angry. No doubt Frenchwomen liked that sort of innuendo, but it only disgusted her.

Yet it was really very strange that Madame Cagliostra had known, or rather had divined, that she possessed a necklace by which she laid great store. But wasn't there such a thing as telepathy? Isn't it supposed by some people that fortune-tellers simply see into the minds of those who come to them, and then arrange what they see there according to their fancy?

That, of course, would entirely account for all that the fortune-teller had said about her pearls.

Sylvia always felt a little uncomfortable when her pearls were not lying round her pretty neck. The first time she had left them in the hotel bureau, at her new friend's request, was when they had been together to some place of amusement at night, and she had felt quite miserable, quite lost without them. She had even caught herself wondering whether M. Girard was perfectly honest, whether she could trust him not to have her dear pearls changed by some clever jeweler, though, to be sure, she felt she would have known her string of pearls anywhere!

*B*ut what was this that was going on between the other two?

Madame Cagliostra dealt out the pack of cards in a slow, deliberate fashion — and then she uttered a kind of low hoarse cry, and mixed the cards all together, hurriedly.

Getting up from the table, she exclaimed, "I regret, Madame, that I can tell you nothing — nothing at all! I feel ill — very ill!" and, indeed, she had turned, even to Sylvia's young and unobservant eyes, terribly pale.

For some moments the soothsayer stood staring into Anna Wolsky's astonished face.

"I know I've disappointed you, Mesdames, but I hope this will not prevent your telling your friends of my powers. Allow me to assure you that it is not often that I am taken in this way!"

Her voice had dropped to a whisper. She was now gazing down at the pack of cards which lay on the table with a look of horror and oppression on her face.

"I will only charge five francs," she muttered at last, "for I know that I have not satisfied you."

Sylvia sprang to the window. She tore apart the curtains and pulled up the sash.

"No wonder the poor woman feels faint," she said quickly. "It's absurd to sit with a window tight shut in this kind of room, which is little more than a box with three people in it!"

Madame Cagliostra had sunk down into her chair again.

"I must beg you to go away, Mesdames," she muttered, faintly. "Five francs is all I ask of you."

But Anna Wolsky was behaving in what appeared to Sylvia a very strange manner. She walked round to where the fortune-teller was sitting.

"You saw something in the cards which you do not wish to tell me?" she said imperiously. "I do not mind being told the truth. I am not a child."

"I swear I saw nothing!" cried the Frenchwoman angrily. "I am too ill to see anything. The cards were to me perfectly blank!"

In the bright sunlight now pouring into the little room the soothsayer looked ghastly, her skin had turned a greenish white.

"Mesdames, I beg you to excuse me," she said again. "If you do not wish to give me the five francs, I will not exact any fee."

She pointed with a shaking finger to the door, and Sylvia put a five-franc piece down on the table.

But before her visitors had quite groped their way to the end of the short, steep staircase, they heard a cry.

"Mesdames!" then after a moment's pause, "Mesdames, I implore you to come back!"

They looked at one another, and then Anna, putting her finger to her lips, went back up the stairs, alone.

"Well," she said, briefly, "I knew you had something to tell me. What is it?"

"No," said Madame Cagliostra dully. "I must have the other lady here, too. You must both be present to hear what I have to say."

Anna went to the door and called out, "Come up Sylvia! She wants to see us both together."

There was a thrill of excitement, of eager expectancy in Madame Wolsky's voice; and Sylvia, surprised, ran up again into the little room, now full of light, sun, and air.

"Stand side by side," ordered the soothsayer shortly. She stared at them for a moment, and then she said with extreme earnestness: —

"I dare not let you go away without giving you a warning. Your two fates are closely intertwined. Do not leave Paris for awhile, especially do not leave Paris together. I see you both running into terrible danger! If you do go away — and I greatly fear that you will do so — then I advise you, together and separately, to return to Paris as soon as possible."

"One question I must ask of you," said Anna Wolsky urgently. "How goes my luck? You know what I mean? I play!"

"It is not your luck that is threatened," replied the fortune-teller, solemnly; "on the contrary, I see wonderful luck; packets of bank-notes and rouleaux of gold! It is not your luck — it is something far, far more important that is in peril. Something which means far more to you even than your luck!"

The Polish woman smiled rather sadly.

"I wonder what that can be?" she exclaimed.

"It is your life!"

"My life?" echoed Anna. "I do not know that I value my life as much as you think I do."

"The English have a proverb, Madame, which says: 'A short life and a merry one.'"

"Can you predict that I shall have, if a short life, then a merry one?"

"Yes," said Madame Cagliostra, "that I can promise you." But there was no smile on her pale face. "And more, I can predict — if you will only follow my advice, if you do not leave Paris for, say" — she hesitated a moment, as if making a silent calculation — "twelve weeks, I can predict you, if not so happy a life, then a long life and a fairly merry one. Will you take my advice, Madame?" she went on, almost threateningly. "Believe me, I do not often offer advice to my clients. It is not my business to do so. But I should have been a wicked woman had I not done so this time. That is why I called you back."

"Is it because of something you have seen in the cards that you tender us this advice?" asked Anna curiously.

But Madame Cagliostra again looked strangely frightened.

"No, no!" she said hastily. "I repeat that the cards told me nothing. The cards were a blank. I could see nothing in them. But, of course, we do not only tell fortunes by cards" — she spoke very quickly and rather confusedly. "There is such a thing as a premonition."

She waited a moment, and then, in a businesslike tone, added, "And now I leave the question of the fee to the generosity of these ladies!"

Madame Wolsky smiled a little grimly, and pulled out a twenty-franc piece.

The woman bowed, and murmured her thanks.

When they were out again into the roughly paved little street, Anna suddenly began to laugh.

"Now, isn't that a typical Frenchwoman? She really did feel ill, she really saw nothing in my cards, and, being an honest woman, she did not feel that she could ask us to pay! Then, when we had gone away, leaving only five francs, her thrift got the better of her honesty; she felt she had thrown away ten good francs! She therefore called us back, and gave us what she took to be very excellent advice. You see, I had told her that I am a gambler. She knows, as we all know, that to play for money is a foolish thing to do. She is aware that in Paris it is not very easy for a stranger to obtain admittance — especially if that stranger be a respectable woman — to a gambling club. She therefore said to herself, 'I will give this lady far more than ten francs' worth of advice. I will tell her not to go away! As long as she remains in Paris she cannot lose her money. If she goes to Dieppe, Trouville, anyplace where there is a Casino, she will lose her money. Therefore I am giving her invaluable advice — worth far more than the ten francs which she ought to be made to give me, and which she shall be made to give me!'"

"I suppose you are right," said Sylvia thoughtfully. "And yet — and yet — she certainly spoke very seriously, did she not, Anna? She seemed quite honestly — in fact, terribly afraid that we should go away together."

"But there is no idea of our going away together," said Madame Wolsky, rather crossly. "I only wish there were! You are going on to Switzerland to join your friends, and as for me, in spite of Madame Cagliostra's mysterious predictions, I shall, of course, go to some place — I think it will be Dieppe (I like the Dieppe Casino the best) — where I can play. And the memory of you, my dear little English friend, will be my mascot. You heard her say that I should be fortunate — that I should have an extraordinary run of good fortune?"

"Yes," said Sylvia, "but do not forget" — she spoke with a certain gravity; death was a very real thing to her, for she had seen in the last two years two deathbeds, that of her father, that of her husband — "do not forget, Anna, that she told you you would not live long if you went away."

"She was quite safe in saying that to me," replied the other hastily. "People who play — those who get the gambling fever into their system when they are still young — do not, as a rule, live very long. Their emotions are too strong, too often excited! Play should be reserved for the old — the old get so quickly deadened, they do not go through the terrible moments younger people do!"

Chapter III

On the morning after her visit to Madame Cagliostra, Sylvia Bailey woke later than usual. She had had a disturbed night, and it was pleasant to feel that she could spend a long restful day doing nothing, or only taking part in one of the gay little expeditions which make Paris to a stranger the most delightful of European capitals.

She opened wide both the windows of her room, and from outside there floated in a busy, happy murmur, for Paris is an early city, and nine o'clock there is equivalent to eleven o'clock in London.

She heard the picturesque street cries of the flower-sellers in the Avenue de l'Opéra — "Beflower yourselves, gentlemen and ladies, be-flower yourselves!"

The gay, shrill sounds floated in to her, and, in spite of her bad night and ugly dreams, she felt extraordinarily well and happy.

Cities are like people. In some cities one feels at home at once; others remain, however well acquainted we become with them, always strangers.

Sylvia Bailey, born, bred, married, widowed in an English provincial town, had always felt strange in London. But with Paris, — dear, delight-ful, sunny Paris, — she had become on the closest, the most affectionately intimate terms from the first day. She had only been here a month, and yet she already knew with familiar knowledge the quarter in which was situated her quiet little hotel, that wonderful square mile — it is not more — which has as its center the Paris Opera House, and which includes the Rue de la Paix and the beginning of each of the great arteries of modern Paris.

And that was not all. Sylvia Bailey knew something of the France of the past. The quiet, clever, old-fashioned Frenchwoman by whom she had been educated had seen to that. She could wander through the narrow streets on the other side of the Seine, and reconstitute the amazing, moving, tragic things which happened there during the great Revolution.

She was now half sorry to think that in ten days or so she had promised to join some acquaintances in Switzerland. Luckily her trustee and would-be lover, Bill Chester, proposed to come out and join the party there. That was something to look forward to, for Sylvia was very fond of him, though he sometimes made her angry by his fussy ways. Chester had not approved of her going to Paris by herself, and he would certainly have shaken his head had he known of yesterday's visit to Madame Cagliostra.

And then Sylvia Bailey began to think of her new friend: of Anna Wolsky. She was sorry, very sorry, that they were going to part so soon. If only Anna would consent to come on with her to Switzerland! But alas! there was no chance of that, for there are no Casinos, no gambling, in the land of William Tell.

There came a knock at the door, and Madame Wolsky walked in. She was dressed for a journey.

"I have to go out of town this morning," she said, "but the place I am going to is quite near, and I shall be back this afternoon."

"Where are you going?" asked Sylvia, naïvely. "Or is it a secret?"

"No, it is not a secret." Anna smiled provokingly. "I am going to go to a place called Lacville. I do not suppose you have ever heard of Lacville, Sylvia?"

The other shook her head.

"I thought not," cried Anna, suddenly bursting out laughing. Then, "Good-bye!" she exclaimed, and she was gone before Sylvia could say anything else.

Lacville? There had been a sparkle, a look of life, of energy in Anna's face. Why was Anna Wolsky going to Lacville? There was something about the place concerning which she had chosen to be mysterious, and yet she had made no secret of going there.

Mrs. Bailey jumped out of bed, and dressed rather more quickly than usual.

It was a very hot day. In fact, it was unpleasantly hot. How delightful it would be to get into the country even for an hour. Why should she not also make her way to Lacville?

She opened the "Guide-Book to Paris and its Environs," of which she had made such good use in the last month, and looked up "Lacville" in the index.

Situated within a drive of the beautiful Forest of Montmorency, the pretty little town of Lacville is still famed for its healing springs and during the summer months of the year is much frequented by Parisians. There are frequent trains from the Gare du Nord.

No kind fairy whispered the truth to Sylvia — namely that this account is only half, nay, a quarter, or an eighth, of the truth.

Lacville is the spendthrift, the gambler — the austere would call her the chartered libertine — of the group of pretty country towns which encircle Paris; for Lacville is in the proud possession of a Gambling Concession which has gradually turned what was once the quietest of inland watering-places into a miniature Monte Carlo.

The vast majority of intelligent, cultivated English and American visitors to Paris remain quite unaware that there is, within half an hour of the French capital, such a spot; the minority, those tourists who do make their way to the alluring little place, generally live to regret it.

But Sylvia knew nothing, nay, less than nothing, of all this, and even if she had known, it would not have stayed her steps today.

She put on her hat and hurried down to the office. There M. Girard would doubtless tell her of a good train to Lacville, and if it were a small place she might easily run across Anna Wolsky.

M. Girard was a very busy man, yet he always found time for a talk with any foreign client of his hotel.

"I want to know," said Sylvia, smiling in spite of herself, for the hotel-keeper was such a merry-looking little man, and so utterly different from any English hotel-keeper she had ever seen! — "I want to know, M. Girard, which is the best way to a place called Lacville? Have you ever been there?"

"Lacville?" echoed M. Girard delightedly; but there came a rather funny look over his shrewd, round face. "Yes, indeed, I have been there, Madame! Not this season yet, but often last summer, and I shall be going there shortly again. I have a friend there — indeed, he is more than a friend, he is a relation of mine, who keeps the most select hotel at Lacville. It is called the Villa du Lac. Is Madame thinking of going to Lacville instead of to Switzerland?"

Sylvia shook her head. "Oh, no! But Madame Wolsky is there today, and I should have gone with her if I had been ready when she came down. It has turned so hot that I feel a few hours in the country would be pleasant, and I am quite likely to meet her, for I suppose Lacville is not a very large place, M. Girard?"

The hotel-keeper hesitated; he found it really difficult to give a true answer to this simple question.

"Lacville?" he repeated; "well — Dame! Lacville is Lacville! It is not like anything Madame has ever seen. On that I would lay my life. First, there is a most beautiful lake — that is, perhaps, the principal attraction; — then the villas of Lacville — ah! they are ravishingly lovely, and then there is also" — he fixed his black eyes on her — "a Casino."

"A Casino?" echoed Sylvia. She scarcely knew what a Casino was.

"But to see the Casino properly Madame must go at night, and it would be well if Madame were accompanied by a gentleman. I do not think Madame should go by herself, but if Madame really desires to see Lacville properly my wife and I will make a great pleasure to ourselves to accompany her there one Sunday night. It is very gay, is Lacville on Sunday night — or, perhaps," added M. Girard quickly, "Madame, being English, would prefer a Saturday night? Lacville is also very gay on Saturday nights."

"But is there anything going on there at night?" asked Sylvia, astonished. "I thought Lacville was a country place."

"There are a hundred and twenty trains daily from the Gare du Nord to Lacville," said the hotel-keeper dryly. "A great many Parisians spend the evening there each day. They do not start till nine o'clock in the evening, and they are back, having spent a very pleasant, or sometimes an unpleasant, soirée, before midnight."

"A hundred and twenty trains!" repeated Sylvia, amazed. "But why do so many people want to go to Lacville?"

Again the hotel-keeper stared at her with a questioning look. Was it possible that pretty Madame Bailey did not know what was the real attraction of Lacville? Yet it was not his business to run the place down — as a matter of fact, he and his wife had invested nearly a thousand pounds of their hard-earned savings in their relation's hotel, the Villa du Lac. If Madame Bailey really wanted to leave salubrious, beautiful Paris for the summer, why should she not go to Lacville instead of to dull, puritanical, stupid Switzerland?

These thoughts rushed through the active brain of M. Girard with amazing quickness.

"Many people go to Lacville in order to play baccarat," he said lightly. And then Sylvia knew why Anna Wolsky had gone to Lacville.

"But apart from the play, Lacville is a little paradise, Madame," he went on enthusiastically. "It is a beauteous spot, just like a scene in an opera. There is the romantic lake, edged with high, shady trees and princely villas — and then the gay, the delightful Casino!"

"And is there a train soon?"

"I will look Madame out a train this moment, and I will also give her one of my cousin Polperro's cards. Madame has, of course, heard of the Empress Eugénie? Well, the Villa du Lac once belonged to one of the Empress's gentlemen-in-waiting. The very highest nobility stay at the Villa du Lac with my cousin. At this very moment he has Count Paul de Virieu, the brother-in-law of a duke, among his clients —"

M. Girard had noticed the British fondness for titles.

"You see, Madame, my cousin was chef to the Emperor of Brazil's sister — this has given him a connection among the nobility. In the winter he has an hotel at Mentone," he was looking up the train while he chatted happily.

"There is a train every ten minutes," he said at last, "from the Gare du Nord. Or, if Madame prefers it, she could walk up from here to the Square of the Trinité and take the tramway; but it is quicker and pleasanter to go by train — unless, indeed, Madame wishes to offer herself the luxury of an automobile. That, alas! I fear would cost Madame twenty to thirty francs."

"Of course I will go by train," said Sylvia, smiling, "and I will lunch at your cousin's hotel, M. Girard."

It would be quite easy to find Anna, or so she thought, for Anna would be at the Casino. Sylvia felt painfully interested in her friend's love of gambling. It was so strange that Anna was not ashamed of it.

And then as she drove to the great railway terminus, from which a hundred and twenty trains start daily for Lacville, it seemed to Sylvia that the whole of Paris was placarded with the name of the place she was now about to visit for the first time!

On every hoarding, on every bare piece of wall, were spread large, flamboyant posters showing a garish but not unattractive landscape. There was the sun sparkling on a wide stretch of water edged with high trees, and gay with little sailing boats, each boat with its human freight of two lovers. Jutting out into the blue lake was a great white building, which Sylvia realized must be the Casino. And under each picture ran the words "Lacville-les-Bains" printed in very black letters.

When she got to the Gare du Nord the same advertisement stared down at her from the walls of the station and of the waiting-rooms.

It was certainly odd that she had never heard of Lacville, and that the place had never been mentioned to her by any of those of her English acquaintances who thought they knew Paris so well.

The Lacville train was full of happy, chattering people. In her first-class carriage she had five fellow-travelers — a man and woman and three children. They looked cheerful, prosperous people, and soon the husband and wife began talking eagerly together.

"I really think," said the lady suddenly, "that we might have chosen some other place than Lacville in which to spend today! There are many places the children would have enjoyed more."

"But there is no place," said her husband in a jovial tone, "where I can spend an amusing hour in the afternoon."

"Ah, my friend, I feared that was coming!" exclaimed his wife, shaking her head. "But remember what happened the last time we were at Lacville – I mean the afternoon when you lost seventy francs!"

"But you forget that other afternoon!" answered the man eagerly. "I mean the afternoon when I made a hundred francs, and bought you and the children a number of delightful little gifts with the money!"

Sylvia was amused. How quaint and odd French people were! She could not imagine such an interchange of words between an English husband and wife, especially before a stranger. And then her amusement was further increased, for the youngest child, a boy of about six, cried out that he also wished to go to the Casino with his dear papa.

"No, no, my sweet cabbage, that will happen quite soon enough, when thou art older! If thou art in the least like thy father, there will certainly come a time when thou also wilt go and lose well-earned money at the Tables," said his mother tenderly.

"But if I win, then I shall buy thee a present," said the sweet cabbage coaxingly.

Sylvia looked out of the window. These happy, chattering people made her feel lonely, and even a little depressed.

The country through which the train was passing was very flat and ugly – in fact, it could scarcely be called country at all. And when at last they drew up into the large station of what was once a quiet, remote village where Parisian invalids, too poor to go elsewhere, came to take medicinal waters, she felt a pang of disappointment. Lacville, as seen from the railway, is an unattractive place.

"Is this Madame's first visit to Lacville?" asked her fellow-traveler, helping her out of the railway carriage. "If so, Madame would doubtless like to make her way to the lake. Would she care to accompany us thither?"

Sylvia hesitated. She almost felt inclined to go back to Paris by the next train. She told herself that there was no hope of finding Anna in such a large place, and that it was unlikely that this dreary-looking town would offer anything in the least pleasant or amusing on a very hot day.

But "It will be enchanting by the lake!" she heard someone say eagerly. And this chance remark made up her mind for her. After all, she might as well go and see the lake, of which everyone who mentioned Lacville spoke so enthusiastically.

Down the whole party swept along a narrow street, bordered by high white houses, shabby cafés, and little shops. Quite a crowd had left the station, and they were all now going the same way.

A turn in the narrow street, and Sylvia uttered a low cry of pleasure and astonishment!

Before her, like a scene in a play when the curtain is rung up, there suddenly appeared an immense sunlit expanse of water, fringed by high trees, and bordered by quaint, pretty châlets and villas, fantastic in shape, and each surrounded by a garden, which in many cases ran down to the edge of the lake.

To the right, stretching out over the water, its pinnacles and minarets reflected in blue translucent depths, rose what looked like a great white marble palace.

"Is it not lovely?" said the Frenchman eagerly. "And the water of the lake is so shallow, Madame, there is no fear of anyone being drowned in it! That is such an advantage when one has children."

"And it is a hundred times more charming in the afternoon," his wife chimed in, happily, "for then the lake is so full of little sailing-boats that you can hardly see the water. Oh, it is gay then, very gay!"

She glanced at Mrs. Bailey's pretty grey muslin dress and elegant parasol.

"I suppose Madame is going to one of the great restaurants? As for us, we shall make our way into a wood and have our luncheon there. It is expensive going to a restaurant with children."

She nodded pleasantly, with the easy, graceful familiarity which foreigners show in their dealings with strangers; and, shepherding their little party along, the worthy pair went briskly off by the broad avenue which girdles the lake.

Again Sylvia felt curiously alone. She was surrounded on every side by groups of merry-looking people, and already out on the lake there floated tiny white-sailed boats, each containing a man and a girl.

Everyone seemed to have a companion or companions; she alone was solitary. She even found herself wondering what she was doing there in a foreign country, by herself, when she might have been in England, in her own pleasant house at Market Dalling!

She took out of her bag the card which the landlord of the Hôtel de l'Horloge had pressed upon her. "Hôtel Pension, Villa du Lac, Lacville."

She went up rather timidly to a respectable-looking old bourgeois and his wife. "Do you know," she asked, "where is the Villa du Lac?"

"Certainly, Madame," answered the old man amiably. "It is there, close to you, not a hundred yards away. That big white house to our left." And then, with that love of giving information which possesses so many Frenchman, he added:

"The Villa du Lac once belonged to the Marquis de Para, who was gentleman-in-waiting to the Empress Eugénie. He and his family lived on here long after the war in fact" — he lowered his voice — "till the Concession was granted to the Casino. You know what I mean? The Gambling Concession. Since then the world of Lacville has become rather mixed, as I have reason to know, for my wife and I have lived here fifteen years. The Marquis de Para sold his charming villa. He was driven away, like so many other excellent people. So the Villa du Lac is now an hotel, where doubtless Madame has friends?"

Sylvia bowed and thanked him. Yes, the Villa du Lac even now looked like a delightful and well-kept private house, rather than like an hotel. It stood some way back — behind high wrought-steel and gilt gates — from the sandy road which lay between it and the lake, and the stone-paved courtyard was edged with a line of green tubs, containing orange trees.

Sylvia walked through the gates, which stood hospitably open, and when she was halfway up the horseshoe stone-staircase which led to the front door, a man, dressed in the white dress of a French chef, and bearing an almost ludicrous resemblance to M. Girard, came hurrying out.

"Madame Bailey?" he exclaimed joyously, and bowing very low. "Have I the honor of greeting Madame Bailey? My cousin telephoned to me that you might be coming, Madame, to déjeuner!" And as Sylvia smiled in assent: "I am delighted, I am honored, by the visit of Madame Bailey!"

Sylvia laughed outright. She really could not help it! It was very nice and thoughtful of M. Girard to have telephoned to his cousin. But how dreadful it would have been if she had gone straight back to Paris from the station. All these kind people would have had their trouble for nothing.

M. Polperro was a shrewd Southerner, and he had had the sense to make but few alterations to the Villa du Lac. It therefore retained something of the grand air it had worn in the days when it had been the property of a Court official. The large, cool, circular hall into which the hotel-keeper ushered Sylvia was charming, as were the long, finely decorated reception-rooms on either side.

The dining room, filled with small oval tables, to which M. Polperro next led his honored guest, had been built out since the house had become an hotel. It commanded a view of the lake on the one side, and of the large, shady garden of the villa on the other.

"I have arranged for Madame a little table in what we call the lake window," observed M. Polperro. "As yet Lacville is very empty. Paris is so delightful," he sighed, "but very soon, when the heat comes, Lacville will be quite full," he smiled joyously. "I myself have a very choice clientèle — I do not deal with rubbish." He drew himself up proudly. "My clients come back to me year after year. Already I have six visitors, and in ten days my pension will be *au grand complet*. It is quality, not quantity, that I desire, Madame. If ever you know anyone who wishes to come to Lacville you may safely recommend them — I say it with my hands on my heart," and he suited his action to his words — "to the Villa du Lac."

How delightful it all was to Sylvia Bailey! No wonder her feeling of depression and loneliness vanished.

As she sat down, and looked out of the bay window which commanded the whole length of the gleaming, sun-flecked lake, she told herself that, pleasant as was Paris, Lacville on a hot day was certainly a hundred times pleasanter than Paris.

And the Casino? Sylvia fixed her blue eyes on the white, fairylike group of buildings, which were so attractive an addition to the pretty landscape.

Surely one might spend a pleasant time at Lacville and never play for money? Though she was inclined to feel that in this matter of gambling English people are curiously narrow. It was better to be philosophical about it, like that excellent Frenchwoman in the train, who had not grudged her husband a little amusement, even if it entailed his losing what she had described as "hard-earned money."

Though she had to wait nearly half an hour for her meal, the time passed quickly; and when at last déjeuner was served to her well and deftly by a pleasant-faced young waitress dressed in Breton costume, each item of the carefully-prepared meal was delicious. M. Polperro had not been chef to a Princess for nothing.

Sylvia Bailey was not greedy, but like most healthy people she enjoyed good food, and she had very seldom tasted quite such good food as that which was served to her at the Hôtel du Lac on this memorable June day.

She had almost finished her luncheon when a fair young man came in and sat down at a small table situated at the other end of the dining room, close to the window overlooking the garden of the Villa du Lac.

Chapter IV

*A*s the young man came into the dining room he glanced over to where Mrs. Bailey was sitting and then he looked away, and, unfolding his table napkin, paid no more attention to the only other occupant of the room.

Now this was a very trifling fact, and yet it surprised our young Englishwoman; she had become accustomed to the way in which Frenchmen, or perhaps it would be more true to say Parisians, stare at a pretty woman in the streets, in omnibuses, and in shops. As for the dining room of the Hôtel de l'Horloge, it always seemed full of eyes when she and Anna Wolsky were having lunch or dinner there.

Now, for the first time, she found herself close to a Frenchman without feeling either uncomfortably or amusingly aware of a steady, unwinking stare. It was quite an odd sensation to find herself thus neglected!

Without actually looking round, Sylvia, out of the corner of her blue eye, could see this exceptional Frenchman. He was dressed in white flannels, and he wore rather bright pink socks and a pink tie to match. He must be, she decided, something of a dandy. Though still a young man, he was rather bald, and he had a thick fair moustache. He looked bored and very grave; she could not help wondering why he was staying at Lacville.

M. Polperro suddenly appeared at the door. "Would M. le Comte prefer scrambled eggs or an omelet?" he asked obsequiously, and "M. le Comte" lifted his head and answered shortly, but with a smile, "Scrambled eggs, my good Polperro."

Doubtless this was the gentleman who was brother-in-law of the French Duke mentioned by M. Girard. He spoke to the chef with the kindly familiarity born of long knowledge.

After having given the Count his scrambled eggs, the young waitress came over to where Sylvia was sitting. "Would Madame like to have her coffee in the garden?" she asked; and Sylvia said that she would.

How enchanting was the garden of the Villa du Lac, and how unlike any hotel garden she had ever seen! The smooth, wide lawn was shaded with noble cedars and bright green chestnut trees; it was paradise compared with the rather stuffy little Hôtel de l'Horloge and the dusty Paris streets.

M. Polperro himself brought Sylvia's coffee. Then he stayed on talking to her, for like all clever hotel-keepers the Southerner had the gift of making those who were staying in his house feel as if they were indeed his guests rather than his clients.

"If Madame should ever care to make a little stay at Lacville, how happy Madame Polperro and I would be!" he exclaimed. "I have a beautiful room overlooking the lake which I could give Madame. It was reserved for a Russian Princess, but now she is not coming —"

"Perhaps I will come and stay here some day," said Sylvia, and she really felt as if she would like to come and stay in the Villa du Lac. "But I am going to Switzerland next week, so it will have to be the next time I come to France in the summer."

"Does Madame play?" asked M. Polperro, insinuatingly.

"I?" said Sylvia, laughing. "No, indeed! Of course, I play bridge — all English people play bridge — but I have never gambled, if you mean that, monsieur, in my life."

"I am delighted to hear Madame say so," said M. Polperro, heartily. "People now talk of Lacville as if there was only the Casino and the play. They forget the beautiful walks, the lovely lake, and the many other attractions we have to offer! Why, Madame, think of the Forest of Montmorency? In old days it was quite a drive from Lacville, but now a taxi or an automobile will get you there in a few minutes! Still the Casino is very attractive too; and all *my* clients belong to the Club!"

Sylvia stayed on for nearly an hour in the delightful, peaceful garden, and then, rather regretfully, she went up the lichen-covered steps which led into the hall. How deliciously cool and quiet it was there.

She paid her bill; it seemed very moderate considering how good her lunch had been, and then slowly made her way out of the Villa du Lac, down across the stone-flagged courtyard to the gate, and so into the sanded road.

Crossing over, she began walking by the edge of the lake; and once more loneliness fell upon her. The happy-looking people who passed her laughing and talking together, and the more silent couples who floated by on the water in the quaint miniature sailing boats with which the surface of the lake was now dotted, were none of them alone.

Suddenly the old parish church of Lacville chimed out the hour — it was only one o'clock — amazingly early still!

Someone coming across the road lifted his hat. Could it be to her? Yes, for it was the young man who had shared with her, for a time, the large dining room of the Villa du Lac.

Again Sylvia was struck by what she could only suppose were the stranger's good manners, for instead of staring at her, as even the good-humored bourgeois with whom she had traveled from Paris that morning had done, the Count — she remembered he was a Count — turned sharply to the right and walked briskly along to the turning which led to the Casino.

The Casino? Why, of course, it was there that she must look for Anna Wolsky. How stupid of her not to have thought of it! And so, after waiting a moment, she also joined the little string of people who were wending their way towards the great white building.

After having paid a franc for admission, Sylvia found herself in the hall of the Casino of Lacville. An eager attendant rushed forward to relieve her of the dust-cloak and parasol which she was carrying.

"Does Madame wish to go straight to the Room of the Games?" he inquired eagerly.

Sylvia bent her head. It was there, or so she supposed, that Anna would be.

Feeling a thrill of keen curiosity, she followed the man through a prettily-decorated vestibule, and so into a large room, overlooking the lake, where already a crowd of people were gathered round the green baize tables.

The Salle des Jeux at Lacville is a charming, conservatorylike apartment, looking, indeed, as if it were actually built out on the water.

But none of the people were looking at the beautiful scene outside. Instead, each group was intent on the table, and on the game being played thereon — a game, it may be mentioned, which has a certain affinity with Roulette and Petits Chevaux, though it is neither the one nor the other.

Sylvia looked about her timidly; but no one took the slightest notice of her, and this in itself was rather strange. She was used to exciting a good deal of attention wherever she went in France, but here, at Lacville, everyone seemed blind to her presence. It was almost as if she were invisible! In a way this was a relief to her; but at the same time, she found it curiously disconcerting.

She walked slowly round each gambling table, keeping well outside the various circles of people sitting and standing there.

Strange to say Anna Wolsky was not among them. Of that fact Sylvia soon became quite sure.

At last a servant in livery came up to her. "Does Madame want a seat?" he asked officiously. "If so, I can procure Madame a seat in a very few moments."

But Sylvia, blushing, shook her head. She certainly had no wish to sit down.

"I only came in to look for a friend," she said, hesitatingly; "but my friend is not here."

And she was making her way out of the Salle des Jeux, feeling rather disconsolate and disappointed, when suddenly, in the vestibule, she saw Madame Wolsky walking towards her in the company of a middle-aged man.

"Then that is settled?" Sylvia heard Anna say in her indifferent French. "You will fill up all the formalities, and by the time I arrive the card of membership will be ready for me? This kind of thing" – she waved her hand towards the large room Sylvia had just left – "is no use to me at all! I only like *le Grand Jeu*"; and a slight smile came over her dark face.

The man who was with her laughed as if she had made a good joke; then bowing, he left her.

"Sylvia!"

"Anna!"

Mrs. Bailey fancied that the other was not particularly sorry to have been followed.

"So you came after me? Well! Well! I never should have thought to have seen my dear Puritan, Sylvia Bailey, in such a place as the Casino of Lacville?" said the Polish lady laughing. "However, as you are here, let us enjoy ourselves. Would you like to risk a few francs?"

Together they had gone back into the Salle des Jeux, and Anna drew Sylvia towards the nearest table.

"This is a child's game!" she exclaimed, contemptuously. "I cannot understand how all these clever Parisians can care to come out here and lose their money every Saturday and Sunday, to say nothing of other days!"

"But I suppose some of these people make money?" questioned Sylvia. She thought she saw a great deal of money being won, as well as lost, on the green cloth of the table before her.

"Oh yes, no doubt a few may make money at this game! But I have just been arranging, with the aid of the owner of the Pension where I am going to stay when I come here, to join the Club."

And then, realizing that Sylvia did not understand, she went on.

"You see, my dear child, there are two kinds of play here – as there are, indeed, at almost every Casino in France. There is *this* game, which is, as I say, a child's game — a game at which you can make or lose a few francs; and then there is Baccarat!"

She waited a moment.

"Yes?" said Sylvia questioningly.

"Baccarat is played here in what they call the Club, in another part of the building. As there is an entrance fee to the Club, there is never such a crowd in the Baccarat Room as there is here. And those who belong to the Club 'mean business,' as they say in your dear country. They come, that is, to play in the way that I understand and that I enjoy play!"

A little color rose to Anna Wolsky's sallow cheeks; she looked exhilarated, excited at the thoughts and memories her words conjured up.

Sylvia also felt curiously excited. She found the scene strangely fascinating — the scene presented by this crowd of eager men and women, each and all absorbed in this mysterious game which looked anything but a child's game, though Anna had called it so.

But as they were trying to make their way through the now dense crowd of people, the middle-aged man who had been with Anna when Sylvia had first seen her just now hurried up to them.

"Everything is arranged, Madame!" he exclaimed. "Here is your membership card. May I have the pleasure of taking you myself to the Club? Your friend can come too. She does not want to play, does she?"

He looked inquisitively at Sylvia, and his hard face softened. He had your true Frenchman's pleasure in charm and beauty. "Madame, or is it Mademoiselle? —"

"Madame!" answered Anna, smiling.

"— Madame can certainly come in and look on for a few moments, even though she be not a member of the Club."

They turned and followed him up a broad, shallow staircase, into a part of the Casino where the very atmosphere seemed different from that surrounding the public gaming tables.

Here, in the Club, all was hushed and quiet, and underfoot was a thick carpet.

There were very few people in the Baccarat Room, some twelve men, and four or five ladies who were broken up into groups, and talking with one another in the intimate, desultory fashion in which people talk who meet daily in pursuit of some common interest or hobby.

And then, all at once, Sylvia Bailey saw that among them, but standing a little apart, was the Count — was not his name de Virieu?

He turned round, and as he saw her she thought that a look of surprise, almost of annoyance, flitted over his impassive face. Then he moved away from where he could see her.

A peculiar-looking old gentleman, who seemed on kindly terms with everyone in the room, pulled a large turnip watch out of his pocket. "It is nearly half-past one!" he exclaimed fussily. "Surely, it is time that we began! Who takes the Bank today?"

"I will," said the Comte de Virieu, coming forward.

Five minutes later play was in full swing. Sylvia did not in the least understand the game of Baccarat, and she would have been surprised indeed had she been told that the best account of it ever written is that which describes it as "neither a recreation nor an intellectual exercise, but simply a means for the rapid exchange of money well suited to persons of impatient temperament."

With fascinated eyes, Sylvia watched Anna put down her gold pieces on the green cloth. Then she noted the cards as they were dealt out, and listened, it must be admitted, uncomprehendingly, to the mysterious words which told how the game was going. Still she sympathized very heartily with her friend when Anna's gold pieces were swept away, and she rejoiced as heartily when gold was added to Anna's little pile.

They both stood, refusing the seats which were pressed upon them.

Suddenly Sylvia Bailey, looking up from the green cloth, saw the eyes of the man who held the Bank fixed full upon her.

The Comte de Virieu did not gaze at the young English woman with the bold, impersonal stare to which she had become accustomed — his glance was far more thoughtful, questioning, and in a sense kindly. But his eyes seemed to pierce her through and through, and suddenly her heart began to beat very fast. Yet no color came into her face — indeed, Sylvia grew pale.

She looked down at the table, but even so she remained conscious of that piercing gaze turned on her, and with some surprise she found herself keenly visualizing the young man's face.

Alone among all the people in the room, the Comte de Virieu looked as if he lived a more or less outdoor life; his face was tanned, his blue eyes were very bright, and the hands dealing out the cards were well-shaped and muscular. Somehow he looked very different, she could hardly explain how or why, from the men round him.

At last she moved round, so as to avoid being opposite to him.

Yes, she felt more comfortable now, and slowly, almost insensibly, the glamour of play began to steal over Sylvia Bailey's senses. She began to understand the at once very simple and, to the uninitiated, intricate game of Baccarat — to long, as Anna Wolsky longed, for the fateful nine, eight, five, and four to be turned up.

She had fifty francs in her purse, and she ached to risk a gold piece.

"Do you think I might put down ten francs?" she whispered to Anna.

And the other laughed, and exclaimed, "Yes, of course you can!"

Sylvia put down a ten-franc piece, and a moment later it had become twenty francs.

"Leave it on," murmured Anna, "and see what happens —"

Sylvia followed her friend's advice, and a larger gold piece was added to the two already there.

She took up the forty francs with a curious thrill of joy and fear.

But then an untoward little incident took place. One of the liveried men-servants stepped forward. "Has Madame got her card of membership?" he inquired smoothly.

Sylvia blushed painfully. No, she had not got a card of membership — and there had been an implied understanding that she was only to look on, not play.

She felt terribly ashamed — a very unusual feeling for Sylvia Bailey — and the gold pieces she held in her hand, for she had not yet put them in her purse, felt as if they burned her.

But she found a friend, a defender in an unexpected quarter. The Count rose from the table. He said a few words in a low tone to the servant, and the man fell back.

"Of course, this young lady may play," he addressed Anna, "and as Banker I wish her all good luck! This is probably her first and her last visit to Lacville." He smiled pleasantly, and a little sadly. Sylvia noticed that he had a low, agreeable voice.

"Take her away, Madame, when she has won a little more! Do not give her time to lose what she has won."

He spoke exactly as if Sylvia was a child. She felt piqued, and Madame Wolsky stared at him rather haughtily. Still, she was grateful for his intervention.

"We thank you, Monsieur," she said stiffly. "But I think we have been here quite long enough."

He bowed, and again sat down.

"I will now take you a drive, Sylvia. We have had sufficient of this!"

Anna walked towards the door, and many were the curious glances now turned after the two friends.

"It will amuse you to see something of Lacville. As that gentleman said, I do not suppose you will ever come here again. And, as I shall spend most of my time in the Casino, I can very well afford to spare a little while out of it today!"

They made their way out of the great white building, Sylvia feeling oppressed, almost bewildered, by her first taste of gambling.

It was three o'clock, and very hot. They hailed one of the little open carriages which are among the innocent charms of Lacville.

"First you will go round the lake," said Madame Wolsky to the driver, "and then you will take us to the Pension Malfait, in l'Avenue des Acacias."

Under shady trees, bowling along sanded roads lined with pretty villas and châlets, they drove all round the lake, and more and more the place impressed Sylvia as might have done a charming piece of scene-painting.

All the people they passed on the road, in carriages, in motorcars, and on foot, looked happy, prosperous, gay, and without a care in the world; and where in the morning there had been one boat, there were now five sailing on the blue, gleaming waters fringed with trees and flowering shrubs.

At last they once more found themselves close to the Casino. A steady stream of people was now pouring in through the great glass doors.

"This sort of thing will go on up till about nine this evening!" said Anna, smiling grimly. "Think, my dear — a hundred and twenty trains daily! That room in the Casino where I first saw you will be crammed to suffocation within an hour, and even the Club will be well filled, though I fancy the regular habitués of the club are rather apt to avoid Saturday and Sunday at Lacville. I myself, when living here, shall try to do something else on those two days. By the way — how dreadful that I should forget! — have you had a proper *déjeuner?*" she looked anxiously at Sylvia.

Sylvia laughed, and told something of her adventures at the Villa du Lac.

"The Villa du Lac? I have heard of it, but surely it's an extremely expensive hotel? The place I've chosen for myself is farther away from the Casino; but the distance will force me to take a walk every day, and that will be a very good thing. Last time I was at Monte Carlo I had a lodging right up in Monaco, and I found that a very much healthier plan than to live close to the Casino," Anna spoke quite seriously. "The Pension Malfait is really extraordinarily cheap for a place near Paris. I am only going to pay fifty-five francs a week, *tout compris!*"

They had now turned from the road encircling the lake, and were driving through leafy avenues which reminded Sylvia of a London suburb where she had once stayed.

The châlets and villas by which they passed were not so large nor so prosperous-looking as those that bordered the lake, but still many of them were pretty and fantastic-looking little houses, and the gardens were gay with flowers.

"I suppose no one lives here in the winter!" said Sylvia suddenly.

She had noticed, for in some ways she was very observant though in other ways strangely unseeing, that all the flowers were of the bedding-out varieties; there were luxuriant creepers, but not a single garden that she passed had that indefinable look of being an old or a well-tended garden.

"In the winter? Why, in the winter Lacville is an absolute desert," said Anna laughing. "You see, the Casino only has a summer Concession; it cannot open till April 15. Of course there are people who will tell you that Lacville is the plague-pit of Paris, but that's all nonsense! Lacville is neither better nor worse than other towns near the capital!"

The carriage had now drawn up before a large, plain, white house, across which was painted in huge, black letters, "Hôtel-Pension Malfait."

"This is the place I have found!" exclaimed Anna. "Would you care to come in and see the room I've engaged from next Monday week?"

Sylvia followed her into the house with curiosity and interest. Somehow she did not like the Pension Malfait, though it was clear that it had once been a handsome private mansion standing in large grounds of its own. The garden, however, had now been cut down to a small strip, and the whole place formed a great contrast to the gay and charming Villa du Lac.

What garden there was seemed uncared for, though an attempt had been made to make it look pretty with the aid of a few geraniums and marguerites.

M. Malfait, the proprietor of the Pension, whom Sylvia had already seen with Anna at the Casino, now came forward in the hall, and Sylvia compared him greatly to his disadvantage, to the merry M. Polperro.

"Madame has brought her friend?" he said eagerly, and staring at Sylvia as he spoke. "I hope that Madame's friend will come and stay with us too? I have a charming room which I could give this lady; but later on we shall be very full — full all the summer! The hot weather is a godsend for Lacville; for it drives the Parisians out from their unhealthy city."

He beckoned to his wife, a disagreeable-looking woman who was sitting in a little glass cage made in an angle of the square hall.

"Madame Wolsky has brought this good lady to see our Pension!" he exclaimed, "and perhaps she is also coming to stay with us —"

In vain Sylvia smilingly shook her head. She was made to go all over the large, rather gloomy house, and to peep into each of the bare, ugly bedrooms.

That which Anna had engaged had a window looking over the back of the house; Sylvia thought it singularly cheerless. There was, however, a good armchair and a writing-table on which lay a new-looking blotter. It was the only bedroom containing such a luxury.

"An English lady was staying here not very long ago," observed M. Malfait, "and she bought that table and left it to me as a little gift when she went away. That was very gracious on her part!"

They glanced into the rather mournful-looking *salon*, of which the windows opened out on the tiny garden. And then M. Malfait led them proudly into the dining room, with its one long table, running down the middle, on which at intervals were set dessert dishes filled with the nuts, grapes, and oranges of which Sylvia had already become so weary at the Hôtel de l'Horloge.

"My clientèle," said M. Malfait gravely, "is very select and *chic*. Those of my guests who frequent the Casino all belong to the Club!"

He stated the fact proudly, and Sylvia was amused to notice that in this matter he and mine host at the Villa du Lac apparently saw eye to eye. Both were eager to dissociate themselves from the ordinary gambler who lost or won a few francs in those of the gambling rooms open to the general public.

"Well," said Anna at last, "I suppose we had better leave now, but we might as well go on driving for about an hour, and then, when it is a little cooler, we will go back to Paris and be there in time for tea."

The driver was as good-natured as everyone else at Lacville seemed to be. He drove his fares away from the town, and so to the very outskirts of Lacville, where there were many charming bits of wild woodland and gardens up for sale.

"Even five years ago," he said, "much of this was forest, Mesdames; but now — well, Dame! — you can understand people are eager to sell. There are rumors that the Concession may be withdrawn from the Casino — that would be terrible, some say it would kill Lacville! It would be all the same to me, I should always find work elsewhere. But it makes everyone eager to sell — those, I mean, who have land at Lacville. There are others," continued the man — he had turned round on his seat, and the horse was going at a foot's pace — "who declare that it would be far better for the town — that there would be a more solid population established here — you understand, Mesdames, what I mean? The Lacville tradesmen would be as pleased, quite as pleased, or so some of them say; but, all the same, they are selling their land!"

When the two friends finally got back to the Hôtel de l'Horloge, Sylvia Bailey found that a letter, which had not been given to her that morning, contained the news that the English friends whom she had been expecting to join in Switzerland the following week had altered their plans, and were no longer going abroad.

Chapter V

Sylvia could hardly have said how it came about that she found herself established in the Villa du Lac only a week after her first visit to Lacville! But so it was, and she found the change a delightful one from every point of view.

Paris had suddenly become intolerably hot. As is the way with the Siren city when June is halfway through, the asphalt pavements radiated heat; the air was heavy, laden with strange, unpleasing odors; and even the trees, which form such delicious oases of greenery in the older quarters of the town were powdered with grey dust.

Also Anna Wolsky had become restless — quite unlike what she had been before that hour spent by her and by Sylvia Bailey in the Club at Lacville; she had gone back there three times, refusing, almost angrily, the company of her English friend. For a day or two Sylvia had thought seriously of returning to England, but she had let her pretty house at Market Dalling till the end of August; and, in spite of the heat, she did not wish to leave France.

Towards the end of the week Anna suddenly exclaimed:

"After all, why shouldn't you come out to Lacville, Sylvia? You can't go to Switzerland alone, and you certainly don't want to go on staying in Paris as Paris is now! I do not ask you to go to the Pension Malfait, but come to the Villa du Lac. You will soon make acquaintances in that sort of place — I mean," she added, "in your hotel, not in the town. We could always spend the mornings together —"

"— And I, too, could join the Club at the Casino," interjected Sylvia, smiling.

"No, no, I don't want you to do that!" exclaimed Anna hastily.

And then Sylvia, for some unaccountable reason, felt rather irritated. It was absurd of Anna to speak to her like that! Bill Chester, her trustee, and sometime lover, always treated her as if she was a child, and a rather naughty child, too; she would not allow Anna Wolsky to do so.

"I don't see why not!" she cried. "You yourself say that there is no harm in gambling if one can afford it."

*T*his was how Sylvia Bailey came to find herself an inmate of the Villa du Lac at Lacville; and when once the owner of the Hôtel de l'Horloge had understood that in any case she meant to leave Paris, he had done all in his power to make her going to his relation, mine host of the Villa du Lac, easy and agreeable.

Sylvia learnt with surprise that she would have to pay very little more at the Villa du Lac than she had done at the Hôtel de l'Horloge; on the other hand, she could not there have the use of a sitting room, for the good reason that there were no private sitting rooms in the villa. But that, so she told herself, would be no hardship, and she could spend almost the whole of the day in the charming garden.

The two friends arrived at Lacville late in the afternoon, and on a Monday, that is on the quietest day of the week. And when Anna had left Sylvia at the Villa du Lac, driving off alone to her own humbler *pension*, the young Englishwoman, while feeling rather lonely, realized that M. Polperro had not exaggerated the charm of his hostelry.

Proudly mine host led Mrs. Bailey up the wide staircase into the spacious, airy room which had been prepared for her. "This was the bedchamber of Madame la Comtesse de Para, the friend of the Empress Eugénie" he said.

The windows of the large, circular room, mirror-lined, and still containing the fantastic, rather showy decorations which dated from the Second Empire, overlooked the broad waters of the lake. Even now, though it was still daylight, certain romantic-natured couples had lit paper lanterns and hung them at the prows of their little sailing-boats.

The scene had a certain fairylike beauty and stillness.

"Madame will find the Villa du Lac far more lively now" exclaimed M. Polperro cheerfully. "Last week I had only M. le Comte Paul de Virieu — no doubt Madame has heard of his brother-in-law, the Duc d'Eglemont?"

Sylvia smiled. "Yes, he won the Derby, a famous English race," she said; and then, simply because the landlord's love of talking was infectious, "And does the Count own horses, too?" she asked.

"Oh, no, Madame. He loves them, yes, and he is a fine horseman, but Count Paul, alas! has other things that interest and occupy him more than horses!"

After M. Polperro had bowed himself out, Sylvia sat down close to one of the open windows and looked out over the enchanting, and to her English eyes, unusual panorama spread out before her.

Yes, she had done well to come here, to a place of which, no doubt, many of her English friends would have thoroughly disapproved! But, after all, what was wrong about Lacville? Where, for the matter of that, was the harm of playing for money if one could afford to lose it?

Sylvia had hardly ever met so kind or so intelligent a woman as was her new friend, Anna Wolsky: and Anna — she made no secret of it at all — allowed playing for money to be her one absorbing interest in life.

As she thought of the Polish woman Sylvia felt sorry that she and her friend were in different *pensions*. It would have been so nice to have had her here, in the Villa du Lac. She felt rather lost without Anna, for she had become accustomed to the other's pleasant, stimulating companionship.

M. Polperro had said that dinner was at half-past seven. Sylvia got up from her chair by the window. She moved back into the room and put on a pretty white lace evening dress which she had not worn since she had been in France.

It would have been absurd to have appeared in such a gown in the little dining room of the Hôtel de l'Horloge, which opened into the street; but the Villa du Lac was quite different.

As she saw herself reflected in one of the long mirrors let into the wall, Sylvia blushed and half-smiled. She had suddenly remembered the young man who had behaved, on that first visit of hers to the Villa du Lac, so much more discreetly than had all the other Frenchmen with whom she had been brought in temporary contact. She was familiar, through newspaper paragraphs, with the name of his brother-in-law, the French duke who had won the Derby. The Duc d'Eglemont, that was the racing French duke who had carried off the blue riband of the British Turf — the other name was harder to remember — then it came to her. Count Paul de Virieu. How kind and courteous he had been to her and her friend in the Club. She remembered him very vividly. Yes, though not exactly good-looking, he had fine eyes, and a clever, if not a very happy, face.

And then, on going down the broad, shallow staircase, and so through the large, oval hall into the dining room, Sylvia Bailey saw that the man of whom she had been thinking was there, sitting very near to where she herself was now told that she was to sit. In the week that had gone by since Sylvia had paid her first visit to Lacville, the Villa had gradually filled up with people eager, like herself, to escape from the heat and dust of Paris, and the pleasant little table by the window had been appropriated by someone else.

When the young Englishwoman came into the dining room, the Comte de Virieu got up from his chair, and clicking his heels together, bowed low and gravely.

She had never seen a man do that before. And it looked so funny! Sylvia felt inclined to burst out laughing. But all she did was to nod gravely, and the Count, sitting down, took no further apparent notice of her.

There were a good many people in the large room; parties of two, three, and four, talking merrily together, as is the way with French people at their meals. No one was alone save the Comte de Virieu and herself. Sylvia wondered if he felt as lonely as she did.

Towards the end of dinner the host came in and beamed on his guests; then he walked across to where Mrs. Bailey sat by herself. "I hope Madame is satisfied with her dinner," he said pleasantly. "Madame must always tell me if there is anything she does not like."

He called the youngest of the three waitresses. "Félicie! You must look very well after Madame," he said solemnly. "Make her comfortable, attend to her slightest wish" — and then he chuckled — "This is my niece," he said, "a very good girl! She is our adopted daughter. Madame will only have to ask her for anything she wants."

Sylvia felt much happier, and no longer lonely. It was all rather absurd — but it was all very pleasant! She had never met an hotel keeper like little Polperro, one at once so familiar and so inoffensive in manner.

"Thank you so much," she said, "but I am more than comfortable! And after dinner I shall go to the Casino to meet my friend, Madame Wolsky."

After they had finished dinner most of M. Polperro's guests streamed out into the garden; and there coffee was served to them on little round iron tables dotted about on the broad green lawn and sanded paths.

One or two of the ladies spoke a kindly word to Sylvia as they passed by her, but each had a friend or friends, and she was once more feeling lonely and deserted when suddenly Count Paul de Virieu walked across to where she was sitting by herself.

Again he clicked his heels together, and again he bowed low. But already Sylvia was getting used to these strange foreign ways, and she no longer felt inclined to laugh; in fact, she rather liked the young Frenchman's grave, respectful manner.

"If, as I suppose, Madame, seeing that you have come back to Lacville —"

Sylvia looked up with surprise painted on her fair face, for the Count was speaking in English, and it was extremely good, almost perfect English.

"— and you wish to join the Club at the Casino, I hope, Madame, that you will allow me to have the honor of proposing you as a member."

He waited a moment, and then went on: "It is far better for a lady to be introduced by someone who is already a member, than for the affair to be managed" — he slightly lowered his voice — "by an hotel keeper. I am well known to the Casino authorities. I have been a member of the Club for some time —"

He stood still gazing thoughtfully down into her face.

"But I am not yet sure that I shall join the Club," said Sylvia, hesitatingly.

He looked — was it relieved or sorry?

"I beg your pardon, Madame! I misunderstood. I thought you told M. Polperro just now in the dining room that you were going to the Casino this evening."

Sylvia felt somewhat surprised. It was odd that he should have overheard her words to M. Polperro, amid all the chatter of their fellow-guests.

"Yes, I am going to the Casino," she said frankly, "but only to meet a friend of mine there, the lady with whom I was the other day when you so kindly interfered to save us, or rather to save *me*, from being ignominiously turned out of the Club." And then she added, a little shyly, "Won't you sit down?"

Again the Comte de Virieu bowed low before her, and then he sat down.

"I fear you will not be allowed to go into the Club this time unless you become a member. They have to be very strict in these matters; to allow a stranger in the Club at all is a legal infraction. The Casino authorities might be fined for doing so."

"How well you speak English!" exclaimed Sylvia, abruptly and irrelevantly.

"I was at school in England," he said, simply, "at a Catholic College called Beaumont, near Windsor; but now I do not go there as often as I should like to do."

And then, scarcely knowing how it came about, Sylvia fell into easy, desultory, almost intimate talk with this entire stranger. But there was something very agreeable in his simple serious manners.

After a while Sylvia suddenly remembered that the Count had thrown his cigarette away before speaking to her.

"Won't you smoke?" she said.

"Are you sure you don't mind, Madame?"

"No, of course I don't mind!" and she was just going to add that her husband had been a great smoker, when some feeling she could not have analyzed to herself made her alter her words to "My father smoked all day long —"

The Count got up and went off towards the house. Sylvia supposed he had gone to get his cigarette-case; but a moment later he came back and sat down by her again. And then very soon out came the host's pretty little niece with a shawl over her arm. "I have brought Madame a shawl," said the girl, smiling, "for it's getting a little cold," and Sylvia felt touched. How very kind French people were — how kind and how thoughtful!

It struck half-past eight. Mrs. Bailey and the Comte de Virieu had been talking for quite a long time.

Sylvia jumped up. "I must go now," she cried, a little regretfully. "I promised to meet my friend in the hall of the Casino at half-past eight. She must be there waiting for me, now."

"If you will allow me to do so, I will escort you to the Casino," said the Count.

Sylvia ran upstairs to put on her hat and gloves. On the table which did duty for a dressing-table there was a small nosegay of flowers in a glass of water. It had not been there before she had come down to dinner.

As she put on a large black tulle hat she told herself with a happy smile that Lacville was an enchanting, a delightful place, and that she already felt quite at home here!

The Comte de Virieu was waiting for her in the hall.

"I think I ought to introduce myself to you, Madame," he said solemnly. "My name is Paul de Virieu."

"And mine is Sylvia Bailey," she said, a little breathlessly.

As they were hurrying along the short piece of road which led to the lane in which the Casino of Lacville is situated, the Count said suddenly, "Will you pardon me, Madame, if I take the liberty of saying that you should arrange for your friend to call for you on those evenings that you intend to spend at the Casino? It is not what English people call 'proper' for you to go to the Casino alone, or only accompanied by a stranger — for I, alas! am still a stranger to you."

There was no touch of coquetry or flirtation in the voice in which he said those words. Sylvia blushed violently, but she did not feel annoyed, only queerly touched by his solicitude for — well, she supposed it was for her reputation.

"You see, Madame," he went on soberly, "you look very young — I mean, pardon me, you *are* very young, and I will confess to you that the first time I saw you I thought you were a 'Miss.' Of course, I saw at once that you were English."

"An English girl would hardly have come all by herself to Lacville!" said Sylvia a little flippantly.

"Oh, Madame, English young ladies do such strange things!"

Sylvia wondered if the Count were not overparticular. Was Lacville the sort of place in which a woman could not walk a few yards by herself? It looked such a happy, innocent sort of spot.

"Perhaps I do not make myself clear," went on Count Paul.

He spoke very quickly, and in a low voice, for they were now approaching the door of the Casino. "Not very long ago a lady had her hand-bag snatched from her within a few yards of the police station, in the center of the town. Everyone comes here to make or to lose money —"

"But most of the people look so quiet and respectable," she said smiling.

"That is true, but there are the exceptions. Lacville contains more exceptions than do most places, Madame."

They were now in the hall of the Casino. Yes, there was Anna Wolsky looking eagerly at the great glass doors.

"Anna? Anna? Here I am! I'm so sorry I'm late!"

Sylvia turned to introduce the Comte de Virieu to Madame Wolsky, but he was already bowing stiffly, and before she could speak he walked on, leaving Mrs. Bailey with her friend.

"I see you've already made one acquaintance, Sylvia," said the Polish lady dryly.

"That's the man who was so kind the last time we were here together. He is staying at the Villa du Lac," Sylvia answered, a little guiltily. "His name is Count Paul de Virieu."

"Yes, I am aware of that; I know him by sight quite well," Anna said quickly.

"And he has offered to propose me as a member of the Club if I wish to join," added Sylvia.

"*I* shall propose you — of course!" exclaimed Anna Wolsky. "But I do not think it is worth worrying about your membership tonight. We can spend the evening downstairs, in the public Salle des Jeux. I should not care to leave you alone there, even on a Monday evening."

"You talk as if I were sugar or salt that would melt!" said Sylvia, a little vexed.

"One has to be very careful in a place like Lacville," said Anna shortly. "There are all sorts of queer people gathered together here on the look-out for an easy way of making money." She turned an affectionate look on her friend. "You are not only very pretty, my dear Sylvia, but you look what the people here probably regard as being of far more consequence, that is, opulent."

"So I am," said Sylvia gaily, "opulent and very, very happy, dear Anna! I am so glad that you brought me here, and first made me acquainted with this delightful place! I am sure Switzerland would not have been half as amusing as Lacville —"

*T*he public gambling room was much quieter and emptier than it had been on the Saturday when Sylvia had first seen it. But all the people playing there, both those sitting at the table and those who stood in serried ranks behind them, looked as if they were engaged on some serious undertaking.

They did not appear, as the casual holiday crowd had done, free from care. There was comparatively little talking among them, and each round of the monotonous game was got through far quicker than had been the case the week before. Money was risked, lost, or gained, with extraordinary swiftness and precision.

A good many of the people there, women as well as men, glanced idly for a moment at the two newcomers, but they soon looked away again, intent on their play.

Sylvia felt keenly interested. She could have stopped and watched the scene for hours without wanting to play herself; but Anna Wolsky soon grew restless, and started playing. Even risking a few francs was better to her than not gambling at all!

"It's an odd thing," she said in a low voice, "but I don't see here any of the people I'm accustomed to see at Monte Carlo. As a rule, whenever one goes to this kind of place one meets people one has seen before. We gamblers are a caste — a sect part!"

"I can't bear to hear you call yourself a gambler," said Sylvia in a low voice.

Anna laughed good-humoredly.

"Believe me, my dear, there is not the difference you apparently think there is between a gambler and the man who has never touched a card."

Anna Wolsky looked round her as she spoke with a searching glance, and then she suddenly exclaimed,

"Yes, I do know someone here after all! That funny-looking couple over there were at Aix-les-Bains all last summer."

"Which people do you mean?" asked Sylvia eagerly.

"Don't you see that long, thin man who is so queerly dressed — and his short, fat wife? A dreadful thing happened to them — a great friend of theirs, a Russian, was drowned in Lac Bourget. It made a great deal of talk in Aix at the time it happened."

Sylvia Bailey looked across the room. She was able to pick out in a moment the people Anna meant, and perhaps because she was in good spirits tonight, she smiled involuntarily at their rather odd appearance.

Standing just behind the *croupier* — whose task it is to rake in and to deal out the money — was a short, stout, dark woman, dressed in a bright purple gown, and wearing a pale blue bonnet particularly unbecoming to her red, massive face. She was not paying much attention to the play, though now and again she put a five-franc piece onto the green baize. Instead, her eyes were glancing round restlessly this way and that, almost as if she were seeking for someone.

Behind her, in strong contrast to herself, was a tall, thin, lanky man, to Sylvia's English eyes absurdly as well as unsuitably dressed in a grey alpaca suit and a shabby Panama hat. In his hand he held open a small book, in which he noted down all the turns of the game. Unlike his short, stout wife, this tall, thin man seemed quite uninterested in the people about him, and Sylvia could see his lips moving, his brows frowning, as if he were absorbed in some intricate and difficult calculation.

The couple looked different from the people about them; in a word, they did not look French.

"The man — their name is Wachner — only plays on a system," whispered Anna. "He is in fact what I call a System Maniac. That is why he keeps noting down the turns in his little book. That sort of gambler ought never to leave Monte Carlo. It is only at Monte Carlo — that is to say, at Roulette — that such a man ever gets a real chance of winning anything. I should have expected them to belong to the Club, and not to trouble over this kind of play!"

Even as she spoke, Anna slightly inclined her head, and the woman at whom they were both looking smiled broadly, showing her strong white teeth as she did so; and then, as her eyes traveled from Anna Wolsky to Anna's companion, they became intent and questioning.

Madame Wachner, in spite of her unwieldy form, and common, showy clothes, was fond of beautiful things, and especially fond of jewels. She was wondering whether the pearls worn by the lovely young Englishwoman standing opposite were real or sham.

The two friends did not stay very long in the Casino on that first evening. Sylvia drove Anna to the Pension Malfait, and then she came back alone to the Villa du Lac.

*B*efore drawing together the curtains of her bedroom windows, Sylvia Bailey stood for some minutes looking out into the warm moonlit night.

On the dark waters of the lake floated miniature argosies, laden with lovers seeking happiness – aye, and perhaps finding it, too.

The Casino was outlined with fairy lamps; the scene was full of glamour, and of mysterious beauty. More than ever Sylvia was reminded of an exquisite piece of scene painting, and it seemed to her as if she were the heroine of a romantic opera – and the hero, with his ardent eyes and melancholy, intelligent face, was Count Paul de Virieu.

She wondered uneasily why Anna Wolsky had spoken of the Count as she had done – was it with dislike or only contempt?

Long after Sylvia was in bed she could hear the tramping made by the feet of those who were leaving the Casino and hurrying towards the station; but she did not mind the sound. All was so strange, new, and delightful, and she fell asleep and dreamt pleasant dreams.

Chapter VI

*O*n waking the next morning, Sylvia Bailey forgot completely for a moment where she was.

She looked round the large, airy room, which was so absolutely unlike the small bedroom she had occupied in the Hôtel de l'Horloge, with a sense of bewilderment and surprise.

And then suddenly she remembered! Why of course she was at Lacville; and this delightful, luxurious room had been furnished and arranged for the lady-in-waiting and friend of the Empress Eugénie. The fact gave an added touch of romance to the Hôtel du Lac.

A ray of bright sunlight streamed in through the curtains she had pinned together the night before. And her traveling clock told her that it was not yet six. But Sylvia jumped out of bed, and, drawing back the curtains, she looked out, and across the lake.

The now solitary expanse of water seemed to possess a new beauty in the early morning sunlight, and the white Casino, of which the minarets were reflected in its blue depths, might have been a dream palace. Nothing broke the intense stillness but the loud, sweet twittering of the birds in the trees which surrounded the lake.

But soon the spell was broken. When the six strokes of the hour chimed out from the old parish church which forms the center of the town of Lacville, as if by enchantment there rose sounds of stir both indoors and out.

A woman came out of the lodge of the Villa du Lac, and slowly opened the great steel and gilt gates.

Sylvia heard the rush of bath water, even the queer click-click of a shower bath. M. Polperro evidently insisted on an exceptional standard of cleanliness for his household.

Sylvia felt fresh and well. The languor induced by the heat of Paris had left her. There seemed no reason why she should not get up too, and even go out of doors if so the fancy pleased her.

She had just finished dressing when there came curious sounds from the front of the Villa, and again she went over to her window.

A horse was being walked up and down on the stones of the courtyard in front of the horseshoe stairway which led up to the hall door. It was not yet half-past six. Who could be going to ride at this early hour of the morning?

Soon her unspoken question was answered; for the Comte de Virieu, clad in riding breeches and a black jersey, came out of the house, and close on his heels trotted M. Polperro, already wearing his white chef's cap and apron.

Sylvia could hear his "M'sieur le Comte" this, and "M'sieur le Comte" that, and she smiled a little to herself. The owner of the Hôtel du Lac was very proud of his noble guest.

The Comte de Virieu was also laughing and talking; he was more animated than she had yet seen him. Sylvia told herself that he looked very well in his rather odd riding dress.

Waving a gay adieu to mine host, he vaulted into the saddle, and then rode out of the gates, and so sharply to the left.

Sylvia wondered if he were going for a ride in the Forest of Montmorency, which, in her lying guide-book, was mentioned as the principal attraction of Lacville.

There came a knock at the door, and Sylvia, calling out "Come in!" was surprised, and rather amused, to see that it was M. Polperro himself who opened it.

"I have come to ask if Madame has slept well," he observed, "and also to know if she would like an English breakfast? If yes, it shall be laid in the dining room, unless Madame would rather have it up here."

"I would much rather come downstairs to breakfast," said Sylvia; "but I do not want anything yet, M. Polperro. It will do quite well if I have breakfast at half-past eight or nine."

She unpacked her trunks, and as she put her things away it suddenly struck her that she meant to stay at Lacville for some time. It was an interesting, a new, even a striking experience, this of hers; and though she felt rather lost without Anna Wolsky's constant presence and companionship, she was beginning to find it pleasant to be once more her own mistress.

She sat down and wrote some letters — the sort of letters that can be written or not as the writer feels inclined. Among them was a duty letter to her trustee, Bill Chester, telling him of her change of address, and of her change of plan.

The people with whom she had been going to Switzerland were friends of Bill Chester too, and so it was doubtful now whether he would go abroad at all.

And all the time Sylvia was writing there was at the back of her mind a curious, unacknowledged feeling that she was waiting for something to happen, that there was something pleasant for her to look forward to. . . .

And when at last she went down into the dining room, and Paul de Virieu came in, Sylvia suddenly realized, with a sense of curious embarrassment, what it was she had been waiting for and looking forward to. It was her meeting with the Comte de Virieu.

"I hope my going out so early did not disturb you," he said, in his excellent English. "I saw you at your window."

Sylvia shook her head, smiling.

"I had already been awake for at least half an hour," she answered.

"I suppose you ride? Most of the Englishwomen I knew as a boy rode, and rode well."

"My father was very anxious I should ride, and as a child I was well taught, but I have not had much opportunity of riding since I grew up."

Sylvia reddened faintly, for she fully expected the Count to ask her if she would ride with him, and she had already made up her mind to say "No," though to say "Yes" would be very pleasant!

But he did nothing of the sort. Even at this early hour of their acquaintance it struck Sylvia how unlike the Comte de Virieu's manner to her was to that of the other young men she knew. While his manner was deferential, even eager, yet there was not a trace of flirtation in it.

Also the Count had already altered all Sylvia Bailey's preconceived notions of Frenchmen.

Sylvia had supposed a Frenchman's manner to a woman to be almost invariably familiar, in fact, offensively familiar. She had had the notion that a pretty young woman — it would, of course, have been absurd for her to have denied, even to herself, that she was very pretty — must be careful in her dealing with foreigners, and she believed it to be a fact that a Frenchman always makes love to an attractive stranger, even on the shortest acquaintance!

This morning, and she was a little piqued that it was so, Sylvia had to admit to herself that the Comte de Virieu treated her much as he might have done some old lady in whom he took a respectful interest. . . .

And yet twice during the half-hour her breakfast lasted she looked up to see his blue eyes fixed full on her with an earnest, inquiring gaze, and she realized that it was not at all the kind of gaze Paul de Virieu would have turned on an old lady.

They got up from their respective tables at the same moment. He opened the door for her, and then, after a few minutes, followed her out into the garden.

"Have you yet visited the *potager?*" he asked, deferentially.

Sylvia looked at him, puzzled. *"Potager"* was quite a new French word to her.

"I think you call it the kitchen-garden." A smile lit up his face. "The people who built the Villa du Lac a matter of fifty years ago were very fond of gardening. I think it might amuse you to see the *potager.* Allow me to show it you."

They were now walking side by side. It was a delicious day, and the dew still glistened on the grass and leaves. Sylvia thought it would be very pleasant, and also instructive, to see a French kitchen-garden.

"Strange to say when I was a child I was often at the Villa du Lac, for the then owner was a distant cousin of my mother. He and his kind wife allowed me to come here for my convalescence after a rather serious illness when I was ten years old. My dear mother did not like me to be far from Paris, so I was sent to Lacville."

"What a curious place to send a child to!" exclaimed Sylvia.

"Ah, but Lacville was extremely different from what it is now, Madame. True, there was the lake, where Parisians used to come out each Sunday afternoon to fish and boat in a humble way, and there were a few villas built round the lake. But you must remember that in those prehistoric days there was no Casino! It is the Casino which has transformed Lacville into what we now see."

"Then we have reason to bless the Casino!" cried Sylvia, gaily.

They had now left behind them the wide lawn immediately behind the Villa du Lac, and were walking by a long, high wall. The Count pushed open a narrow door set in an arch in the wall, and Sylvia walked through into one of the largest and most delightful kitchen-gardens she had ever seen.

It was brilliant with color and scent; the more homely summer flowers filled the borders, while, at each place where four paths met, a round, stone-rimmed basin, filled with water to the brim, gave a sense of pleasant coolness.

The farther end of the walled garden was bounded by a stone orangery, a building dating from the eighteenth century, and full of the stately grace of a vanished epoch.

"What a delightful place!" Sylvia exclaimed. "But this garden must cost M. Polperro a great deal of money to keep up —"

The Comte de Virieu laughed.

"Far from it! Our clever host hires out his *potager* to a firm of market gardeners, part of the bargain being that they allow him to have as much fruit and vegetables as he requires throughout the year. Why, the *potager* of the Villa du Lac supplies the whole of Lacville with fruit and flowers! When I was a child I thought this part of the garden paradise, and I spent here my happiest hours."

"It must be very odd for you to come back and stay in the Villa now that it is an hotel."

"At first it seemed very strange," he answered gravely. "But now I have become quite used to the feeling."

They walked on for awhile along one of the narrow flower-bordered paths.

"Would you care to go into the orangery?" he said. "There is not much to see there now, for all the orange trees are out of doors. Still, it is a quaint, pretty old building."

The orangery of the Villa du Lac was an example of that at once artificial and graceful eighteenth-century architecture which, perhaps because of its mingled formality and delicacy, made so distinguished and attractive a setting to feminine beauty. It remained, the only survival of the dependencies of a château sacked and burned in the Great Revolution, more than half a century before the Villa du Lac was built.

The high doors were wide open, and Sylvia walked in. Though all the pot-plants and half-hardy shrubs were sunning themselves in the open-air, the orangery did not look bare, for every inch of the inside walls had been utilized for growing grapes and peaches.

There was a fountain set in the center of the stone floor, and near the fountain was a circular seat.

"Let us sit down," said Paul de Virieu suddenly. But when Sylvia Bailey sat down he did not come and sit by her, instead he so placed himself that he looked across at her slender, rounded figure, and happy smiling face.

"Are you thinking of staying long at Lacville, Madame?" he asked abruptly.

"I don't know," she answered hesitatingly. "It will depend on my friend Madame Wolsky's plans. If we both like it, I daresay we shall stay three or four weeks."

There fell what seemed to Sylvia a long silence between them. The Frenchman was gazing at her with a puzzled, thoughtful look.

Suddenly he got up, and after taking a turn up and down the orangery, he came and stood before her.

"Mrs. Bailey!" he exclaimed. "Will you permit me to be rather impertinent?"

Sylvia reddened violently. The question took her utterly by surprise. But the Comte de Virieu's next words at once relieved, and yes, it must be admitted, chagrined her.

"I ask you, Madame, to leave Lacville! I ask permission to tell you frankly and plainly that it is not a place to which you ought to have been brought."

He spoke with great emphasis.

Sylvia looked up at him. She was bewildered, and though not exactly offended, rather hurt.

"But why?" she asked plaintively. "Why should I not stay at Lacville?"

"Oh, well, there can be no harm in your staying on a few days if you are desirous of doing so. But Lacville is not a place where I should care for my own sister to come and stay." He went on, speaking much quicker — "Indeed, I will say more! I will tell you that Lacville may seem a paradise to you, but that it is a paradise full of snakes."

"Snakes?" repeated Sylvia slowly. "You mean, of course, human snakes?"

He bowed gravely.

"Every town where reigns the Goddess of play attracts reptiles, Madame, as the sun attracts lizards! It is not the game that does so, or even the love of play in the Goddess's victims; no, it is the love of gold!"

Sylvia noticed that he had grown curiously pale.

"Lacville as a gambling center counts only next to Monte Carlo. But whereas many people go to Monte Carlo for health, and for various forms of amusement, people only come here in order to play, and to see others play. The Casino, which doubtless appears to you a bright, pretty place, has been the scene and the cause of many a tragedy. Do you know how Paris regards Lacville?" he asked searchingly.

"No — yes," Sylvia hesitated. "You see I never heard of Lacville till about a week ago." Innate honesty compelled her to add, "But I have heard that the Paris trades-people don't like Lacville."

"Let me tell you one thing," the Count spoke with extraordinary seriousness. "Every tradesman in Paris, without a single exception, has signed a petition imploring the Government to suspend the Gambling Concession!"

"What an extraordinary thing!" exclaimed Sylvia, and she was surprised indeed.

"Pardon me, it is not at all extraordinary. A great deal of the money which would otherwise go into the pockets of these tradesmen goes now to enrich the anonymous shareholders of the Casino of Lacville! Of course, Paris hotel-keepers are not in quite the same position as are the other Parisian trades-people. Lacville does not do them much harm, for the place is so near Paris that foreigners, if they go there at all, generally go out for the day. Only the most confirmed gambler cares actually to *live* at Lacville."

He looked significantly at Sylvia, and she felt a wave of hot color break over her face.

"Yes, I know what you must be thinking, and it is, indeed, the shameful truth! I, Madame, have the misfortune to be that most miserable and most God-forsaken of living beings, a confirmed gambler."

The Count spoke in a tone of stifled pain, almost anger, and Sylvia gazed up at his stern, sad face with pity and concern filling her kind heart.

"I will tell you my story in a few words," he went on, and then he sat down by her, and began tracing with his stick imaginary patterns on the stone floor.

"I was destined for what I still regard as the most agreeable career in the world — that of diplomacy. You see how I speak English? Well, Madame, I speak German and Spanish equally well. And then, most unhappily for me, my beloved mother died, and I inherited from her a few thousand pounds. I felt very miserable, and I happened to be at the moment idle. A friend persuaded me to go to Monte Carlo. That fortnight, Madame, changed my life — made me what the English call 'an idle good-for-nothing.' Can you wonder that I warn you against staying at Lacville?"

Sylvia was touched, as well as surprised, by his confidences. His words breathed sincerity, and the look of humiliation and pain on his face had deepened. He looked white and drawn.

"It is very kind of you to tell me this, and I am very much obliged to you for your warning," she said in a low tone.

But the Comte de Virieu went on as if he hardly heard her words.

"The lady with whom you first came to Lacville — I mean the Polish lady — is well known to me by sight. For the last three years I have seen her at Monte Carlo in the winter, and at Spa and Aix-les-Bains in the summer. Of course I was not at all surprised to see her turn up here, but I confess, Madame, that I was very much astonished to see with her a" — he hesitated a moment — "a young English lady. You would, perhaps, be offended if I were to tell you exactly what I felt when I saw you at the Casino!"

"I do not suppose I should be offended," said Sylvia softly.

"I felt, Madame, as if I saw a lily growing in a field of high, rank, evil-smelling — nay, perhaps I should say, poisonous — weeds."

"But I cannot go away now!" cried Sylvia. She was really impressed — very uncomfortably impressed — by his earnest words. "It would be most unkind to my friend, Madame Wolsky. Surely, it is possible to stay at Lacville, and even to play a little, without anything very terrible happening?" She looked at him coaxingly, anxiously, as a child might have done.

But Sylvia was not a child; she was a very lovely young woman. Comte Paul de Virieu's heart began to beat.

But, bah! This was absurd! His day of love and love-making lay far, far behind him. He rose and walked towards the door.

In speaking to her as he had forced himself to speak, the Frenchman had done an unselfish and kindly action. Sylvia's gentle and unsophisticated charm had touched him deeply, and so he had given her what he knew to be the best possible advice.

"I am not so foolish as to pretend that the people who come and play in the Casino of Lacville are all confirmed gamblers," he said, slowly. "We French take our pleasures lightly, Madame, and no doubt there is many an excellent Parisian bourgeois who comes here and makes or loses his few francs, and gets no harm from it. But, still, I swore to myself that I would warn you of the danger —"

They went out into the bright sunshine again, and Sylvia somehow felt as if she had made a friend — a real friend — in the Comte de Virieu. It was a curious sensation, and one that gave her more pleasure than she would have cared to own even to herself.

Most of the men she had met since she became a widow treated her as an irresponsible being. Many of them tried to flirt with her for the mere pleasure of flirting with so pretty a woman; others, so she was resentfully aware, had only become really interested in her when they became aware that she had been left by her husband with an income of two thousand pounds a year. She had had several offers of marriage since her widowhood, but not one of the men who had come and said he loved her had confessed as much about himself as this stranger had done.

She was the more touched and interested because the Frenchman's manner was extremely reserved. Even in the short time she had been at the Villa du Lac, Sylvia had realized that though the Count was on speaking terms with most of his fellow-guests, he seemed intimate with none of the people whose happy chatter had filled the dining room the night before.

Just before going back into the Villa, Sylvia stopped short; she fixed her large ingenuous eyes on the Count's face.

"I want to thank you again," she said diffidently, "for your kindness in giving me this warning. You know we in England have a proverb, 'Forewarned is forearmed.' Well, believe me, I will not forget what you have said, and — and I am grateful for your confidence. Of course, I regard it as quite private."

The Count looked at her for a moment in silence, and then he said very deliberately,

"I am afraid the truth about me is known to all those good enough to concern themselves with my affairs. I am sure, for instance, that your Polish friend is well aware of it! You see before you a man who has lost every penny he owned in the world, who does not know how to work, and who is living on the charity of relations."

Sylvia had never heard such bitter accents issue from human lips before.

"The horse you saw me ride this morning," he went on in a low tone, "is not my horse; it belongs to my brother-in-law. It is sent for me every day because my sister loves me, and she thinks my health will suffer if I do not take exercise. My brother-in-law did not give me the horse, though he is the most generous of human beings, for he feared that if he did I should sell it in order that I might have more money for play."

There was a long, painful pause, then in a lighter tone the Count added, "And now, au revoir, Madame, and forgive me for having thrust my private affairs on your notice! It is not a thing I have been tempted ever to do before with one whom I have the honor of knowing as slightly as I know yourself."

Sylvia went upstairs to her room. She was touched, moved, excited. It was quite a new experience with her to come so really near to any man's heart and conscience.

Life is a secret and a tangled skein, full of loose, almost invisible threads. This curiously intimate, and yet impersonal conversation with one who was not only a stranger, but also a foreigner, made her realize how little we men and women really know of one another. How small was her knowledge, for instance, of Bill Chester — though, to be sure, of him there was perhaps nothing to know. How really little also she knew of Anna Wolsky! They had become friends, and yet Anna had never confided to her any intimate or secret thing about herself. Why, she did not even know Anna's home address!

Sylvia felt that there was now a link which hardly anything could break between herself and this Frenchman, whom she had never seen till a week ago. Even if they never met again after today, she would never forget that he had allowed her to see into the core of his sad, embittered heart. He had lifted a corner of the veil which covered his conscience, and he had done this in order that he might save her, a stranger, from what he knew by personal experience to be a terrible fate!

Chapter VII

*T*wo hours later Sylvia Bailey was having luncheon with Anna Wolsky in the Pension Malfait.

The two hostelries, hers and Anna's, were in almost absurd contrast the one to the other. At the Villa du Lac everything was spacious, luxurious, and quiet. M. Polperro's clients spent, or so Sylvia supposed, much of their time in their own rooms upstairs, or else in the Casino, while many of them had their own motors, and went out on long excursions. They were cosmopolitans, and among them were a number of Russians.

Here at the Pension Malfait, the clientèle was French. All was loud talking, bustle, and laughter. The large house contained several young men who had daily work in Paris. Others, like Madame Wolsky, were at Lacville in order to indulge their passion for play, and quite a number of people came in simply for meals.

Among these last, rather to Sylvia's surprise, were Monsieur and Madame Wachner, the middle-aged couple whom Anna Wolsky had pointed out as having been at Aix-les-Bains the year before, at the same time as she was herself.

The husband and wife were now sitting almost exactly opposite Anna and Sylvia at the narrow table d'hôte, and again a broad, sunny smile lit up the older woman's face when she looked across at the two friends.

"We meet again!" she exclaimed in a guttural voice, and then in French, addressing Madame Wolsky, "This is not very much like Aix-les-Bains, is it, Madame?"

Anna shook her head.

"Still it is a pretty place, Lacville, and cheaper than one would think." She leant across the table, and continued in a confidential undertone: "As for us — my husband and I — we have taken a small villa; he has grown so tired of hotels."

"But surely you had a villa at Aix?" said Anna, in a surprised tone.

"Yes, we had a villa there, certainly. But then a very sad affair happened to us —" she sighed. "You may have heard of it?" and she fixed her small, intensely bright eyes inquiringly on Anna.

Anna bent her head.

"Yes, I heard all about it" she said gravely. "You mean about your friend who was drowned in the lake? It must have been a very distressing thing for you and your husband."

"Yes, indeed! He never can bear to speak of it."

And Sylvia, looking over at the man sitting just opposite to herself, saw a look of unease come over his sallow face. He was eating his omelet steadily, looking neither to the right nor to the left.

"Ami Fritz!" cried his wife, turning suddenly to him, and this time she spoke English, "Say, 'How d'you do,' to this lady! You will remember that we used to see 'er at Aix, in the Casino there?"

"Ami Fritz" bowed his head, but remained silent.

"Yes," his wife went on, volubly, "that sad affair made Aix very unpleasant to us! After that we spent the winter in various pensions, and then, instead of going back to Aix, we came 'ere. So far, I am quite satisfied with Lacville."

Though she spoke with a very bad accent and dropped her aitches, her English was quick and colloquial.

"Lacville is a cozy, 'appy place!" she cried, and this time she smiled full at Sylvia, and Sylvia told herself that the woman's face, if very plain, was like a sunflower, — so broad, so kindly, so good-humored!

When déjeuner was over, the four had coffee together, and the melancholy Monsieur Wachner, who was so curiously unlike his bright, vivacious wife, at last broke into eager talk, for he and Anna Wolsky had begun to discuss different gambling systems. His face lighted up; it was easy to see what interested and stimulated this long, lanky man whose wife addressed him constantly as "Ami Fritz."

"Now 'e is what the English call 'obby-'orse riding," she exclaimed, with a loud laugh. "To see 'im in all 'is glory you should see my Fritz at Monte Carlo!" she was speaking to Sylvia. "There 'as never been a system invented in connection with that devil-game, Roulette, that L'Ami Fritz does not know, and that 'e 'as not — at some time or other — played more to 'is satisfaction than to mine!" But she spoke very good-humoredly. "'E cannot ring many changes on Baccarat, and I do not often allow 'im to play downstairs. No, no, that is too dangerous! That is for children and fools!"

Sylvia was still too ignorant of play to understand the full significance of Madame Wachner's words, but she was vaguely interested, though she could not understand one word of the eager talk between Anna and the man.

"Let us leave them at it!" exclaimed the older woman, suddenly. "It will be much nicer in the garden, Madame, for it is not yet too 'ot for out of doors. By the way, I forgot to tell you my name. That was very rude of me! My name is Wachner — Sophie Wachner, at your service."

"And my name is Bailey — Sylvia Bailey."

"Ah, I thought so — you are a Mees!"

"No," said Sylvia gravely, "I am a widow."

Madame Wachner's face became very serious.

"Ah," she said, sympathetically, "that is sad — very sad for one so young and so beautiful!"

Sylvia smiled. Madame Wachner was certainly a kindly, warm-hearted sort of woman.

They walked out together into the narrow garden, and soon Madame Wachner began to amuse her companion by lively, shrewd talk, and they spent a pleasant half hour pacing up and down.

The Wachners seemed to have traveled a great deal about the world and especially in several of the British Colonies.

It was in New Zealand that Madame Wachner had learnt to speak English: "My 'usband, 'e was in business there," she said vaguely.

"And you?" she asked at last, fixing her piercing eyes on the pretty Englishwoman, and allowing them to travel down till they rested on the milky row of perfectly-matched pearls.

"Oh, this is my first visit to France," answered Sylvia, "and I am enjoying it very much indeed."

"Then you 'ave not gambled for money yet?" observed Madame Wachner. "In England they are too good to gamble!" She spoke sarcastically, but Sylvia did not know that.

"I never in my life played for money till last week, and then I won thirty francs!"

"Ah! Then now surely you will join the Club?"

"Yes," said Sylvia a little awkwardly. "I suppose I shall join the Club. You see, my friend is so fond of play."

"I believe you there!" cried the other, familiarly. "We used to watch Madame Wolsky at Aix — my 'usband and I. It seems so strange that there we never spoke to 'er, and that now we seem to know 'er already so much better than we did in all the weeks we were together at Aix! But there" — she sighed a loud, heaving sigh — "we 'ad a friend — a dear young friend — with us at Aix-les-Bains."

"Yes, I know," said Sylvia, sympathizingly.

"You know?" Madame Wachner looked at her quickly. "What is it that you know, Madame?"

"Madame Wolsky told me about it. Your friend was drowned, was he not? It must have been very sad and dreadful for you and your husband."

"It was terrible!" said Madame Wachner vehemently. "Terrible!"

*T*he hour in the garden sped by very quickly, and Sylvia was rather sorry when it came to be time to start for the Casino.

"Look here!" cried Madame Wachner suddenly. "Why should not L'Ami Fritz escort Madame Wolsky to the Casino while you and I take a pretty drive? I am so tired of that old Casino — and you will be so tired of it soon, too!" she exclaimed in an aside to Sylvia.

Sylvia looked questioningly at Anna.

"Yes, do take a drive, dear. You have plenty of time, for I intend to spend all this afternoon and evening at the Casino," said Madame Wolsky, quickly, in answer to Sylvia's look. "It will do quite well if you come there after you have had your tea. My friend will never go without her afternoon tea;" she turned to Madame Wachner.

"I, too, love afternoon tea!" cried Madame Wachner, in a merry tone. "Then that is settled! You and I will take a drive, and then we will 'ave tea and then go to the Casino."

Mrs. Bailey accompanied her friend upstairs while Anna put on her things and got out her money.

"You will enjoy a drive on this hot day, even with that funny old woman," said Madame Wolsky, affectionately. "And meanwhile I will get your membership card made out for the Club. If you like to do so, you might have a little gamble this evening. But I do not want my sweet English friend to become as fond of play as I am myself" — there crept a sad note into her voice. "However, I do not think there is any fear of that!"

When the two friends came downstairs again, they found Monsieur and Madame Wachner standing close together and speaking in a low voice. As she came nearer to them Sylvia saw that they were so absorbed in each other that they did not see her, and she heard the man saying in a low, angry voice, in French: "There is nothing to be done here at all, Sophie! It is foolish of us to waste our time like this!" And then Madame Wachner answered quickly, "You are always so gloomy, so hopeless! I tell you there *is* something to be done. Leave it to me!"

Then, suddenly becoming aware that Sylvia was standing beside her, the old woman went on: "My 'usband, Madame, always says there is nothing to be done! You see, 'e is tired of 'is last system, and 'e 'as not yet invented another. But, bah! I say to 'im that no doubt luck will come today. 'E may find Madame Wolsky a mascot." She was very red and looked disturbed.

"I 'ave asked them to telephone for an open carriage," Madame Wachner added, in a better-humored tone. "It will be here in three or four minutes. Shall we drive you first to the Casino?" This question she asked of her husband.

"No," said Monsieur Wachner, harshly, "certainly not! I will walk in any case."

"And I will walk too," said Anna, who had just come up. "There is no need at all for us to take you out of your way. You had better drive at once into the open country, Sylvia."

And so they all started, Madame Wolsky and her tall, gaunt, morose companion, walking, while Sylvia and Madame Wachner drove off in the opposite direction.

The country immediately round Lacville is not pretty; the little open carriage was rather creaky, and the horse was old and tired, and yet Sylvia Bailey enjoyed her drive very much.

Madame Wachner, common-looking, plain, almost grotesque in appearance though she was, possessed that rare human attribute, vitality.

Sometimes she spoke in French, sometimes in English, changing from the one to the other with perfect ease; and honestly pleased at having escaped a long, dull, hot afternoon in the Casino, the older woman set herself to please and amuse Sylvia. She thoroughly succeeded. A clever gossip, she seemed to know a great deal about all sorts of interesting people, and she gave Sylvia an amusing account of Princess Mathilde Bonaparte, whose splendid château they saw from their little carriage.

Madame Wachner also showed the most sympathetic interest in Sylvia and Sylvia's past life. Soon the Englishwoman found herself telling her new acquaintance a great deal about her childhood and girlhood — something even of her brief, not unhappy, married life. But she shrank back, both mentally and physically, when Madame Wachner carelessly observed, "Ah, but soon you will marry again; no doubt you are already engaged?"

"Oh, no!" Sylvia shook her head.

"But you are young and beautiful. It would be a crime for you not to get married again!" Madame Wachner persisted; and then, "I love beauty," she cried enthusiastically. "You did not see me, Madame, last week, but I saw you, and I said to my 'usband, 'There is a very beautiful person come to Lacville, Fritz!' 'E laughed at me. 'Now you will be satisfied — now you will 'ave something to look at,' 'e says. And it is quite true! When I come back that night I was very sorry to see you not there. But we will meet often now," she concluded pleasantly, "for I suppose, Madame, that you too intend to play?"

That was the second time she had asked the question.

"I shall play a little," said Sylvia, blushing, "but of course I do not want to get into the habit of gambling."

"No, indeed, that would be terrible! And then there are not many who can afford to gamble and to lose their good money." She looked inquiringly at Sylvia. "But, there," she sighed — her fat face became very grave — "it is extraordinary 'ow some people manage to get money — I mean those 'oo are determined to play!"

And then, changing the subject, Madame Wachner suddenly began to tell her new acquaintance all about the tragic death by drowning of her and her husband's friend at Aix-les-Bains the year before. She now spoke in French, but with a peculiar guttural accent.

"I never talk of it before Fritz," she said quickly, "but, of course, we both often think of it still. Oh, it was a terrible thing! We were devoted to this young Russian friend of ours. He and Fritz worked an excellent system together — the best Fritz ever invented — and for a little while they made money. But his terribly sad death broke our luck" — she shook her head ominously.

"How did it happen?" said Sylvia sympathetically.

And then Madame Wachner once again broke into her h-less English.

"They went together in a boat on Lake Bourget — it is a real lake, that lake, not like the little fishpond 'ere. A storm came on, and the boat upset. Fritz did his best to save the unfortunate one, but 'e could not swim. You can imagine my sensations? I was in a summer-'ouse, trembling with fright. Thunder, lightning, rain, storm, all round! Suddenly I see Fritz, pale as death, wet through, totter up the path from the lake. 'Where is Sasha?' I shriek out to 'im. And 'e shake 'is 'ead despairingly — Sasha was in the lake!"

The speaker stared before her with a look of vivid terror on her face. It was almost as if she saw the scene she was describing — nay, as if she saw the pale, dead face of the drowned man. It gave her companion a cold feeling of fear.

"And was it long before they found him?" asked Sylvia in a low tone.

"They never did find 'im," said Madame Wachner, her voice sinking to a whisper. "That was the extraordinary thing — Sasha's body was never found! Many people thought the money 'e 'ad on 'is person weighed 'im down, kept 'im entangled in the weeds at the bottom of the lake. Did not your friend tell you it made talk?"

"Yes," said Sylvia.

"'E 'ad not much money on 'is person," repeated Madame Wachner, "but still there was a good deal more than was found in 'is bedroom. That, of course, was 'anded over to the authorities. They insisted on keeping it."

"But I suppose his family got it in the end?" said Sylvia.

"No. 'E 'ad no family. You see, our friend was a Russian nobleman, but he had also been a Nihilist, so 'e 'ad concealed 'is identity. It was fortunate for us that we 'ad got to know an important person in the police; but for that we might 'ave 'ad much worry" — she shook her head. "They were so much annoyed that poor Sasha 'ad no passport. But, as I said to them — for Fritz quite lost 'is 'ead, and could say nothing — not 'alf, no, not a quarter of the strangers in Aix 'as passports, though, of course, it is a good and useful thing to 'ave one. I suppose, Madame, that *you* 'ave a passport?"

She stopped short, and looked at Sylvia with that eager, inquiring look which demands an answer even to the most unimportant question.

"A passport?" repeated Sylvia Bailey, surprised. "No, indeed! I've never even seen one. Why should I have a passport?"

"When you are abroad it is always a good thing to 'ave a passport," said Madame Wachner quickly. "You see, it enables you to be identified. It gives your address at 'ome. But I do not think that you can get one now — no, it is a thing that one must get in one's own country, or, at any rate," she corrected herself, "in a country where you 'ave resided a long time."

"What is your country, Madame?" asked Sylvia. "Are you French? I suppose Monsieur Wachner is German?"

Madame Wachner shook her head.

"Oh, 'e would be cross to 'ear that! No, no, Fritz is Viennese — a gay Viennese! As for me, I am" — she waited a moment — "well, Madame, I am what the French call *'une vraie cosmopolite'* — oh, yes, I am a true citizeness of the world."

Chapter VIII

*T*hey had been driving a considerable time, and at last the coachman, turning round on his seat, asked where they wished to go next.

"I ask you to come and 'ave tea with me," said Madame Wachner turning to Sylvia. "We are not very far from the Châlet des Muguets, and I 'ave some excellent tea there. We will 'ave a rest, and tell the man to come back for us in one hour. What do you think of that, Madame?"

"It is very kind of you," said Sylvia gratefully; and, indeed, she did think it very kind. It would be pleasant to rest a while in the Wachner's villa and have tea there.

Sylvia was in the mood to enjoy every new experience, however trifling, and she had never been in a French private house.

"Au Châlet des Muguets," called out Madame Wachner to the driver.

He nodded and turned his horse round.

Soon they were making their way along newly-made roads, cut through what had evidently been, not so very long before, a great stretch of forest land.

"The good people of Lacville are in a hurry to make money," observed Madame Wachner in French. "I am told that land here has nearly trebled in value the last few years, though houses are still cheap."

"It seems a pity they should destroy such beautiful woods," said Sylvia regretfully, remembering what the Comte de Virieu had said only that morning.

The other shrugged her shoulders, "I do not care for scenery — no, not at all!" she exclaimed complacently.

The carriage drew up with a jerk before a small white gate set in low, rough, wood palings. Behind the palings lay a large, straggling, and untidy garden, relieved from absolute ugliness by some high forest trees which had been allowed to remain when the house in the center of the plot of ground was built.

Madame Wachner stepped heavily out of the carriage, and Sylvia followed her, feeling amused and interested. She wondered very much what the inside of the funny little villa she saw before her would be like. In any case, the outside of the Châlet des Muguets was almost ludicrously unlike the English houses to which she was accustomed.

Very strange, quaint, and fantastic looked the one-storey building, standing far higher than any bungalow Sylvia had ever seen, in a lawn of high, rank grass.

The walls of the Châlet des Muguets were painted bright pink, picked out with sham brown beams, which in their turn were broken at intervals by large blue china lozenges, on which were painted the giant branches of lilies-of-the-valley which gave the villa its inappropriate name!

The chocolate-colored row of shutters were now closed to shut out the heat, for the sun beat down pitilessly on the little house, and the whole place had a curiously deserted, unlived-in appearance.

Sylvia secretly wondered how the Wachners could bear to leave the garden, which might have been made so pretty with a little care, in such a state of neglect and untidiness. Even the path leading up to the side of the house, where jutted out a mean-looking door, was covered with weeds.

But Madame Wachner was evidently very pleased with her temporary home, and quite satisfied with its surroundings.

"It is a pretty 'ouse, is it not?" she asked in English, and smiling broadly. "And only one thousand francs, furnished, for the 'ole season!"

Sylvia quickly made a mental calculation. Forty pounds? Yes, she supposed that was very cheap — for Lacville.

"We come in May, and we may stay till October," said Madame Wachner, still speaking in a satisfied tone. "I made a bargain with a woman from the town. She comes each morning, cooks what I want, and does the 'ousework. Often we 'ave our déjeuner out and dine at 'ome, or we dine close to the Casino — just as we choose. Food is so dear in France, it makes little difference whether we stay at 'ome or not for meals."

They were now close to the chocolate-colored door of the Châlet, and Madame Wachner, to Sylvia Bailey's surprise and amusement, lifted a corner of the shabby outside mat, and took from under it a key. With it she opened the door. "Walk in," she said familiarly, "and welcome, Madame, to my 'ome!"

Sylvia found herself in a bare little hall, so bare indeed that there was not even a hat and umbrella stand there.

Her hostess walked past her and opened a door which gave into a darkened room.

"This is our dining room," she said proudly. "Walk in, Madame. It is 'ere we had better 'ave tea, perhaps."

Sylvia followed her. How dark, and how very hot it was in here! She could see absolutely nothing for some moments, for she was blinded by the sudden change from the bright light of the hall to the dim twilight of the closely-shuttered room.

Then gradually she began to see everything — or rather the little there was to be seen — and she felt surprised, and a little disappointed.

The dining room was more than plainly furnished; it was positively ugly.

The furniture consisted of a round table standing on an unpolished parquet floor, of six cane chairs set against the wall, and of a walnut-wood buffet, on the shelves of which stood no plates, or ornaments of any description. The walls were distempered a reddish-pink color, and here and there the color had run in streaky patches.

"Is it not charming?" exclaimed Madame Wachner. "And now I will show you our pretty little salon!"

Sylvia followed her out into the hall, and so to the left into the short passage which ran down the center of the tiny house.

The drawing room of the Châlet des Muguets was a little larger than the dining room, but it was equally bare of anything pretty or even convenient. There was a small sofa, covered with cheap tapestry, and four uncomfortable-looking chairs to match; on the sham marble mantelpiece stood a gilt and glass clock and two chandeliers. There was not a book, not a paper, not a flower.

Both rooms gave Sylvia a strange impression that they were very little lived in. But then, of course, the Wachners were very little at home.

"And now I will get tea," said Madame Wachner triumphantly.

"Will you not let me help you?" asked Sylvia, timidly. "I love making tea — every Englishwoman loves making tea." She had no wish to be left in this dull, ugly little drawing room by herself.

"Oh, but your pretty dress! Would it not get 'urt in the kitchen?" cried Madame Wachner deprecatingly.

But she allowed Sylvia to follow her into the bright, clean little kitchen, of which the door was just opposite the drawing room.

"What a charming little *cuisine!*" cried Sylvia smiling. She was glad to find something that she could honestly praise, and the kitchen was, in truth, the pleasantest place in the house, exquisitely neat, with the brass *batterie de cuisine* shining and bright. "Your day servant must be an exceptionally clean woman."

"Yes," said Madame Wachner, in a rather dissatisfied tone, "she is well enough. But, oh, those French people, how eager they are for money! Do you suppose that woman ever stays one minute beyond her time? No, indeed!"

Even as she spoke she was pouring water into a little kettle, and lighting a spirit lamp. Then, going to a cupboard, she took out two cups and a cracked china teapot.

Sylvia did her part by cutting some bread and butter, and, as she stood at the white table opposite the kitchen window, she saw that beyond the small piece of garden which lay at the back of the house was a dense chestnut wood, only separated from the Châlet des Muguets by a straggling hedge.

"Does the wood belong to you, too?" she asked.

Madame Wachner shook her head.

"Oh! no," she said, "that is for sale!"

"You must find it very lonely here at night," said Sylvia, musingly, "you do not seem to have any neighbors either to the right or left."

"There is a villa a little way down the road," said Madame Wachner quickly. "But we are not nervous people — and then we 'ave nothing it would be worth anybody's while to steal."

Sylvia reminded herself that the Wachners must surely have a good deal of money in the house if they gambled as much as Anna Wolsky said they did. Her hostess could not keep it all in the little bag which she always carried hung on her wrist.

And then, as if Madame Wachner had seen straight into her mind, the old woman said significantly. "As to our money, I will show you where we keep it. Come into my bedroom; perhaps you will take off your hat there; then we shall be what English people call 'cozy.'"

Madame Wachner led the way again into the short passage, and so into a large bedroom, which looked, like the kitchen, on to the back garden.

After the kitchen, this bedroom struck Sylvia as being the pleasantest room in the Châlet des Muguets, and that although, like the dining room and drawing room, it was extraordinarily bare.

There was no chest of drawers, no dressing-table, no cupboard to be seen. Madame Wachner's clothes hung on pegs behind the door, and there was a large brass-bound trunk in a corner of the room.

But the broad, low bed looked very comfortable, and there was a bathroom next door.

Madame Wachner showed her guest the bathroom with great pride.

"This is the 'English comfortable,'" she said, using the quaint phrase the French have invented to express the acme of domestic luxury. "My 'usband will never allow me to take a 'ouse that has no bathroom. 'E is very clean about 'imself" — she spoke as if it was a fact to be proud of, and Sylvia could not help smiling.

"I suppose there are still many French houses without a bathroom," she said.

"Yes," said Madame Wachner quickly, "the French are not a clean people," — she shook her head scornfully.

"I suppose you keep your money in that box?" said Sylvia, looking at the brass-bound trunk.

"No, indeed! *This* is where I keep it!"

Madame Wachner suddenly lifted her thin alpaca skirt, and Sylvia, with astonishment, saw that hung round her capacious waist were a number of little wash-leather bags. "My money is all 'ere!" exclaimed Madame Wachner, laughing heartily. "It rests — oh, so cozily — against my petticoat."

They went back into the kitchen. The water was boiling, and Sylvia made the tea, Madame Wachner looking on with eager interest.

"La! La! it will be strong! I only put a pinch for ourselves. And now go into the dining room, and I will bring the teapot there to you, Madame!"

"No, no," said Sylvia laughing, "why should we not drink our tea here, in this pretty kitchen?"

The other looked at her doubtfully. "Shall we?"

"Yes, of course!" cried Sylvia.

They drew up two rush-bottomed chairs to the table and sat down.

Sylvia thoroughly enjoyed this first taste of Madame Wachner's hospitality. The drive and the great heat had made her feel tired and languid, and the tea did her good.

"I will go and see if the carriage is there," said Madame Wachner at last.

While her hostess was away, Sylvia looked round her with some curiosity.

What an extraordinary mode of life these people had chosen for themselves! If the Wachners were rich enough to gamble, surely they had enough money to live more comfortably than they were now doing? It was clear that they hardly used the dining room and drawing room of the little villa at all. When Sylvia had been looking for the butter, she had not been able to help seeing that in the tiny larder there was only a small piece of cheese, a little cold meat, and a couple of eggs on a plate. No wonder Monsieur Wachner had heartily enjoyed the copious, if rather roughly-prepared, meal at the Pension Malfait.

"Yes, the carriage is there," said Madame Wachner bustling back. "And now we must be quick, or L'Ami Fritz will be cross! Do you know that absurd man actually still thinks 'e is master, and yet we 'ave been married — oh, I do not know 'ow many years! But he always loves seeing me even after we 'ave been separated but two hours or so!"

Together they went out, Madame Wachner carefully locking the door and hiding the key where she had found it, under the mat outside.

Sylvia could not help laughing.

"I really wonder you do that," she observed. "Just think how easy it would be for anyone to get into the house!"

"Yes, that is true, but there is nothing to steal. As I tell you, we always carry our money about with us," said Madame Wachner. She added in a serious tone, "and I should advise you to do so too, my dear young friend."

Chapter IX

A quarter of an hour's sharp driving brought Sylvia and Madame Wachner to the door of the Casino. They found Madame Wolsky in the hall waiting for them.

"I couldn't think what had happened to you!" she exclaimed in an anxious tone. "But here is your membership card, Sylvia. Now you are free of the Baccarat tables!"

Monsieur Wachner met his wife with a frowning face. He might be pleased to see Madame Wachner, but he showed his pleasure in an odd manner. Soon, however, the secret of his angry look was revealed, for Madame Wachner opened the leather bag hanging from her wrist and took out of it a hundred francs.

"Here, Fritz," she cried, gaily. "You can now begin your play!"

Sylvia Bailey felt very much amused. So poor "Ami Fritz" was not allowed to gamble unless his wife were there to see that he did not go too far. No wonder he had looked impatient and eager, as well as cross! He had been engaged — that was clear — in putting down the turns of the game, and in working out what were no doubt abstruse calculations connected with his system.

The Club was very full, and it was a little difficult at that hour of the late afternoon to get near enough to a table to play comfortably; but a stranger had kindly kept Anna Wolsky's place for her.

"I have been quite lucky," she whispered to Sylvia. "I have made three hundred francs, and now I think I will rest a bit! Slip in here, dear, and I will stand behind you. I do not advise you to risk more than twenty francs the first time; on the other hand, if you feel *en veine*, if the luck seems persistent — it sometimes is when one first plays with gold — then be bold, and do not hesitate!"

Sylvia, feeling rather bewildered, slipped into her friend's place, and Anna kept close behind her.

With a hand that trembled a little, she put a twenty-franc piece down on the green table. After doing so she looked up, and saw that the Comte de Virieu was standing nearly opposite to her, on the other side of the table.

His eyes were fixed on her, and there was a very kind and indulgent, if sad, smile on his face. As their glances met he leant forward and also put a twenty-franc piece on the green cloth close to where Sylvia's money lay.

The traditional words rang out: *"Faites vos jeux, Messieurs, Mesdames! Le jeu est fait! Rien ne va plus!"*

And then Sylvia saw her stake and that of the Count doubled. There were now four gold pieces where two had been.

"Leave your money on, and see what happens," whispered Anna. "After all you are only risking twenty francs!"

And Sylvia obediently followed the advice.

Again there came a little pause; once more the words which she had not yet learnt to understand rang out in the croupier's monotonous voice.

She looked round her; there was anxiety and watchful suspense on all the eager faces. The Comte de Virieu alone looked indifferent.

A moment later four gold pieces were added to the four already there.

"You had better take up your winnings, or someone may claim them," muttered Anna anxiously.

"Oh, but I don't like to do that," said Sylvia.

"Of course you must!"

She put out her hand and took up her four gold pieces, leaving those of the Count on the table. Then suddenly she put back the eighty francs on the cloth, and smiled up at him; it was a gay little shame-faced smile. "Please don't be cross with me, kind friend," — that is what Sylvia's smile seemed to say to Paul de Virieu — "but this is so *very* exciting!"

He felt stirred to the heart. How sweet, how confidingly simple she looked! And — and how very beautiful. He at once loved and hated to see her there, his new little *"amie Anglaise!"*

"Are you going to leave the whole of it on this time?" whispered Anna.

"Yes, I think I will. It's rather fun. After all, I'm only risking twenty francs!" whispered back Sylvia.

And once more she won.

"What a pity you didn't start playing with a hundred francs! Think of how rich you would be now," said Anna, with the true gambler's instinct. "But it is clear, child, that you are going to do well this evening, and I shall follow your luck! Take the money off now, however."

Sylvia waited to see what the Count would do. Their eyes asked and answered the same question. He gave an imperceptible nod, and she took up her winnings — eight gold pieces!

It was well that she had done so, for the next deal of the cards favored the banker.

Then something very surprising happened to Sylvia.

Someone — she thought it was Monsieur Wachner — addressed the croupier whose duty it was to deal out the cards, and said imperiously, *"A Madame la main!"*

Hardly knowing what she was doing, Sylvia took up the cards which had been pushed towards her. A murmur of satisfaction ran round the table, for there lay what even she had learnt by now was the winning number, a nine of hearts, and the second card was the king of clubs.

Again and again, she turned up winning numbers — the eight and the ace, the five and the four, the six and the three — every combination which brought luck to the table and confusion to the banker.

Eyes full of adoring admiration, aye and gratitude, were turned on the young Englishwoman. Paul de Virieu alone did not look at her. But he followed her play.

"Now put on a hundred francs," said Anna, authoritatively.

Sylvia looked at her, rather surprised by the advice, but she obeyed it. And still the Comte de Virieu followed her lead.

That made her feel dreadfully nervous and excited — it would be so terrible to make him lose too!

Neither of them lost. On the contrary, ten napoleons were added to the double pile of gold.

And then, after that, it seemed as if the whole table were following Sylvia's game.

"That pretty Englishwoman is playing for the first time!" — so the word went round. And they all began backing her luck with feverish haste.

The banker, a good-looking young Frenchman, stared at Sylvia ruefully. Thanks to her, he was being badly punished. Fortunately, he could afford it.

At the end of half an hour, feeling tired and bewildered by her good fortune, Mrs. Bailey got up and moved away from the table, the possessor of £92. The Comte Virieu had won exactly the same amount.

Now everybody looked pleased except the banker. For the first time a smile irradiated Monsieur Wachner's long face.

As for Madame Wachner, she was overjoyed. Catching Sylvia by the hand, she exclaimed, in her curious, woolly French, "I would like to embrace you! But I know that English ladies do not like kissing in public. It is splendid – splendid! Look at all the people you have made happy."

"But how about the poor banker?" asked Sylvia, blushing.

"Oh, 'e is all right. 'E is very rich."

Madame Wolsky, like the Count, had exactly followed her friend's play, but not as soon as he had done. Still, she also had made over £80.

"Two thousand francs!" she cried, joyfully. "That is very good for a beginning. And you?" she turned to Monsieur Wachner.

He hesitated, and looked at his wife deprecatingly.

"L'Ami Fritz," said Madame Wachner, *"will* play 'is system, Mesdames. However, I am glad to say that today he soon gave it up in honor of our friend here. What 'ave you made?" she asked him.

"Only eight hundred francs," he said, his face clouding over. "If you had given me more than that hundred francs, Sophie, I might have made five thousand in the time."

"Bah!" she said. "That does not matter. We must not risk more than a hundred francs a day – you know how often I've told you that, Fritz." She was now speaking in French, very quickly and angrily.

But Sylvia hardly heard. She could not help wondering why the Count had not come up and congratulated her. The thought that she had brought him luck was very pleasant to her.

He had left off playing, and was standing back, near one of the windows. He had not even glanced across to the place where she stood. This aloofness gave Sylvia a curious little feeling of discomfiture. Why, several strangers had come up and cordially thanked her for bringing them such luck.

"Let us come out of this place and 'ave some ices," exclaimed Madame Wachner, suddenly. "When l'Ami Fritz 'as a stroke of luck 'e often treats 'is old wife to an ice."

The four went out of the Casino and across the way to an hotel, which, as Madame Wachner explained to her two new friends, contained the best restaurant in Lacville. The sun was sinking, and, though it was still very hot, there was a pleasant breeze coming up from the lake.

Sylvia felt excited and happy. How wonderful – how marvelous – to make nearly £100 out of a twenty-franc piece! That was what she had done this afternoon.

And then, rather to her surprise, after they had all enjoyed ices and cakes at Madame Wachner's expense, Anna Wolsky and l'Ami Fritz declared they were going back to the Casino.

"I don't mean to play again tonight," said Sylvia, firmly. "I feel dreadfully tired," and the excitement had indeed worn her out. She longed to go back to the Hôtel du Lac.

Still, she accompanied the others to the Club, and together with Madame Wachner, she sat down some way from the tables. In a very few minutes they were joined by the other two, who had by now lost quite enough gold pieces to make them both feel angry with themselves, and, what was indeed unfair, with poor Sylvia.

"I'm sure that if you had played again, and if we had followed your play, we should have added to our winnings instead of losing, as we have done," said Anna crossly.

"I'm so sorry," and Sylvia felt really distressed. Anna had never spoken crossly to her before.

"Forgive me!" cried the Polish woman, suddenly softening. "I ought not to have said that to you, dear little friend. No doubt we should all have lost just the same. You know that fortune-teller told me that I should make plenty of money — well, even now I have had a splendid day!"

"Do come back with me and have dinner at the Villa du Lac," said Sylvia eagerly.

They shook hands with the Wachners, and as they walked the short distance from the Casino to the villa, Sylvia told Anna all about her visit to the Châlet des Muguets.

"They seem nice homely people," she said, "and Madame Wachner was really very kind."

"Yes, no doubt; but she is a very strict wife," answered Anna smiling. "The poor man had not one penny piece till she came in, and he got so angry and impatient waiting for her! I really felt inclined to lend him a little money; but I have made it a rule never to lend money in a Casino; it only leads to unpleasantness afterwards."

In the hall of the Villa du Lac the Comte de Virieu was standing reading a paper. He was dressed for dinner, and he bowed distantly as the two ladies came in.

"Why, there is the Comte de Virieu!" exclaimed Anna, in a low, and far from a pleased tone. "I had no idea he was staying here."

"Yes, he is staying here," said Sylvia, blushing uneasily, and quickly she led the way upstairs. It wanted a few minutes to seven.

Anna Wolsky waited till the door of Sylvia's room was shut, and then,

"I cannot help being sorry that you are staying in the same hotel as that man," she said, seriously. "Do not get to know him too well, dear Sylvia. The Count is a worthless individual; he has gambled away two fortunes. And now, instead of working, he is content to live on an allowance made to him by his sister's husband, the Duc d'Eglemont. If I were you, I should keep on very distant terms with him. He is, no doubt, always looking out for a nice rich woman to marry."

Sylvia made no answer. She felt she could not trust herself to speak; and there came over her a feeling of intense satisfaction that Anna Wolsky was not staying here with her at the Villa du Lac.

She also made up her mind that next time she entertained Anna she would do so at the restaurant of which the cooking had been so highly commended by Madame Wachner.

The fact that Madame Wolsky thought so ill of the Comte de Virieu made Sylvia feel uncomfortable all through dinner. But the Count, though he again bowed when the two friends came into the dining room, did not come over and speak to them, as Sylvia had felt sure he would do this evening.

After dinner he disappeared, and Sylvia took Anna out into the garden. But she did not show her the *potager*. The old kitchen-garden already held for her associations which she did not wish to spoil or even to disturb.

Madame Wolsky, sipping M. Polperro's excellent coffee, again mentioned the Count.

"I am exceedingly surprised to see him here at Lacville," she said in a musing voice, "I should have expected him to go to a more *chic* place. He always plays in the winter at Monte Carlo."

Sylvia summoned up courage to protest.

"But, Anna," she exclaimed, "surely the Comte de Virieu is only doing what a great many other people do!"

Anna laughed good-humoredly.

"I see what you mean," she said. "You think it is a case of 'the pot calling the kettle black.' How excellent are your English proverbs, dear Sylvia! But no, it is quite different. Take me. I have an income, and choose to spend it in gambling. I might prefer to have a big house, or perhaps I should say a small house, for I am not a very rich woman. But no, I like play, and I am free to spend my money as I like. The Comte de Virieu is very differently situated! He is, so I've been told, a clever, cultivated man. He ought to be working — doing something for his country's good. And then he is so disagreeable! He makes no friends, no acquaintances. He always looks as if he was doing something of which he was ashamed. He never appears gay or satisfied, not even when he is winning —"

"He does not look as cross as Monsieur Wachner," said Sylvia, smiling.

"Monsieur Wachner is like me," said Anna calmly. "He probably made a fortune in business, and now he and his wife enjoy risking a little money at play. Why should they not?"

"Madame Wachner told me today all about their poor friend who was drowned," said Sylvia irrelevantly.

"Ah, yes, that was a sad affair! They were very foolish to become so intimate with him. Why, they actually had him staying with them at the time! You see, they had a villa close to the lake-side. And this young Russian, it appears, was very fond of boating. It was a mysterious affair, because, oddly enough, he had not been out in the town, or even to the Casino, for four days before the accident happened. There was a notion among some people that he had committed suicide, but that, I fancy, was not so. He had won a large sum of money. Some thought the gold weighed down his body in the water —. But that is absurd. It must have been the weeds."

"Madame Wachner told me that quite a lot of money was found in his room," said Sylvia quickly.

"No, that is not true. About four hundred francs were found in his bedroom. That was all. I fancy the police made themselves rather unpleasant to Monsieur Wachner. The Russian Embassy made inquiries, and it seemed so odd to the French authorities that the poor fellow could not be identified. They found no passport, no papers of any sort —"

"Have you a passport?" asked Sylvia. "Madame Wachner asked me if I had one. But I've never even seen a passport!"

"No," said Anna, "I have not got a passport now. I once had one, but I lost it. One does not require such a thing in a civilized country! But a Russian must always have a passport, it is an absolute law in Russia. And the disappearance of that young man's passport was certainly strange — in fact, the whole affair was mysterious."

"It must have been terrible for Monsieur and Madame Wachner," said Sylvia thoughtfully.

"Oh yes, very disagreeable indeed! Luckily he is entirely absorbed in his absurd systems, and she is a very cheerful woman."

"Yes, indeed she is!" Sylvia could not help smiling. "I am glad we have got to know them, Anna. It is rather mournful when one knows no one at all in a place of this kind."

And Anna agreed, indifferently.

Chapter X

*A*nd then there began a series of long cloudless days for Sylvia Bailey. For the first time she felt as if she was seeing life, and such seeing was very pleasant to her.

Not in her wildest dreams, during the placid days of her girlhood and brief married life, had she conceived of so interesting and so exhilarating an existence as that which she was now leading! And this was perhaps owing in a measure to the fact that there is, if one may so express it, a spice of naughtiness in life as led at Lacville.

In a mild, a very mild, way Sylvia Bailey had fallen a victim to the Goddess of Play. She soon learned to look forward to the hours she and Anna Wolsky spent each day at the baccarat tables. But, unlike Anna, Sylvia was never tempted to risk a greater sum on that dangerous green cloth than she could comfortably afford to lose, and perhaps just because this was so, on the whole she won money rather than lost it.

A certain change had come over the relations of the two women. They still met daily, if only at the Casino, and they occasionally took a walk or a drive together, but Madame Wolsky — and Sylvia Bailey felt uneasy and growing concern that it was so — now lived for play, and play alone.

Absorbed in the simple yet fateful turns of the game, Anna would remain silent for hours, immersed in calculations, and scarcely aware of what went on round her. She and Monsieur Wachner — "L'Ami Fritz," as even Sylvia had fallen into the way of calling him — seemed scarcely alive unless they were standing or sitting round a baccarat table, putting down or taking up the shining gold pieces which they treated as carelessly as if they were counters.

But it was not the easy, idle, purposeless life she was now leading that brought the pretty English widow that strange, unacknowledged feeling of entire content with life.

What made existence at Lacville so exciting and so exceptionally interesting to Sylvia Bailey was her friendship with Comte Paul de Virieu.

There is in every woman a passion for romance, and in Sylvia this passion had been baulked, not satisfied, by her first marriage.

Bill Chester loved her well and deeply, but he was her lawyer and trustee as well as her lover. He had an honest, straightforward nature, and when with her something always prompted Chester to act the part of candid friend, and the part of candid friend fits in very ill with that of lover. To take but one example of how ill his honesty of purpose served him in the matter, Sylvia had never really forgiven him the "fuss" he had made about her string of pearls.

But with the Comte de Virieu she never quite knew what to be at, and mystery is the food of romance.

At the Villa du Lac the two were almost inseparable, and yet so intelligently and quietly did the Count arrange their frequent meetings – their long walks and talks in the large deserted garden, their pleasant morning saunters through the little town – that no one, or so Sylvia believed, was aware of any special intimacy between them.

Sometimes, as they paced up and down the flower-bordered paths of the old kitchen-garden, or when, tired of walking, they made their way into the orangery and sat down on the circular stone bench by the fountain, Sylvia would remember, deep in her heart, the first time Count Paul had brought her there; and how she had been a little frightened, not perhaps altogether unpleasantly so, by his proximity!

She had feared – but she was now deeply ashamed of having entertained such a thought – that he might suddenly begin making violent love to her, that he might perhaps try to kiss her! Were not all Frenchmen of his type rather gay dogs?

But nothing – nothing of the sort had ever been within measurable distance of happening. On the contrary, he always treated her with scrupulous respect, and he never – and this sometimes piqued Sylvia – made love to her, or attempted to flirt with her. Instead, he talked to her in that intimate, that confiding fashion which a woman finds so attractive in a man when she has reason to believe his confidences are made to her alone.

When Bill Chester asked her not to do something she desired to do, Sylvia felt annoyed and impatient, but when Count Paul, as she had fallen into the way of calling him, made no secret of his wish that she should give up play, Sylvia felt touched and pleased that he should care.

Early in their acquaintance the Count had warned her against making casual friendships in the Gambling Rooms, and he even did not like her knowing – this amused Sylvia – the harmless Wachners.

When he saw her talking to Madame Wachner in the Club, Count Paul would look across the baccarat table and there would come a little frown over his eyes — a frown she alone could see.

And as the days went on, and as their intimacy seemed to grow closer and ever closer, there came across Sylvia a deep wordless wish — and she had never longed for anything so much in her life — to rescue her friend from what he admitted to be his terrible vice of gambling. In this she showed rather a feminine lack of logic, for, while wishing to wean him from his vice, she did not herself give up going to the Casino.

She would have been angry indeed had the truth been whispered to her, the truth that it was not so much her little daily gamble — as Madame Wachner called it — that made Sylvia so faithful an attendant at the Club; it was because when there she was still with Paul de Virieu, she could see and sympathize with him when he was winning, and grieve when he was losing, as alas! he often lost.

When they were not at the Casino the Comte de Virieu very seldom alluded to his play, or to the good or ill fortune which might have befallen him that day. When with her he tried, so much was clear to Sylvia, to forget his passion for gambling.

But this curious friendship of hers with Count Paul only occupied, in a material sense, a small part of Sylvia's daily life at Lacville; and the people with whom she spent most of her time were still Anna Wolsky and Monsieur and Madame Wachner, or perhaps it should be said Madame Wachner.

It was not wonderful that Mrs. Bailey liked the cheerful woman, who was so bright and jovial in manner, and who knew, too, how to flatter so cleverly. When with Madame Wachner Sylvia was made to feel that she was not only very pretty, but also immensely attractive, and just now she was very anxious to think herself both.

*L*ate one afternoon — and they all four always met each afternoon at the Casino — Madame Wachner suddenly invited Sylvia and Anna to come back to supper at the Châlet des Muguets.

Anna was unwilling to accept the kindly invitation. It was clear that she did not wish to waste as much time away from the Casino as going to the Wachners' villa would involve. But, seeing that Sylvia was eager to go, she gave way.

Now on this particular afternoon Sylvia was feeling rather dull, and, as she expressed it to herself, "down on her luck," for the Comte de Virieu had gone into Paris for a few hours.

His sister, the Duchesse d'Eglemont, had come up from the country for a few days, and the great pleasure and delight he had expressed at the thought of seeing her had given the young English widow a little pang of pain. It made her feel how little she counted in his life after all.

And so, for the second time, Sylvia visited the odd, fantastic-looking Châlet des Muguets, and under very pleasant auspices.

This evening the bare dining room she had thought so ugly wore an air of festivity. There were flowers on the round table and on the buffet, but, to her surprise, a piece of oilcloth now hid the parquet floor. This puzzled Sylvia, as such trifling little matters of fact often puzzle a fresh young mind. Surely the oilcloth had not been there on her last visit to the villa? She remembered clearly the unpolished parquet floor.

Thanks to the hostess and to Sylvia herself, supper was a bright, merry meal. There was a variety of cold meats, some fine fruit, and a plate of dainty pastry.

They all waited on one another, though Madame Wachner insisted on doing most of the work. But L'Ami Fritz, for once looking cheerful and eager, mixed the salad, putting in even more vinegar than oil, as Mrs. Bailey laughingly confessed that she hated olive oil!

After they had eaten their appetizing little meal, the host went off into the kitchen where Sylvia had had tea on her first visit to the Châlet, and there he made the most excellent coffee for them all, and even Mrs. Bailey, who was treated as the guest of honor, though she knew that coffee was not good for her, was tempted into taking some.

One thing, however, rather dashed her pleasure in the entertainment.

Madame Wachner, forgetting for once her usual tact, suddenly made a violent attack on the Comte de Virieu.

They were all talking of the habitués of the Casino: "The only one I do not like," she exclaimed, in French, "is that Count – if indeed Count he be? He is so arrogant, so proud, so rude! We have known him for years, have L'Ami Fritz and I, for we are always running across him at Monte Carlo and other places. But no, each time we meet he looks at us as if he was a fish. He does not even nod!"

"When the Comte de Virieu is actually playing, he does not know that other people exist," said Anna Wolsky, slowly.

She had looked across at Sylvia and noticed her English friend's blush and look of embarrassment. "I used to watch him two years ago at Monte Carlo, and I have never seen a man more absorbed in his play."

"That is no excuse!" cried Madame Wachner, scornfully. "Besides, that is only half the truth. He is ashamed of the way he is spending his life, and he hates the people who see him doing it! It is shameful to be so idle. A strong young man doing nothing, living on charity, so they say! And he despises all those who do what he himself is not ashamed to do."

And Sylvia, looking across at her, said to herself with a heavy sigh that this was true. Madame Wachner had summed up Count Paul very accurately.

At last there came the sound of a carriage in the quiet lane outside.

"Fritz! Go and see if that is the carriage I ordered to come here at nine o'clock," said his wife sharply; and then, as he got up silently to obey her, she followed him out into the passage, and Sylvia, who had very quick ears, heard her say, in low, vehement tones, "I work and work and work, but you do nothing! Do try and help me — it is for your sake I am taking all this trouble!"

What could these odd words mean? At what was Madame Wachner working?

A sudden feeling of discomfort came over Sylvia. Then the stout, jolly-looking woman was not without private anxieties and cares? There had been something so weary as well as so angry in the tone in which Madame Wachner spoke to her beloved "Ami Fritz."

A moment later he was hurrying towards the gate.

"Sophie," he cried out from the garden, "the carriage is here! Come along — we have wasted too much time already —"

Like Anna Wolsky, Monsieur Wachner grudged every moment spent away from the tables.

Madame Wachner hurried her two guests into her bedroom to put on their hats.

Anna Wolsky walked over to the window.

"What a strange, lonely place to live in!" she said, and drew the lace shawl she was wearing a little more closely about her thin shoulders. "And that wood over there — I should be afraid to live so near a wood! I should think that there might be queer people concealed there."

"Bah! Why should we be frightened, even if there were queer people there!"

"Well, but sometimes you must have a good deal of money in this house."

Madame Wachner laughed.

"When we have so much money that we cannot carry it about, and that, alas! is not very often — but still, when Fritz makes a big win, we go into Paris and bank the money."

"I do not trouble to do that," said Anna, "for I always carry all my money about with me. What do you do?" she turned to Sylvia Bailey.

"I leave it in my trunk at the hotel," said Sylvia. "The servants at the Villa du Lac seem to be perfectly honest — in fact they are mostly related to the proprietor, M. Polperro."

"Oh, but that is quite wrong!" exclaimed Madame Wachner, eagerly. "You should never leave your money in the hotel; you should always carry it about with you — in little bags like this. See!"

Again she suddenly lifted the light alpaca skirt she was wearing, as she had done before, in this very room, on the occasion of Sylvia's first visit to the Châlet. "That is the way to carry money in a place like this!" she said, smiling. "But now hurry, or all our evening will be gone!"

They left the house, and hastened down the garden to the gate, where L'Ami Fritz received his wife with a grumbling complaint that they had been so long.

And he was right, for the Casino was very full. Sylvia made no attempt to play. Somehow she did not care for the Club when Count Paul was not there.

She was glad when she was at last able to leave the others for the Villa du Lac.

Anna Wolsky accompanied her friend to the entrance of the Casino. The Comte de Virieu was just coming in as Sylvia went out; bowing distantly to the two ladies, he hurried through the vestibule towards the Club.

Sylvia's heart sank. Not even after spending a day with his beloved sister could he resist the lure of play!

Chapter XI

*D*uring much of the night that followed Sylvia lay awake, her mind full of the Comte de Virieu, and of the strange friendship which had sprung up between them.

Their brief meeting at the door of the Casino had affected her very painfully. As he had passed her with a distant bow, a look of shame, of miserable unease, had come over Count Paul's face.

Yes, Madame Wachner had summed him up very shrewdly, if unkindly. He was ashamed, not only of the way in which he was wasting his life, but also of the company into which his indulgence of his vice of gambling brought him.

And Sylvia — it was a bitter thought — was of that company. That fact must be faced by her. True, she was not a gambler in the sense that most of the people she met and saw daily at the Casino were gamblers, but that was simply because the passion of play did not absorb her as it did them. It was her good fortune, not any virtue in herself, that set her apart from Anna Wolsky.

And now she asked herself — or rather her conscience asked her — whether she would not do well to leave Lacville; to break off this strange and — yes, this dangerous intimacy with a man of whom she knew so very little, apart from the great outstanding fact that he was a confirmed gambler, and that he had given up all that makes life worth living to such a man as he, in order to drag on a dishonored, purposeless life at one or other of the great gambling centers of the civilized world?

And yet the thought of going away from Lacville was already intolerable to Sylvia. There had arisen between the Frenchman and herself a kind of close, wordless understanding and sympathy which she, at any rate, still called "friendship." But she would probably have assented to Meredith's words, "Friendship, I fancy, means one heart between two."

At last she fell into a troubled sleep, and dreamt a disturbing dream.

She found herself wandering about the Châlet des Muguets, trying to find a way out of the locked and shuttered building. The ugly little rooms were empty. It was winter, and she was shivering with cold. Someone must have locked her in by mistake. She had been forgotten. . . .

"Toc, toc, toc!" at the door. And Sylvia sat up in bed relieved of her nightmare. It was eight o'clock! She had overslept herself. Félicie was bringing in her tea, and on the tray lay a letter addressed in a handwriting Sylvia did not know, and on which was a French stamp.

She turned the pale-grey envelope over doubtfully, wondering if it was really meant for her. But yes — of that there could be no doubt, for it was addressed, "Madame Bailey, Villa du Lac, Lacville-les-Bains."

She opened it to find that the note contained a gracefully-worded invitation to déjeuner for the next day, and the signature ran — "Marie-Anne d'Eglemont."

Why, it must be Paul de Virieu's sister! How very kind of her, and — and how very kind of *him.*

The letter must have been actually written when Count Paul was in Paris with his sister — and yet, when they had passed one another the evening before, he had bowed as distantly, as coldly, as he might have done to the most casual of acquaintances.

Sylvia got up, filled with a tumult of excited feeling which this simple invitation to luncheon scarcely warranted.

But Paul de Virieu came in from his ride also eager, excited, smiling.

"Have you received a note from my sister?" he asked, hurrying towards her in the dining room which they now had to themselves each morning. "When I told her how you and I had become" — he hesitated a moment, and then added the words, "good friends, she said how much she would like to meet you. I know that you and my dear Marie-Anne would like one another —"

"It is very kind of your sister to ask me to come and see her," said Sylvia, a little stiffly.

"I am going back to Paris this evening," he went on, "to stay with my sister for a couple of nights. So if you can come tomorrow to lunch, as I think my sister has asked you to do, I will meet you at the station."

After breakfast they went out into the garden, and when they were free of the house Count Paul said suddenly,

"I told Marie-Anne that you were fond of riding, and, with your permission, she proposes to send over a horse for you every morning. And, Madame — forgive me — but I told her I feared you had no riding habit! You and she, however, are much the same height, and she thinks that she might be able to lend you one if you will honor her by accepting the loan of it during the time you are at Lacville."

Sylvia was bewildered, she scarcely knew how to accept so much kindness.

"If you will write a line to my sister some time today," continued the Count, "I will be the bearer of your letter."

*T*hat day marked a very great advance in the friendship of Sylvia Bailey and Paul de Virieu.

Till that day, much as he had talked to her about himself and his life, and the many curious adventures he had had, for he had traveled a great deal, and was a cultivated man, he had very seldom spoken to her of his relations.

But today he told her a great deal about them, and she found herself taking a very keen, intimate interest in this group of French people whom she had never seen — whom, perhaps, with one exception, she never would see.

How unlike English folk they must be — these relations of Count Paul! For the matter of that, how unlike any people Sylvia had ever seen or heard of.

First, he told her of the sweet-natured, pious young duchess who was to be her hostess on the morrow — the sister whom Paul loved so dearly, and to whom he owed so much.

Then he described, in less kindly terms, her proud narrow-minded, if generous, husband, the French duke who still lived — thanks to the fact that his grandmother had been the daughter of a great Russian banker — much as must have lived the nobles in the Middle Ages — apart, that is, from everything that would remind him that there was anything in the world of which he disapproved or which he disliked.

The Duc d'Eglemont ignored the fact that France was a Republic; he still talked of "the King," and went periodically into waiting on the Duke of Orleans.

Count Paul also told Sylvia of his great-uncle and godfather, the Cardinal, who lived in Italy, and who had — or so his family liked to believe — so nearly become Pope.

Then there were his three old maiden great-aunts, who had all desired to be nuns, but who apparently had not had the courage to do so when it came to the point. They dwelt together in a remote Burgundian château, and they each spent an hour daily in their chapel praying that their dear nephew Paul might be rescued from the evils of play.

And as Paul de Virieu told Sylvia Bailey of all these curious old-world folk of his, Sylvia wondered more and more why he led the kind of existence he was leading now.

*F*or the first time since Sylvia had come to Lacville, neither she nor Count Paul spent any part of that afternoon at the Casino. They were both at that happy stage of — shall we say friendship? — when a man and a woman cannot see too much of one another; when time is as if it were not; when nothing said or done can be wrong in the other's sight; when Love is still a soft and an invisible presence, with naught about him of the exacting tyrant he will so soon become.

Count Paul postponed his departure for Paris till after dinner, and not till she went up to dress did Sylvia sit down to write her answer to the Duchesse d'Eglemont.

For a long while she held her pen in her hand. How was she to address Paul de Virieu's sister? Must she call her "Dear Madame?" Should she call her "Dear Duchesse?" It was really an unimportant matter, but it appeared very important to Sylvia Bailey. She was exceedingly anxious not to commit any social solecism.

And then, while she was still hesitating, still sitting with the pen poised in her hand, there came a knock at the door.

The maid handed her a note; it was from Count Paul, the first letter he had ever written to her.

"Madame," – so ran the note – "it occurs to me that you might like to answer my sister in French, and so I venture to send you the sort of letter that you might perhaps care to write. Each country has its own usages in these matters – that must be my excuse for my apparent impertinence."

And then there followed a prettily-turned little epistle which Sylvia copied, feeling perhaps a deeper gratitude than a far greater service would have won him from her.

Chapter XII

A couple of hours later Sylvia and Count Paul parted at the door of the Casino. He held her hand longer than was usual with him when bidding her good-night; then, dropping it, he lifted his hat and hurried off towards the station.

Sylvia stood in the dusk and looked after him till a turn in the short road hid his hurrying figure from her sight.

She felt very much moved, touched to the core of her heart. She knew just as well as if he had told her why the Comte de Virieu had given up his evening's play tonight. He had left Lacville, and arranged to meet

her in Paris the next day, in order that their names might not be coupled
– as would have certainly been the case if they had traveled together
into Paris the next morning – by M. Polperro and the good-natured,
but rather vulgar Wachners.

As she turned and walked slowly through the Casino, moving as in
a dream, Sylvia suddenly felt herself smartly tapped on the shoulder.

She turned round quickly – then she smiled. It was Madame Wachner.

"Why 'ave you not come before?" her friend exclaimed. "Madame
Wolsky is making such a sensation! Come quick – quick!" and she
hurried the unresisting Sylvia towards the Club rooms. "I come downstairs to see if I could find you," went on Madame Wachner breathlessly.

What could be happening? Sylvia felt the other's excitement to be
contagious. As she entered the gambling room she saw that a large crowd
was gathered round the center Baccarat table.

"A party of young men out from Paris," explained Madame Wachner
in a low tone, "are throwing about their money. It might have been
terrible. But no, it is a great piece of good fortune for Madame Wolsky!"

And still Sylvia did not understand.

They walked together up to the table, and then, with amazement and
a curious feeling of fear clutching at her heart, Sylvia Bailey saw that
Anna Wolsky was holding the Bank.

It was the first time she had ever seen a lady in the Banker's seat.

A thick bundle of notes, on which were arranged symmetrical piles
of gold lay in front of Madame Wolsky, and as was always the case when
she was really excited, Anna's face had become very pale, and her eyes
glistened feverishly.

The play, too, was much higher than usual. This was owing to the
fact that at one end of the table there stood a little group of five young
men in evening dress. They talked and laughed as they flung their money
on the green cloth, and seemed to enjoy the fact that they were the center
of attraction.

"One of them," whispered Madame Wachner eagerly, "had already
lost eight thousand francs when I went downstairs to look for you! See,
they are still losing. Our friend has the devil's own luck tonight! I have
forbidden L'Ami Fritz to play at all. Nothing can stand against her. She
sweeps the money up every time. If Fritz likes, he can go downstairs to
the lower room and play."

But before doing so L'Ami Fritz lingered awhile, watching Madame
Wolsky's wonderful run of luck with an expression of painful envy and
greed on his wolfish countenance.

Sylvia went round to a point where she could watch Anna's face. To
a stranger Madame Wolsky might have appeared almost indifferent; but

there had come two spots of red on her cheeks, and the hand with which she raked up the money trembled.

The words rang out, *"Faites vos jeux, Messieurs, Mesdames."* Then, *"Le jeu est fait! Rien ne va plus!"*

The luck suddenly turned against Anna. She looked up, and found Sylvia's eyes fixed on her. She made a slight motion, as if she wished her friend to go away.

Sylvia slipped back, and walked quietly round the table. Then she stood behind Anna, and once more the luck came back, and the lady banker's pile of notes and gold grew higher and higher. . . .

"This is the first time a woman has held the Bank this month," Sylvia heard someone say.

And then there came an answer, "Yes, and it is by far the best Bank we have had this month — in fact, it's the best play we've had this season!"

At last Anna pushed away her chair and got up.

One of the young men who had lost a good deal of money came up to her and said smilingly.

"I hope, Madame, you are not going away. I propose now to take the Bank; surely, you will allow me to have my revenge?"

Anna Wolsky laughed.

"Certainly!" she answered. "I propose to go on playing for some time longer."

He took the Banker's seat, and the crowd dispersed to the other tables. L'Ami Fritz slipped away downstairs, but his wife stayed on in the Club by Sylvia's side.

Soon the table was as much surrounded as before, for Anna was again winning. She had won as banker, now she won as simple player, and all those about her began to "follow her luck" with excellent results to themselves.

The scene reminded Sylvia of that first evening at the Casino. It was only three weeks ago, and yet how full, how crowded the time had been!

Somehow tonight she did not feel inclined to play. To her surprise and amusement she saw Madame Wachner actually risk a twenty-franc piece. A moment later the stake was doubled, and soon the good lady had won nine gold pieces. Her face flushed with joy like a happy child's.

"Oh, why is not Fritz here?" she exclaimed. "How sorry I am I sent him downstairs! But, never mind, his old wife is making some money for once!"

At last the Banker rose from the table. He was pretty well cleared out. Smiling and bowing to Anna, he said, "Well, Madame, I congratulate you! You must have a very powerful mascot."

Anna shook her head gaily.

"It is pleasant to win from a millionaire," she whispered to Sylvia, "for one knows it does not hurt him! That young man has a share in the profit on every piece of sugar sold in France, and you know how fond the French are of sweet things!"

She turned from the table, followed by Sylvia and Madame Wachner.

"What will you do with all your money?" asked Madame Wachner anxiously.

"I told one of the ushers to have it all turned into notes for me," she answered indifferently. "As to what I shall do with it! — well, I suppose I shall have to go into Paris and bank some of it in a day or two. I shan't play tomorrow. I shall take a rest — I deserve a rest!" She looked extraordinarily excited and happy.

"Shall we drop you at the Pension Malfait?" said Madame Wachner amiably. "It is right on our way home, you know. I, too, have made money —" she chuckled joyously.

Madame Wachner left the two friends standing in the hall while she went to look for her husband in the public gambling room, and as they stood there Sylvia became conscious that they were being stared at with a great deal of interest and curiosity. The news of Anna Wolsky's extraordinary good luck had evidently spread.

"I wish I had come in a little earlier," said Sylvia presently. "I've never seen you take the Bank before. Surely this is the first time you have done so?"

"Yes, this is the first time I have ever been tempted to take the Bank at Lacville. But somehow I suddenly felt as if I should be lucky tonight. You see, I've made a good deal of money the last day or two, and Madame Wachner persuaded me to try my luck."

"I wish you had told me you were thinking of taking the Bank."

"I would have told you," said Anna quietly, "if I had seen you today. But I have been seeing very little of you lately, Sylvia. Why, you are more with Madame Wachner than with me!"

She did not speak unkindly, but Sylvia felt a pang of remorse. She had indeed seen very little of Anna Wolsky during the last few days, but that was not because she had been with Madame Wachner.

"I will come and see you for a little while tonight," she said impetuously, "for I am going to spend tomorrow in Paris — with a friend who is there just now —"

She hurried out the half-truth with a curious feeling of guilt.

"Yes, do come!" cried Anna eagerly. "You can stay with me while the carriage takes the Wachners on home, and then it can call for you on the way back. I should not like you to walk to the Villa du Lac alone at this time of night."

"Ah, but I'm not like you; I haven't won piles of money!" said Sylvia, smiling.

"No, but that makes very little difference in a place like this —"

And then Monsieur and Madame Wachner joined them. L'Ami Fritz looked quite moved out of himself. He seized Anna by the hand. "I congratulate you!" he said heartily. "What a splendid thing to go on winning like that. I wish I had been there, for I might have followed your luck!"

They all four walked out of the Casino. It was a very dark night.

"And what will you do with all that money?" Monsieur Wachner solicitously inquired. "It is a great sum to carry about, is it not?"

"It is far better to carry about one's money than to trust it to anyone but to a well-managed bank," exclaimed his wife, before Anna could answer the question. "As for the hotel-keepers, I would not trust them with one penny. What happened to a friend of ours, eh, Fritz, tell them that?"

They were now packed into an open carriage, and driving towards the Pension Malfait.

"I don't know what you are talking about," said her husband, crossly.

"Yes, you do! That friend of ours who was boarding in one of those small houses in the Condamine at Monte Carlo, and who one day won a lot of money. He gave his winnings to his hotel-keeper to keep for the night. Next day the man said his safe had been broken open by a foreign waiter who had disappeared. Our friend had no redress — none at all! Malfait may be a very good sort of man, but I would not give him your money —" she turned to Anna.

"No, of course not," said Madame Wolsky. "I should never think of entrusting a really large sum of money to a man of whom I know nothing. It is, as you say, very much better to keep one's money on one's person. It's the plan I've always followed. Then, if it is stolen, or if one loses it, one has only oneself to blame."

"It is very exciting taking the Bank," she added, after a pause. "I think I shall take the Bank again next time I play."

The short drive was soon over, and as Anna and Sylvia were going into the Pension Malfait, Madame Wachner called out, "Will you both come to supper tomorrow?"

Sylvia shook her head.

"I am going into Paris for the day," she said, "and I shall feel tired when I get back. But many thanks, all the same."

"Then *you* must come" — Madame Wachner addressed Anna Wolsky. "We also will have a rest from the Casino."

"Very well! I accept gratefully your kind invitation."

"Come early. Come at six, and we can 'ave a cozy chat first."

"Yes, I will!"

After giving directions that they were to be told when the carriage had come back from the Châlet des Muguets, the two friends went up to Anna Wolsky's bedroom.

Sylvia sat down by the open window.

"You need not light a candle, Anna," she said. "It's so pleasant just now, so quiet and cool, and the light would only attract those horrid midges. They seem to me the only things I have to find fault with in Lacville!"

Anna Wolsky came and sat down in the darkness close to the younger woman.

"Sylvia," she said, "dear little Sylvia! Sometimes I feel uneasy at having brought you to Lacville." She spoke in a thoughtful and very serious tone.

"Indeed, you need feel nothing of the kind."

Sylvia Bailey put out her hand and took the other woman's hand in her own. She knew in her heart what Anna meant, but she willfully pretended to misunderstand her.

"You need never think that I run the slightest risk of becoming a gambler," she went on, a little breathlessly. "I was looking at my account-book today, and I find that since I have been here I have lost seventy francs. Two days ago I had won a hundred and ten francs. So you see it is not a very serious matter, is it? Just think of all the fun I've had! It's well worth the money I've lost. Besides, I shall probably win it all back —"

"I was not thinking of the money," said Anna Wolsky slowly.

Sylvia made a restless movement, and took her hand out of Anna's affectionate clasp.

"I'm afraid that you are becoming very fond of the Comte de Virieu," went on Anna, in a low voice but very deliberately. "You must forgive me, Sylvia, but I am older than you are. Have you thought of the consequences of this friendship of yours? I confess that at the beginning I credited that man with the worst of motives, but now I feel afraid that he is in love — in fact I feel sure that he is madly in love with you. Do you know that he never takes his eyes off you in the Club? Often he forgets to pick up his winnings. . . ."

Sylvia's heart began to beat. She wondered if Anna was indeed telling the truth. She almost bent forward and kissed her friend in her gratitude – but all she said was, and that defiantly,

"You can believe me when I say that he has never said a word of love to me. He has never even flirted with me. I give you my word that that is so!"

"Ah, but it is just that fact that makes me believe that he cares. Flirtation is an English art, not a French art, my dear Sylvia. A Frenchman either loves – and when he loves he adores on his knees – or else he has no use, no use at all, for what English people mean by flirtation – the make-believe of love! I should feel much more at ease if the Count had insulted you –"

"Anna!"

"Yes, indeed! I am quite serious. I fear he loves you."

And as Sylvia gave a long, involuntary, happy sigh, Anna went on: "Of course, I do not regard him with trust or with liking. How could I? On the other hand, I do not go as far as the Wachners; they, it is quite clear, evidently know something very much to the Count's discredit."

"I don't believe they do!" cried Sylvia, hotly. "It is mere prejudice on their part! He does not like them, and they know it. He thinks them vulgar sort of people, and he suspects that Monsieur Wachner is German – that is quite enough for him."

"But, after all, it does not really matter what the Wachners think of the Comte de Virieu, or what he thinks of them," said Anna. "What matters is what *you* think of him, and what *he* thinks of you."

Sylvia was glad that the darkness hid her deep, burning blushes from Anna Wolsky.

"You do not realize," said the Polish lady, gravely, "what your life would be if you were married to a man whose only interest in life is play. Mind you, I do not say that a gambler does not make a kind husband. We have an example" – she smiled a little – "in this Monsieur Wachner. He is certainly very fond of his wife, and she is very fond of him. But would you like your husband always to prefer his vice to you?"

Sylvia made no answer.

"But why am I talking like that?" Anna Wolsky started up suddenly. "It is absurd of me to think it possible that you would dream of marrying the Comte de Virieu! No, no, my dear child, this poor Frenchman is one of those men who, even if personally charming, no wise woman would think of marrying. He is absolutely ruined. I do not suppose he has a penny left of his own in the world. He would not have the money to buy you a wedding ring. You would have to provide even that! It would be madness – absolute madness!"

"I do not think," said Sylvia, in a low tone, "that there is the slightest likelihood of my ever marrying the Comte de Virieu. You forget that I have known him only a short time, and that he has never said a word of love to me. As you say, all he cares about is play."

"Surely you must be as well aware as I am that lately he has played a great deal less," said Anna, "and the time that he would have spent at the Club — well, you and I know very well where he has spent the time, Sylvia. He has spent it with you."

"And isn't that a good thing?" asked Sylvia, eagerly. "Isn't it far better that he should spend his time talking to me about ordinary things than in the Casino? Let me assure you again, and most solemnly, Anna, that he never makes love to me —"

"Of course it is a good thing for him that he plays less" — Anna spoke impatiently — "but is it best for you? That is what I ask myself. You have not looked well lately, Sylvia. You have looked very sad sometimes. Oh, do not be afraid, you are quite as pretty as ever you were!"

The tears were running down Sylvia's face. She felt that she ought to be very angry with her friend for speaking thus plainly to her, and yet she could not be angry. Anna spoke so tenderly, so kindly, so delicately.

"Shall we go away from Lacville?" asked Madame Wolsky, suddenly. "There are a hundred places where you and I could go together. Let us leave Lacville! I am sure you feel just as I do — I am sure you realize that the Comte de Virieu would never make you happy."

Sylvia shook her head.

"I do not want to go away," she whispered.

And then Madame Wolsky uttered a short exclamation.

"Ah!" she cried, "I understand. He is the friend you are to meet tomorrow — that is why you are going into Paris!"

Sylvia remained silent.

"I understand it all now," went on Anna. "That is the reason why he was not there tonight. He has gone into Paris so as not to compromise you at Lacville. That is the sort of gallantry that means so little! As if Lacville matters — but tell me this, Sylvia? Has he ever spoken to you as if he desired to introduce his family to you? That is the test, remember — that is the test of a Frenchman's regard for a woman."

There came a knock at the door. "The carriage for Madame has arrived."

They went downstairs, Sylvia having left her friend's last question unanswered.

Madame Wolsky, though generally so undemonstrative, took Sylvia in her arms and kissed her.

"God bless you, my dear little friend!" she whispered, "and forgive all I have said to you tonight! Still, think the matter over. I have lived a great deal of my life in this country. I am almost a Frenchwoman. It is no use marrying a Frenchman unless his family marry you too – and I understand that the Comte de Virieu's family have cast him off."

Sylvia got into the carriage and looked back, her eyes blinded with tears.

Anna Wolsky stood in the doorway of the Pension, her tall, thin figure in sharp silhouette against the lighted hall.

"We will meet the day after tomorrow, is that not so?" she cried out.

And Sylvia nodded. As she drove away, she told herself that whatever happened she would always remain faithful to her affection for Anna Wolsky.

Chapter XIII

*T*he next morning found Paul de Virieu walking up and down platform No. 9 of the Gare du Nord, waiting for Mrs. Bailey's train, which was due to arrive from Lacville at eleven o'clock.

Though he looked as if he hadn't a care in the world save the pleasant care of enjoying the present and looking forward to the future, life was very grey just now to the young Frenchman.

To a Parisian, Paris in hot weather is a depressing place, even under the pleasantest of circumstances, and the Count felt an alien and an outcast in the city where he had spent much of his careless and happy youth.

His sister, the Duchesse d'Eglemont, who had journeyed all the way from Brittany to see him for two or three days, had received him with that touch of painful affection which the kindly and the prosperous so often bestow on those whom they feel to be at once beloved and prodigal.

When with his dear Marie-Anne, Paul de Virieu always felt as though he had been condemned to be guillotined, and as if she were doing everything to make his last days on earth as pleasant as possible.

When he had proposed that his sister should ask his new friend, this English widow he had met at Lacville, to luncheon — nay more, when he had asked Marie-Anne to lend Mrs. Bailey a riding habit, and to arrange that one of the Duc's horses should come over every morning in order that he and Mrs. Bailey might ride together — the kind Duchesse had at once assented, almost too eagerly, to his requests. And she had asked her brother no tiresome, indiscreet questions as to his relations with the young Englishwoman, — whether, for instance, he was really fond of Sylvia, whether it was conceivably possible that he was thinking of marrying her?

And, truth to tell, Paul de Virieu would have found it very difficult to give an honest answer to the question. He was in a strange, debatable state of mind about Sylvia — beautiful, simple, unsophisticated Sylvia Bailey.

He told himself, and that very often, that the young Englishwoman, with her absurd, touching lack of worldly knowledge, had no business to be living in such a place as Lacville, wasting her money at the Baccarat tables, and knowing such queer people as were — well, yes, even Anna Wolsky was queer — Madame Wolsky and the Wachners!

But if Sylvia Bailey had no business to be at Lacville, he, Paul de Virieu, had no business to be flirting with her as he was doing — for though Sylvia was honestly unaware of the fact, the Count was carrying on what he well knew to be a very agreeable flirtation with the lady he called in his own mind his *"petite amie Anglaise,"* and very much he was enjoying the experience — when his conscience allowed him to enjoy it.

Till the last few weeks Paul de Virieu had supposed himself to have come to that time of life when a man can no longer feel the delicious tremors of love. Now no man, least of all a Frenchman, likes to feel that this time has come, and it was inexpressibly delightful to him to know that he had been mistaken — that he could still enjoy the most absorbing and enchanting sensation vouchsafed to poor humanity.

He was in love! In love for the first time for many years, and with a sweet, happy-natured woman, who became more intimately dear to him every moment that went by. Indeed, he knew that the real reason why he had felt so depressed last night and even this morning was because he was parted from Sylvia.

But where was it all to end? True, he had told Mrs. Bailey the truth about himself very early in their acquaintance — in fact, amazingly soon, and he had been prompted to do so by a feeling which defied analysis.

But still, did Sylvia, even now, realize what that truth was? Did she in the least understand what it meant for a man to be bound and gagged, as he was bound and gagged, lashed to the chariot of the Goddess of Chance? No, of course she did not realize it — how could such a woman as was Sylvia Bailey possibly do so?

Walking up and down the long platform, chewing the cud of bitter reflection, Paul de Virieu told himself that the part of an honest man, to say nothing of that of an honorable gentleman, would be to leave Lacville before matters had gone any further between them. Yes, that was what he was bound to do by every code of honor.

And then, just as he had taken the heroic resolution of going back to Brittany with his sister, as Marie-Anne had begged him to do only that morning, the Lacville train steamed into the station — and with the sight of Sylvia's lovely face all his good resolutions flew to the winds.

She stepped down from the high railway carriage, and looked round her with a rather bewildered air, for a crowd of people were surging round her, and she had not yet caught sight of Count Paul.

Wearing a pinkish mauve cotton gown and a large black tulle hat, Sylvia looked enchantingly pretty. And if the Count's critical French eyes objected to the alliance of a cotton gown and tulle hat, and to the wearing of a string of large pearls in the morning, he was in the state of mind when a man of fastidious taste forgives even a lack of taste in the woman to whom he is acting as guide, philosopher, and friend.

He told himself that Sylvia Bailey could not be left alone in a place like Lacville, and that it was his positive duty to stay on there and look after her. . . .

Suddenly their eyes met. Sylvia blushed — Heavens! how adorable she looked when there came that vivid rose-red blush over her rounded cheeks. And she was adorable in a simple, unsophisticated way, which appealed to Paul de Virieu as nothing in woman had ever appealed to him before.

He could not help enjoying the thought of how surprised his sister would be. Marie-Anne had doubtless pictured Mrs. Bailey as belonging to the rather hard, self-assertive type of young Englishwoman of whom Paris sees a great deal. But Sylvia looked girlishly simple, timid, and confiding.

As he greeted her, Paul de Virieu's manner was serious, almost solemn. But nonetheless, while they walked side by side in a quiet, leisurely fashion through the great grey station, Sylvia felt as if she had indeed passed through the shining portals of fairyland.

In the covered courtyard stood the Duchesse's carriage. Count Paul motioned the footman aside and stood bareheaded while Sylvia took her place in the victoria. As he sat down by her side he suddenly observed, "My brother-in-law does not like motorcars," and Sylvia felt secret, shame-faced gratitude to the Duc d'Eglemont, for, thanks to this prejudice of his, the moments now being spent by her alone with Count Paul were trebled.

As the carriage drove with swift, gondolalike motion through the hot streets, Sylvia felt more than ever as if she were in a new, enchanted country — that dear country called Romance, and, as if to prolong the illusion, the Count began to talk what seemed to her the language of that country.

"Every Frenchman," he exclaimed, abruptly, "is in love with love, and when you hear — as you may do sometimes, Madame — that a Frenchman is rarely in love with his own wife, pray answer that this is quite untrue! For it often happens that in his wife a Frenchman discovers the love he has sought elsewhere in vain."

He looked straight before him as he added: "As for marriage — well, marriage is in my country regarded as a very serious matter indeed! No Frenchman goes into marriage as light-heartedly as does the average Englishman, and as have done, for instance, so many of my own English schoolfellows. No, to a Frenchman his marriage means everything or nothing, and if he loved a woman it would appear to him a dastardly action to ask her to share his life if he did not believe that life to be what would be likely to satisfy her, to bring her honor and happiness."

Sylvia turned to him, and, rather marveling at her own temerity, she asked a fateful question:

"But would love ever make the kind of Frenchman you describe give up a way of life that was likely to make his wife unhappy?"

Count Paul looked straight into the blue eyes which told him so much more than their owner knew they told.

"Yes! He might easily give up that life for the sake of a beloved woman. But would he remain always faithful in his renunciation? That is the question which none, least of all himself, can answer!"

The victoria was now crossing one of the bridges which are, perhaps, the noblest possession of outdoor Paris.

Count Paul changed the subject. He had seen with mingled pain and joy how much his last honest words had troubled her.

"My brother-in-law has never cared to move west, as so many of his friends have done," he observed. "He prefers to remain in the old family house that was built by his great-grandfather before the French Revolution."

Soon they were bowling along a quiet, sunny street, edged with high walls overhung with trees. The street bore the name of Babylon.

And indeed there was something almost Babylonian, something very splendid in the vast courtyard which formed the center of what appeared, to Sylvia's fascinated eyes, a grey stone palace. The long rows of high, narrow windows which now encompassed her were all closed, but with the clatter of the horses' hoofs on the huge paving-stones the great house stirred into life.

The carriage drew up. Count Paul jumped out and gave Sylvia his hand. Huge iron doors, that looked as if they could shut out an invading army, were flung open, and after a moment's pause, Paul de Virieu led Sylvia Bailey across the threshold of the historic Hôtel d'Eglemont.

She had never seen, she had never imagined, such pomp, such solemn state, as that which greeted her, and there came across her a childish wish that Anna Wolsky and the Wachners could witness the scene — the hall hung with tapestries given to an ancestor of the Duc d'Eglemont by Louis the Fourteenth, the line of powdered footmen, and the solemn major-domo who ushered them up the wide staircase, at the head of which there stood a slender, white-clad young woman, with a sweet, eager face.

This was the first time Sylvia Bailey had met a duchess, and she was perhaps a little surprised to see how very unpretentious a duchess could be!

Marie-Anne d'Eglemont spoke in a low, almost timid voice, her English being far less good than her brother's, and yet how truly kind and highly-bred she at once showed herself, putting Sylvia at her ease, and appearing to think there was nothing at all unusual in Mrs. Bailey's friendship with Paul de Virieu!

And then, after they had lunched in an octagon room of which each panel had been painted by Van Loo, and which opened on a garden where the green glades and high trees looked as if they must be far from a great city, there suddenly glided in a tiny old lady, dressed in a sweeping black gown and little frilled lace cap.

Count Paul bowing low before her, kissed her waxen-looking right hand.

"My dear godmother, let me present to you Mrs. Bailey," and Sylvia felt herself being closely, rather pitilessly, inspected by shrewd though not unkindly eyes — eyes sunken, dimmed by age, yet seeing more, perhaps, than younger eyes would have seen.

The old Marquise beckoned to Count Paul, and together they slowly walked through into the garden and paced away down a shaded alley. For the first time Sylvia and Marie-Anne d'Eglemont were alone together.

"I wish to thank you for your kindness to my poor Paul," the Duchesse spoke in a low, hesitating voice. "You have so much influence over him, Madame."

Sylvia shook her head.

"Ah! But yes, you have!" She looked imploringly at Sylvia. "You know what I mean? You know what I would ask you to do? My husband could give Paul work in the country, work he would love, for he adores horses, if only he could be rescued from this terrible infatuation, this passion for play."

She stopped abruptly, for the Count and his little, fairylike god-mother had turned round, and were now coming towards them.

Sylvia rose instinctively to her feet, for the tiny Marquise was very imposing.

"Sit down, Madame," she said imperiously, and Sylvia meekly obeyed.

The old lady fixed her eyes with an appraising gaze on her godson's English friend.

"Permit me to embrace you," she exclaimed suddenly. "You are a very pretty creature! And though no doubt young lips often tell you this, the compliments of the old have the merit of being quite sincere!"

She bent down, and Sylvia, to her confusion and surprise, felt her cheeks lightly kissed by the withered lips of Paul de Virieu's godmother.

"Madame Bailey's rouge is natural; it does not come off!" the old lady exclaimed, and a smile crept over her parchment-colored face. "Not but what a great deal of nonsense is talked about the usage of rouge, my dear children! There is no harm in supplementing the niggardly gifts of nature. You, for instance, Marie-Anne, would look all the better for a little rouge!" She spoke in a high, quavering voice.

The Duchesse smiled. Her brother had always been the old Marquise's favorite.

"But I should feel so ashamed if it came off," she said lightly; "if, for instance, I felt one of my cheeks growing pale while the other remained bright red?"

"That would never happen if you used what I have often told you is the only rouge a lady should use, that is, the sap of the geranium blossom — that gives an absolutely natural tint to the skin, and my own dear mother always used it. You remember how Louis XVIII. complimented her on her beautiful complexion at the first Royal ball held after the Restoration? Well, the Sovereign's gracious words were entirely owing to the geranium blossom!"

Chapter XIV

*T*he day after her memorable expedition to Paris opened pleasantly for Sylvia Bailey, though it was odd how dull and lifeless the Villa du Lac seemed to be without Count Paul.

But he would be back tomorrow, and in the morning of the next day they were to begin riding together.

Again and again she went over in retrospect every moment of the two hours she had spent in that great house in the Faubourg St. Germain.

How kind these two ladies had been to her, Paul's gentle sister and his stately little fairylike godmother! But the Duchesse's manner had been very formal, almost solemn; and as for the other — Sylvia could still feel the dim, yet terribly searching, eyes fixed on her face, and she wondered nervously what sort of effect she had produced on the old Marquise.

Meanwhile, she felt that now was the time to see something of Anna Wolsky. The long afternoon and evening stretching before her seemed likely to be very dull, and so she wrote a little note and asked Anna if she would care for a long expedition in the Forest of Montmorency. It was the sort of thing Anna always said bored her, but as she was not going to the Casino a drive would surely be better than doing nothing.

*A*nd now Sylvia, sitting idly by her bedroom window, was awaiting Anna's answer to her note. She had sent it, just before she went down to luncheon, by a commissionaire, to the Pension Malfait, and the answer ought to have come ere now.

After their drive she and Anna might call on the Wachners and offer to take them to the Casino; and with the thought of the Wachners there came over Sylvia a regret that the Comte de Virieu was so fastidious. He seemed to detest the Wachners! When he met them at the Casino, the most he would do was to incline his head coldly towards them. Who could wonder that Madame Wachner spoke so disagreeably of him?

Sylvia Bailey's nature was very loyal, and now she reminded herself that this couple, for whom Count Paul seemed to have an instinctive dislike, were good-natured and kindly. She must ever remember gratefully how helpful Madame Wachner had been during the first few days she and Anna had been at Lacville, in showing them the little ways about the place, and in explaining to them all sorts of things about the Casino.

And how kindly the Wachners had pressed Anna yesterday to have supper with them during Sylvia's absence in Paris!

*T*here came a knock at the door, and Sylvia jumped up from her chair. No doubt this was Anna herself in response to the note.

"Come in," she cried out, in English.

There was a pause, and another knock. Then it was not Anna?

"Entrez!"

The commissionaire by whom Sylvia had sent her note to Madame Wolsky walked into the room. To her great surprise he handed her back her own letter to her friend. The envelope had been opened, and together with her letter was a sheet of common notepaper, across which was scrawled, in pencil, the words, *"Madame Wolsky est partie."*

Sylvia looked up. *"Partie?"* The word puzzled her. Surely it should have been *"Sortie."* Perhaps Anna had gone to Paris for the day to bank her large winnings. "Then the lady was out?" she said to the man.

"The lady has left the Pension Malfait," he said, briefly. "She has gone away."

"There must be some mistake!" Sylvia exclaimed, in French. "My friend would never have left Lacville without telling me."

The commissionaire went on: "But I have brought back a motor-cab as Madame directed me to do."

She paid him, and went downstairs hurriedly. What an extraordinary mistake! It was out of the question that Anna should have left Lacville without telling her; but as the motor was there she might as well drive to the Pension Malfait and find out the meaning of the curt message, and also why her own letter to Anna had been opened.

If Anna had gone into Paris for the day, the only thing to do was to go for a drive alone. The prospect was not exhilarating, but it would be better than staying indoors, or even in the garden by herself, all afternoon.

Sylvia felt rather troubled and uncomfortable as she got into the open motor. Somehow she had counted on seeing Anna today. She remembered her friend's last words to her. They had been kind, tender words, and though Anna did not approve of Sylvia's friendship for Paul de Virieu, she had spoken in a very understanding, sympathetic way, almost as a loving mother might have spoken.

It was odd of Anna not to have left word she was going to Paris for the day. In any case, the Wachners would know when Anna would be back. It was with them that she had had supper yesterday evening –.

While these thoughts were passing disconnectedly through Sylvia's mind, she suddenly saw the substantial figure of Madame Wachner walking slowly along the sanded path by the side of the road.

"Madame Wachner! Madame Wachner!" she cried out eagerly, and the car drew up with a jerk.

That citizeness of the world, as she had called herself, stepped down from the curb. She looked hot and tired. It was a most unusual time for Madame Wachner to be out walking, and by herself, in Lacville.

But Sylvia was thinking too much about Anna Wolsky to trouble about anything else.

"Have you heard that Anna Wolsky is away for the day?" she exclaimed. "I have received such a mysterious message from the Pension Malfait! Do come with me there and find out where she has gone and when she is coming back. Did she say anything about going into Paris when she had supper with you last night?"

With a smile and many voluble thanks Madame Wachner climbed up into the open car, and sat back with a sigh of satisfaction.

She was very stout, though still so vigorous, and her shrewd, determined face now turned smilingly to the pretty, anxious-eyed Englishwoman. But she waited a few moments before answering Sylvia's eager questions. Then,

"I cannot tell you," she said slowly and in French, "what has happened to Madame Wolsky –"

"What has happened to her!" cried Sylvia. "What do you mean, Madame Wachner?"

"Oh, of course, nothing 'as 'appened." Madame Wachner dropped soothingly into English. "All I mean is that Madame Wolsky did not come to us yesterday evening. We stayed in on purpose, but, as English people say so funnily, she never turn up!"

"But she was coming to tea as well as to supper!"

"Yes, we waited for 'er a long time, and I 'ad got such a beautiful little supper! But, alas! she did not come – no, not at all."

"How odd of her! Perhaps she got a telegram which contained bad news –"

"Yes," said Madame Wachner eagerly, "no doubt. For this morning when I go to the Pension Malfait, I 'ear that she 'as gone away! It was for that I was 'urrying to the Villa du Lac to see if you knew anything, dear friend."

"Gone away?" repeated Sylvia, bewildered. "But it is inconceivable that Anna could have left Lacville without telling me — or, for the matter of that, without telling you, too —"

"She 'as taken what you in England call 'French leave,'" said Madame Wachner dryly. "It was not very considerate of 'er. She might 'ave sent us word last night. We would not then 'ave waited to 'ave our nice supper."

"She can't have gone away without telling me," repeated Sylvia. She was staring straight into her companion's red face: Madame Wachner still looked very hot and breathless. "I am sure she would never have done such a thing. Why should she?"

The older woman shrugged her shoulders.

"I expect she will come back soon," she said consolingly. "She 'as left her luggage at the Pension Malfait, and that, after all, does not look as if she 'as gone for evare!"

"Left her luggage?" cried Sylvia, in a relieved tone. "Why, then, of course, she is coming back! I expect she has gone to Paris for a night in order to see friends passing through. How could the Pension Malfait people think she had gone — I mean for good? You know, Madame Wachner" — she lowered her voice, for she did not wish the driver to hear what she was about to say — "you know that Anna won a very large sum of money two nights ago."

Sylvia Bailey was aware that people had been robbed and roughly handled, even in idyllic Lacville, when leaving the Casino after an especial stroke of luck at the tables.

"I do hope nothing has happened to her!"

"'Appened to 'er? What do you mean?" Madame Wachner spoke quite crossly. "Who ever thought of such a thing!" And she fanned herself vigorously with a paper fan she held in her left hand. "As to her winnings — yes, she won a lot of money the night she took the bank. But, remember that she 'as 'ad plenty of time yesterday to lose it all again — ah, yes!"

"But she meant to give up play till Monday," said Sylvia, eagerly. "I feel sure she never went inside the Casino yesterday."

"Oh, but she did. My 'usband saw her there."

"At what time?" asked Sylvia, eagerly.

"Let me see —"

"Of course, it must have been early, as you were back waiting for her late in the afternoon."

"Yes, it must have been early. And once in the Casino! — well, dear friend, you know as well as I do that with Madame Wolsky the money flies! Still, let us suppose she did not lose 'er money yesterday. In that case surely Madame Wolsky would 'ave done well to leave Lacville with 'er gains in 'er pocketbook."

Madame Wachner was leaning back in the car, a ruminating smile on her broad, good-tempered face.

She was thoroughly enjoying the rush through the air. It was very hot, and she disliked walking. Her morose husband very seldom allowed her to take a cab. He generally forced her to walk to the Casino and back.

Something of a philosopher was Madame Wachner, always accepting with eager, out-stretched hands that with which the gods provided her.

And all at once pretty Sylvia Bailey, though unobservant as happy, prosperous youth so often is, conceived the impression that her companion did not at all wish to discuss Anna's sudden departure. Madame Wachner had evidently been very much annoyed by Anna's lack of civility, and surely the least Anna could have done would have been to send a message saying that it was impossible for her to come to supper at the Châlet des Muguets!

"I am quite sure Anna did not mean to be rude, dear Madame Wachner," said Sylvia, earnestly. "You know she may have sent you a letter or a message which miscarried. They are rather careless people at the Pension Malfait."

"Yes, of course, that is always possible," said the other rather coldly.

And then, as they came within sight of the Pension Malfait, Madame Wachner suddenly placed her large, powerful, bare hand on Sylvia's small gloved one.

"Look 'ere, my dear," she said, familiarly, "do not worry about Madame Wolsky. Believe me, she is not worth it."

Sylvia looked at her amazed, and then Madame Wachner broke into French: "She thought of nothing but play — that is the truth! Play, play, play! Other times she was half asleep!"

She waited a moment, then slowly, and in English, she said, "I believe in my 'eart that she 'as gone off to Aix. The play 'ere was not big enough for 'er. And remember that you 'ave good friends still left in Lacville. I do not only speak of me and of my 'usband, but also of another one."

She laughed, if good-naturedly, then a little maliciously.

But Sylvia gave no answering smile. She told herself that Madame Wachner, though kindly, was certainly rather vulgar, not to say coarse. And her words about Madame Wolsky were really unkind. Anna was not such a gambler as was Fritz Wachner.

They were now at the gate of the boarding house.

"We will, at any rate, go in and find out when Anna left, and if she said where she was going," said Sylvia.

"If you do not mind," observed Madame Wachner, "I will remain out here, in the car. They have already seen me this morning at the Pension Malfait. They must be quite tired of seeing me."

Sylvia felt rather disappointed. She would have liked the support of Madame Wachner's cheerful presence when making her inquiries, for she was aware that the proprietors of Anna's pension — M. and Madame Malfait — had been very much annoyed that she, Sylvia, had not joined her friend there.

Madame Malfait was sitting in her usual place — that is, in a little glass cage in the hall — and when she saw Mrs. Bailey coming towards her, a look of impatience, almost of dislike, crossed her thin, shrewd face.

"Bon jour, Madame!" she said curtly. "I suppose you also have come to ask me about Madame Wolsky? But I think you must have heard all there is to hear from the lady whom I see out there in the car. I can tell you nothing more than I have already told her. Madame Wolsky has treated us with great want of consideration. She did not come home last evening. Poor Malfait waited up all night, wondering what could be the matter. And then, this morning, we found a letter in her room saying she had gone away!"

"A letter in her room?" exclaimed Sylvia. "Madame Wachner did not tell me that my friend had left a letter —"

But Madame Malfait went on angrily:

"Madame Wolsky need not have troubled to write! A word of explanation would have been better, and would have prevented my husband sitting up till five o'clock this morning. We quite feared something must have happened to her. But we have a great dislike to any affair with the police, and so we thought we would wait before telling them of her disappearance, and it is indeed fortunate that we did so!"

"Will you kindly show me the letter she left for you?" said Sylvia.

Without speaking, Madame Malfait bent down over her table, and then held out a piece of notepaper on which were written the words:

Madame Malfait, —
    Being unexpectedly obliged to leave Lacville, I enclose herewith 200 francs. Please pay what is owing to you out of it, and distribute the rest among the servants. I will send you word where to forward my luggage in a day or two.

Sylvia stared reflectively at the open letter.

Anna had not even signed her name. The few lines were very clear, written in a large, decided handwriting, considerably larger, or so it seemed to Sylvia, than what she had thought Anna's ordinary hand to be. But then the Englishwoman had not had the opportunity of seeing much of her Polish friend's calligraphy.

Before she had quite finished reading the mysterious letter over a second time, Madame Malfait took it out of her hand.

But Sylvia Bailey was entirely unused to being snubbed — pretty young women provided with plenty of money seldom are snubbed — and so she did not turn away and leave the hall, as Madame Malfait hoped she would do.

"What a strange thing!" she observed, in a troubled tone. "How extraordinary it is that my friend should have gone away like this, leaving her luggage behind her! What can possibly have made her want to leave Lacville in such a hurry? She was actually engaged to have dinner with our friends, Monsieur and Madame Wachner. Did she not send them any sort of message, Madame Malfait? I wish you would try and remember what she said when she went out."

The Frenchwoman looked at her with a curious stare.

"If you ask me to tell you the truth, Madame," she replied, rather insolently, "I have no doubt at all that your friend went to the Casino yesterday and lost a great deal of money — that she became, in fact, *décavée.*"

Then, feeling ashamed, both of her rudeness and of her frankness, she added:

"But Madame Wolsky is a very honest lady, that I will say for her. You see, she left enough money to pay for everything, as well as to provide my servants with handsome gratuities. That is more than the last person who left the Pension Malfait in a hurry troubled to do!"

"But is it not extraordinary that she left her luggage, and that she did not even tell you where she was going?" repeated Sylvia in a worried, dissatisfied tone.

"Pardon me, Madame, that is not strange at all! Madame Wolsky probably went off to Paris without knowing exactly where she meant to stay, and no one wants to take luggage with them when they are looking round for an hotel. I am expecting at any moment to receive a telegram telling me where to send the luggage. You, Madame, if you permit me to say so, have not had my experience — my experience, I mean, in the matter of ladies who play at the Lacville Casino."

There was still a tone of covert insolence in her voice, and she went on, "True, Madame Wolsky has not behaved as badly as she might have done. Still, you must admit that it is rather inconsiderate of her, after engaging the room for the whole of the month of August, to go off like this!"

Madame Malfait felt thoroughly incensed, and did not trouble to conceal the fact. But as Mrs. Bailey at last began walking towards the front door, the landlady of the pension hurried after her.

"Madame will not say too much about her friend's departure, will she?" she said more graciously. "I do not want any embarrassments with the police. Everything is quite *en règle,* is it not? After all, Madame Wolsky had a right to go away without telling anyone of her plans, had she not, Madame?"

Sylvia turned round. "Certainly, she had an entire right to do so," she answered coldly. "But, still, I should be much obliged if you will send me word when you receive the telegram you are expecting her to send you about the luggage."

"*W*ell?" cried Madame Wachner eagerly, as Sylvia silently got into the motor again. "Have you learnt anything? Have they not had news of our friend?"

"They have heard nothing since they found that odd letter of hers," said Sylvia. "You never told me about the letter, Madame Wachner?"

"Ah, that letter! I saw it, too. But it said nothing, absolutely nothing!" exclaimed Madame Wachner.

And Sylvia suddenly realized that in truth Anna's letter did say nothing.

"I should have thought they would have had a telegram today about the luggage."

"So would I," said Sylvia. And then musingly, "I should never, never have expected Anna Wolsky to go off like that. So — so mysteriously —"

"Well, there, I quite disagree with you! It is just what I should have expected her to do!" exclaimed Madame Wachner. "She told me of that visit you both made to the soothsayer. Perhaps she made up in her mind to follow that person's advice. Our friend was always a little mysterious, was she not? Did she ever talk to you of her family, of her friends?" She looked inquisitively at her companion.

"Yes — no," said Sylvia, hesitating. "I do not think poor Anna has many relations. You see, she is a widow. I believe her father and mother are dead."

"Ah, that is very sad! Then you do not know of anyone to write to about her?"

"I?" said Sylvia. "No, of course I don't know of anyone to write to. How could I? I haven't known her very long, you know, Madame Wachner. But we became friends almost at once."

The motor was still stationary. The driver turned round for orders. Sylvia roused herself.

"Can I drive you back to the Châlet des Muguets?" she asked. "Somehow I don't feel inclined to take a drive in the forest now."

"If you do not mind," said Madame Wachner, "I should prefer to be driven to the station, for l'Ami Fritz had to go to Paris." She laughed ruefully. "To fetch money, as usual! His system did not work at all well yesterday — poor Fritz!"

"How horrid!" said Sylvia. "It must be very disappointing to your husband when his system goes wrong."

"Yes, very," answered the wife dryly. "But when one system fails — well, then he at once sets himself to inventing another! I lose a great deal more in the lower room playing with francs than Fritz does at baccarat playing with gold. You see, a system has this good about it — the player generally comes out even at the end of each month."

"Does he, indeed?"

But Sylvia was not attending to what the other was saying. She was still absorbed in the thought of her friend, and of the mystery of her friend's sudden departure from Lacville.

When at last they reached the station, Madame Wachner turned and grasped Sylvia by the hand.

"We must not let you become low-spirited!" she exclaimed. "It is a great pity your kind friend has gone away. But doubtless you will soon be going away, too?"

And, as Sylvia made no answer, "Perhaps it would be well not to say too much concerning Madame Wolsky having left like this. She might come back any moment, and then she would not like it if there had been a fuss made about it! If I were you I would tell nobody — I repeat emphatically *nobody.*"

Madame Wachner stared significantly at Sylvia. "You do not know what the police of Lacville are like, my dear friend. They are very unpleasant people. As you were Anna's only friend in the place, they might give you considerable trouble. They would ask you where to look for her, and they would torment you incessantly. If I were you I would say as little as possible."

Madame Wachner spoke very quickly, almost breathlessly, and Sylvia felt vaguely uncomfortable. There was, of course, only one person to whom she was likely to mention the fact, and that was Paul de Virieu.

Was it possible that Madame Wachner wished to warn her against telling him of a fact which he was sure to discover for himself in the course of a day or two?

Chapter XV

*A*s Sylvia drove away alone from the station, she felt exceedingly troubled and unhappy.

It was all very well for Madame Wachner to take the matter of Anna Wolsky's disappearance from Lacville so philosophically. The Wachners' acquaintance with Madame Wolsky had been really very slight, and they naturally knew nothing of the Polish woman's inner nature and temperament.

Sylvia told herself that Anna must have been in great trouble, and that something very serious must have happened to her, before she could have gone away like this, without saying anything about it.

If poor Anna had changed her mind, and gone to the Casino the day before, she might, of course, have lost all her winnings and more. Sylvia reminded herself that it stood to reason that if one could make hundreds of pounds in an hour or two, then one might equally lose hundreds of pounds in the same time. But somehow she could hardly believe that her friend had been so foolish.

Still, how else to account for Anna's disappearance, her sudden exit from Lacville? Anna Wolsky was a proud woman, and Sylvia suspected that if she had come unexpectedly to the end of her resources, she would have preferred to go away rather than confide her trouble to a new friend.

Tears slowly filled Sylvia Bailey's blue eyes. She felt deeply hurt by Anna's strange conduct.

Madame Wachner's warning as to saying as little as possible of the other's departure from Lacville had made very little impression on Sylvia, yet it so far affected her that, instead of telling Monsieur Polperro of the fact the moment she was back at the Villa du Lac, she went straight up to her own room. But when there she found that she could settle down to nothing – neither to a book nor to letters.

Since her husband's death Sylvia Bailey's social circle had become much larger, and there were a number of people who enjoyed inviting and meeting the pretty, wealthy young widow. But just now all these friends of hers in faraway England seemed quite unreal and, above all, quite uninteresting.

Sylvia told herself with bitter pain, and again the tears sprang to her eyes, that no one in the wide world really cared for her. Those people who had been going to Switzerland had thrown her over without a thought. Anna Wolsky, who had spoken as if she really loved her only a day or two ago, and who had made that love her excuse for a somewhat impertinent interference in Sylvia's private affairs, had left Lacville without even sending her word that she was leaving!

True, she had a new and a delightful friend in Count Paul de Virieu. But what if Anna had been right? What if Count Paul were a dangerous friend, or, worse still, only amusing himself at her expense? True, he had taken her to see his sister; but that, after all, might not mean very much.

Sylvia Bailey went through a very mournful hour. She felt terribly depressed and unhappy, and at last, though there was still a considerable time to dinner, she went downstairs and out into the garden with a book.

And then, in a moment, everything was changed. From sad, she became happy; from mournful and self-pitying, full of exquisite content.

Looking up, Sylvia had seen the now familiar figure of Count Paul de Virieu hurrying towards her.

How early he had left Paris! She had understood that he meant to come back by the last train, or more probably tomorrow morning.

"Paris was so hot, and my sister found that friends of hers were passing through, so I came back earlier than I meant to do," he said a little lamely; and then, "Is anything the matter?"

He looked with quick, anxious concern into her pale face and red-lidded eyes. "Did you have a bad night at the tables?"

Sylvia shook her head.

"Something so strange – so unexpected – has happened." Her mouth quivered. "Anna Wolsky has left Lacville!"

"Left Lacville?" Count Paul repeated, in almost as incredulous a tone as that in which Sylvia herself had said the words when the news had been first brought her. "Have you and she quarreled, Mrs. Bailey? You permit?" He waited till she looked up and said listlessly, "Yes, please do," before lighting his cigarette.

"quarreled? Oh, no! She has simply gone away without telling me!"

The Comte de Virieu looked surprised, but not particularly sorry.

"That's very strange," he said. "I should have thought your friend was not likely to leave Lacville for many weeks to come."

His acute French mind had already glanced at all the sides of the situation, and he was surprised at the mixed feelings which filled his heart. With the Polish woman gone, his young English friend was not likely to stay on at such a place as Lacville alone.

"But where has Madame Wolsky gone?" he asked quickly. "And why has she left? Surely she is coming back?" (Sylvia could certainly stay on a few days alone at Lacville, if her friend was coming back.)

But what was this that Mrs. Bailey was saying in so plaintive a tone?

"That's the extraordinary thing about it! I haven't the slightest idea where Anna is, or why she has left Lacville." In spite of herself her voice trembled. "She did not give me the slightest warning of what she was thinking of doing; in fact, only a few days ago, when we were talking of our future plans, I tried to persuade her to come back to England with me on a long visit."

"Tell me all that happened," he said, sitting down and speaking in the eager, kindly way he seemed to keep for Sylvia alone.

And then Sylvia told him. She described the coming of the messenger, her journey to the Pension Malfait, and she repeated, as far as was possible, the exact words of her friend's curiously-worded, abrupt letter to Madame Malfait.

"They all think," she said at last, "that Anna went to the Casino and lost all her money — both the money she made, and the money she brought here; and that then, not liking to tell even me anything about it, she made up her mind to go away."

"They *all* think this?" repeated Count Paul, meaningly. "Whom do you mean by *all*, Mrs. Bailey?"

"I mean the people at the Pension Malfait, and the Wachners —"

"Then you saw the Wachners today?"

"I met Madame Wachner as I was going to the Pension Malfait," said Sylvia, "and she went there with me. You see, the Wachners asked Anna to have supper with them yesterday, and they waited for her ever so long, but she never came. That makes it clear that she must have left Lacville some time in the early afternoon. I wish — I cannot help wishing — that I had not gone into Paris yesterday, Count Paul."

And then suddenly she realized how ungracious her words must sound.

"No, no," she cried, impetuously. "Of course, I do not mean that! I had a very, very happy time, and your sister was very kind and sweet to me. But it makes me unhappy to think that Anna may have been worried and anxious about money with me away —"

There was a pause, and then, in a very different voice, Sylvia Bailey asked the Comte de Virieu a question that seemed to him utterly irrelevant.

"Do you believe in fortune-tellers?" she asked abruptly. "Are you superstitious?"

"Like everyone else, I have been to such people," he answered indifferently. "But if you ask my true opinion — well, no; I am quite skeptical! There may be something in what these dealers in hope sometimes say, but more often there is nothing. In fact, you must remember that a witch generally tells her client what she believes her client wishes to hear."

"Madame Wachner is inclined to think that Anna left Lacville because of something which a fortune-teller told her — indeed told both of us — before we came here." Mrs. Bailey was digging the point of her parasol in the grass.

"Tiens! Tiens!" he exclaimed. "That is an odd idea! Pray tell me all about it. Did you and your friend consult a fashionable necromancer, or did you content yourselves with going to a cheap witch?"

"To quite a cheap witch."

Sylvia laughed happily; she was beginning to feel really better now. She rather wondered that she had never told Count Paul about that strange visit to the fortune-teller, but she had been taught, as are so many Englishwomen of her type, to regard everything savoring of superstition as not only silly and weak-minded, but also as rather discreditable.

"The woman called herself Madame Cagliostra," she went on gaily, "and she only charged five francs. In the end we did pay her fifteen. But she gave us plenty for our money, I assure you — in fact, I can't remember half the things she said!"

"And to you was prophesied — ?" Count Paul leant forward and looked at her fixedly.

Sylvia blushed.

"Oh, she told me all sorts of things! As you say they don't really know anything; they only guess. One of the things that she told me was that it was possible, in fact, quite likely, that I should never go back to England — I mean at all! And that if I did so, I should go as a stranger. Wasn't that absurd?"

"Quite absurd," said Count Paul, quietly. "For even if you married again, Madame; if you married a Frenchman, for instance, you would still wish to go back to your own country sometimes — at least, I suppose so."

"Of course I should." And once more Sylvia reddened violently.

But this time Count Paul felt no pleasure in watching the flood of carmine staining not only the smooth, rounded cheek, but the white forehead and neck of his fair English friend.

Sylvia went on speaking, a little quickly.

"She said almost the same thing to Anna. Wasn't that odd? I mean she said that Anna would probably never go back to her own country. But what was really very strange was that she did not seem to be able to see into Anna's future at all. And then — oh well, she behaved very oddly. After we had gone she called us back —" Sylvia stopped for a moment.

"Well?" said Count Paul eagerly. "What happened then?"

He seldom allowed himself the pleasure of looking into Sylvia's blue eyes. Now he asked for nothing better than that she should go on talking while he went on looking at her.

"She made us stand side by side — you must understand, Count, that we had already paid her and gone away — when she called us back. She stared at us in a very queer sort of way, and said that we must not leave Paris, or if we did leave Paris, we must not leave together. She said that if we did so we should run into danger."

"All rather vague," observed the Count. "And, from the little I know of her, I should fancy Madame Wolsky the last woman in the world to be really influenced by that kind of thing."

He hardly knew what he was saying. His only wish was that Sylvia would go on talking to him in the intimate, confiding fashion she was now doing. Heavens! How wretched, how lonely he had felt in Paris after seeing her off the day before!

"Oh, but at the time Anna was very much impressed," said Sylvia, quickly. "Far more than I was — I know it made her nervous when she was first playing at the tables. And when she lost so much money the first week we were here she said to me, 'That woman was right. We ought not to have come to Lacville!' But afterwards, when she began to be so wonderfully lucky, she forgot all about it, or, rather, she only remembered that the woman had said to her that she would have a great run of luck."

"Then the woman said that, too," remarked Count Paul, absently.

(What was it his godmother had said? "I felicitate you on your conquest, naughty Paul!" and he had felt angry, even disgusted, with the old lady's cynical compliment. She had added, meaningly, "Why not turn over a new leaf? Why not marry this pretty creature? We should all be pleased to see you behave like a reasonable human being.")

But Sylvia was answering him.

"Yes, the woman said that Anna would be very lucky."

The Comte de Virieu thought for a moment, and then withdrew his eyes from his friend's face.

"I presume you have already telephoned to the hotel in Paris where you first met Madame Wolsky?"

"Why, it never occurred to me to do that!" cried Sylvia. "What a good idea!"

"Wait," he said. "I will go and do it for you."

But five minutes later he came back, shaking his head. "I am sorry to say the people at the Hôtel de l'Horloge know nothing of Madame Wolsky. They have had no news of her since you and she both left the place. I wonder if the Wachners know more of her disappearance than they have told you?"

"What *do* you mean?" asked Sylvia, very much surprised.

"They're such odd people," he said, in a dissatisfied voice. "And you know they were always with your friend. When you were not there, they hardly ever left her for a moment."

"But I thought I had told you how distressed they are about it? How they waited for her last evening and how she never came? Oh no, the Wachners know nothing," declared Sylvia confidently.

Chapter XVI

*T*here is something very bewildering and distressing in the sudden disappearance or even the absence of a human being to whose affectionate and constant presence one has become accustomed. And as the hours went by, and no letter or message arrived from Anna Wolsky, Sylvia became seriously troubled, and spent much of her time walking to and from the Pension Malfait.

Surely Anna could not have left Paris, still less France, without her luggage? All sorts of dreadful possibilities crowded on Sylvia's mind; Anna Wolsky might have met with an accident: she might now be lying unidentified in a Paris hospital. . . .

At last she grew so uneasy about her friend that she felt she must do something!

Mine host of the Villa du Lac was kind and sympathetic, but even he could suggest no way of finding out where Anna had gone.

And then Sylvia suddenly bethought herself that there was one thing she could do which she had not done: she could surely go to the police of Lacville and ask them to make inquiries in Paris as to whether there had been an accident of which the victim in any way recalled Anna Wolsky.

To her surprise, M. Polperro shook his head very decidedly.

"Oh no, do not go to the police!" he said in an anxious tone. "No, no, I do not advise you to do that! Heaven knows I would do anything in reason to help you, Madame, to find your friend. But I beg of you not to ask me to go for you to the police!"

Sylvia was very much puzzled. Why should M. Polperro be so unwilling to seek the help of the law in so simple a matter as this?

"I will go myself," she said.

And just then — they were standing in the hall together — the Comte de Virieu came up.

"What is it you will do yourself, Madame?" he asked, smiling.

Sylvia turned to him eagerly.

"I feel that I should like to speak to the police about Anna Wolsky," she exclaimed. "It is the first thing one would do in England if a friend suddenly disappeared — in fact, the police are always looking for people who have gone away in a mysterious manner. You see, I can't help being afraid, Count Paul" — she lowered her voice — "that Anna has met with some dreadful accident. She hasn't a friend in Paris! Suppose she is lying now in some hospital, unable to make herself understood? I only wish that I had a photograph of Anna that I could take to them."

"Well, there is a possibility that this may be so. But remember it is even more probable that Madame Wolsky is quite well, and that she will be annoyed at your taking any such step to find her."

"Yes," said Sylvia, slowly. "I know that is quite possible. And yet — and yet it is so very unlike Anna not to send me a word of explanation! And then, you know in that letter she left in her room at the Pension Malfait she positively promised to send a telegram about her luggage. Surely it is very strange that she has not done that?"

"Well, if you really wish the police communicated with," said the Comte de Virieu, "I will go to the police station here, with pleasure."

"Why should we not go together?" asked Sylvia, hesitatingly.

"By all means. But think over what we are to say when we get there. If your friend had not left the letter behind her, then, of course it would be our positive duty to communicate with the police. But I cannot help being afraid —" He stopped abruptly.

"Of what are you afraid?" asked Sylvia eagerly.

"I am afraid that Madame Wolsky may be very much offended by your interference in the matter."

"Oh, no!" cried Sylvia. "Indeed, in that you are quite mistaken! I know Anna would never be offended by anything I could do. She was very fond of me, and so am I of her. But in any case I am willing to risk it. You see" — her voice broke, quivered — "I am really very unhappy about Anna —"

"When would you like to go to the Commissioner of Police?" asked the Count.

"Is there any reason why we should not go now?"

"No. Let us go at once. I only had the feeling that you might hear from her any moment."

Together they walked up into the little town of Lacville. To each any expedition in which the other took part had become delightful. They were together now more than they had ever been before. No, Count Paul could not be sorry that Sylvia's friend had left Lacville. He had no wish for her return.

At last they came to a rather mean-looking white house; out of one of the windows hung a tricolor flag.

"Here we are!" he said briefly.

"It doesn't look a very imposing place," said Sylvia smiling.

But all the same, as the Count rang the bell Sylvia suddenly felt as if she would like to run away! After all, what should she say to the Commissioner of Police? Would he think her interference in Anna's affairs strange and uncalled for? But she kept her thoughts to herself.

They were shown into a room where a tired-looking man bent over a large, ink-stained table littered over with papers.

"Monsieur? Madame?" he glanced up inquiringly, and gave them a searching look. But he did not rise from the table, as Sylvia expected him to do. "What can I do for you?" he said. "I am at your service," and again he stared with insistent curiosity at the couple before him, at the well-dressed young Englishwoman and at her French companion.

The Count explained at some length why they had come.

And then at last the Commissioner of Police got up.

"Madame has now been at Lacville three weeks?" — and he quickly made a note of the fact on a little tablet he held in his hand. "And her friend, a Polish lady named Wolsky, has left Lacville rather suddenly? Madame has, however, received a letter from her friend explaining that she had to leave unexpectedly?"

"No," said Sylvia, quickly, "the letter was not sent to me; it was left by my friend in her bedroom at the Pension Malfait. You see, the strange thing, Monsieur, is that Madame Wolsky left all her luggage. She took absolutely nothing with her, excepting, of course, her money. And as yet nothing has come from her, although she promised to telegraph where her luggage was to be sent on to her! I come to you because I am afraid that she had met with some accident in the Paris streets, and I thought you would be able to telephone for us to the Paris Police."

She looked very piteously at the French official, and his face softened, a kindly look came over it.

"Well, Madame," he said, "I will certainly do everything I can. But I must ask you to provide me first with a few more particulars about your friend."

"I will tell you everything I know. But I really do not know very much."

"Her age?" said the Commissioner.

"I do not know her age, but I suppose she is about thirty."

"The place of her birth?"

Sylvia shook her head.

"What is her permanent address? Surely you know with whom you could communicate the news of an accident having happened to her?"

"I am afraid I don't even know that." Sylvia began to feel rather foolish. But − but was it so strange after all? Who among the people she was now living with knew anything of her faraway English home? If anything happened to herself, for instance? Even Count Paul would not know to whom to write. It was an odd, rather an uncomfortable thought.

The Commissioner went to a drawer and pulled out from it a portfolio filled with loose pieces of paper.

"Malfait? Malfait? Malfait?" he muttered interrogatively to himself. And at last he found what he was looking for. It was a large sheet, on which was inscribed in large round letters "Pension Malfait." There were many close lines of writing under the words. He looked down and read through all that was there.

"The Pension Malfait has a good reputation!" he exclaimed, in a relieved tone. "I gather from what you say, Monsieur," − he gave a quick shrewd look at the Count − "that Madame and her friend did not play in a serious sense at the Casino − I mean, there was no large sum of money in question?"

Count Paul hesitated − but Sylvia thought that surely it were better to tell the truth.

"Yes," she said, "my friend did play, and she played rather high. She must have had a large sum of money in her possession when she left Lacville, unless she lost it all on the last day. But I was in Paris, and so I don't know what she did."

The Commissioner looked grave.

"Ah, but that alters the case very much!" he said. "I must request you to come with me to the Pension Malfait. We had better pursue our inquiries there. If this Madame Wolsky had a large sum of money in notes and gold, it becomes very important that we should know where she is."

They all three left the shabby little house together, and Sylvia could not help wondering what would happen there while they were gone. But the Commissioner solved her doubts by turning the key in the door.

The Count hailed a cab, and they all got into it. Then followed a curious little drive. The Commissioner made polite conversation with Mrs. Bailey. He spoke of the beauties of Lacville. "And Madame," he said, pleasantly, "is staying at the Villa du Lac? It is a charming house, with historic associations."

Sylvia was surprised. She remembered clearly that she had not told the police official where she was staying.

When they reached the Pension Malfait they were kept waiting a few moments, but at last M. Malfait appeared in the hall. He received them with obsequious amiability.

Still, even Sylvia could not but be aware that he was extremely angry, and she herself felt wretchedly uncomfortable. What if Anna Wolsky were all right after all? Would she not blame her for having made such a fuss?

"Everything is quite *en règle,*" M. Malfait said smoothly when the purport of their presence was explained to him in a few curt words by the Commissioner of Police.

"You see, Monsieur le Commissaire, it is quite simple. The lady left us a letter explaining why she was obliged to go away. I do not know why Madame" — he turned to Sylvia — "thought it necessary to go to you? We have been perfectly open about the whole matter. We are respectable people, and have absolutely nothing to hide. Madame Wolsky's boxes are there, in her bedroom; I might have let the room twice over since she left, but no, I prefer to wait, hoping that the lady — the very charming lady — will come back."

"By the way, where is the letter which she left?" said the Commissioner in a businesslike voice. "I should like to see that letter."

"Where is the letter?" repeated Monsieur Malfait vaguely. Then in a loud voice, he said, "I will ask my wife for the letter. She looks after the correspondence."

Madame Malfait came forward. She looked even more annoyed than her husband had looked when he had seen by whom Sylvia was accompanied.

"The letter?" she repeated shortly. "Mon Dieu! I do not know where I have put it. But by this time I almost know it by heart. It was a pleasing letter, for it spoke very warmly of our establishment. But where is the letter?" she looked round her, as if she expected to find it suddenly appear.

"Ah! I remember to whom I showed it last! It was to that agreeable friend of Madame Wolsky" — she put an emphasis on the word "agreeable," and stared hard at Sylvia as she did so. "It was to that Madame Wachner I last showed it. Perhaps she put it in her pocket, and forgot to give it me back. I know she said she would like her husband to see it. Monsieur and Madame Wachner often take their meals here. I will ask them if they have the letter."

"Well, at any rate, we had better open Madame Wolsky's trunks; that may give us some clue," said the Commissioner in a weary voice.

And, to Sylvia's confusion and distress, they all then proceeded to the bedroom where she had last seen her friend, and there Monsieur Malfait broke the locks of Anna Wolsky's two large trunks.

But the contents of Anna's trunks taught them nothing. They were only the kind of objects and clothes that a woman who traveled about the world a great deal would naturally take with her. Everything, however, was taken out, turned over, and looked at.

"If your friend possessed a passport," said the police official in a dissatisfied tone, "she has evidently taken it with her. There is nothing of any consequence at all in those boxes. We had better shut them up again, and leave them."

But when they came down again into the hall, he suddenly asked Monsieur Malfait, "Well, where is the letter?" He had evidently forgotten Madame Malfait's involved explanation.

"I will send you the letter tomorrow," said Monsieur Malfait smoothly. "The truth is, we handed it to a lady who was also a friend of Madame Wolsky, and she evidently forgot to give it back to us. We will find out whether she has kept it."

On the way back the Commissioner of Police said gaily,

"It is quite clear that Madame" — he turned and bowed courteously to Sylvia — "knows very little of Lacville, Monsieur le Comte! Why, people are always disappearing from Lacville! My time would indeed be full were I to follow all those who go away in a hurry — not but what I have been only too delighted to do this for Madame and for Monsieur le Comte."

He then bowed to the Count and stared smilingly at Sylvia.

"I am pleased to think," he went on playfully, "that Madame herself is not likely to meet with any unpleasant adventure here, for the Villa du Lac is a most excellent and well-conducted house. Be assured, Madame, that I will find out in the next few hours if your friend has met with an accident in the Paris streets."

He left them at the gate of the Villa.

When the Commissioner had quite disappeared, the Count observed, "Well, we have done what you wished. But it has not had much result, has it?"

Sylvia shook her head disconsolately.

"No, Count Paul. I am afraid I made a mistake in going to the police. The Malfaits are evidently very angry with me! And yet — and yet, you know in England it's the first thing that people do."

Count Paul laughed kindly.

"It is a matter of absolutely no consequence. But you see, you never quite understand, my dear friend, that Lacville is a queer place, and that here, at any rate, the hotel-keepers are rather afraid of the police. I was even glad that the Commissioner did not ask to look over *your* boxes, and did not exact a passport from you!"

More seriously he added, "But I see that you are dreadfully anxious about Madame Wolsky, and I myself will communicate with the Paris police about the matter. It is, as you say, possible, though not probable, that she met with an accident after leaving you."

Chapter XVII

A long week went by, and still no news, no explanation of her abrupt departure from Lacville, was received from Anna Wolsky; and the owners of the Pension Malfait were still waiting for instructions as to what was to be done with Madame Wolsky's luggage, and with the various little personal possessions she had left scattered about her room.

As for Sylvia, it sometimes seemed to her as if her Polish friend had been obliterated, suddenly blotted out of existence.

But as time went on she felt more and more pained and discomfited by Anna's strange and heartless behavior to herself. Whatever the reason for Madame Wolsky's abrupt departure, it would not have taken her a moment to have sent Sylvia Bailey a line — if only to say that she could give no explanation of her extraordinary conduct.

Fortunately there were many things to distract Sylvia's thoughts from Anna Wolsky. She now began each morning with a two hours' ride with Paul de Virieu. She had a graceful seat, and had been well taught; only a little practice, so the Count assured her, was needed to make her into a really good horsewoman, the more so that she was very fearless.

Leaving the flat plain of Lacville far behind them, they would make their way into the Forest of Montmorency, and through to the wide valley, which is so beautiful and so little known to most foreign visitors to Paris.

The Duchesse d'Eglemont had sent her maid to Lacville with the riding habit she was lending Sylvia, and by a word M. Polperro let fall, the Englishwoman realized, with mingled confusion and amusement, that the hotel-keeper supposed her to be an old and intimate friend of Count Paul's sister.

The other people in the hotel began to treat her with marked cordiality.

And so it came to pass that outwardly the Polish lady's disappearance came to be regarded even by Sylvia as having only been a ripple on the pleasant, lazy, agreeable life she, Count Paul, and last, not least, the Wachners, were all leading at Lacville.

In fact, as the days went on, only Mrs. Bailey herself and that kindly couple, Madame Wachner and her silent husband, seemed to remember that Anna had ever been there. During the first days, when Sylvia had been really very anxious and troubled, she had had cause to be grateful to the Wachners for their sympathy; for whereas Paul de Virieu seemed only interested in Anna Wolsky because she, Sylvia, herself was interested, both Madame Wachner and her morose, silent husband showed real concern and distress at the mysterious lack of news.

Whenever Sylvia saw them, and she saw them daily at the Casino, either Madame Wachner or L'Ami Fritz would ask her in an eager, sympathetic voice, "Have you had news of Madame Wolsky?"

And then, when she shook her head sadly, they would express — and especially Madame Wachner would express — increasing concern and surprise at Anna's extraordinary silence.

"If only she had come to us as she arranged to do!" the older woman exclaimed more than once in a regretful tone. "Then, at any rate, we should know something; she would not have concealed her plans from us entirely; we were, if new friends, yet on such kind, intimate terms with the dear soul!"

And now, as had been the case exactly a week ago, Sylvia was resting in her room. She was sitting just as she had then sat, in a chair drawn up close to the window. There had been no ride that morning, for Paul de Virieu had been obliged to go into Paris for the day.

Sylvia felt dull and listless. She had never before experienced that aching longing for the presence of another human being which in our civilized life is disguised under many names, but which in this case, Sylvia herself called by that of "friendship."

Moreover, she had received that morning a letter which had greatly disturbed her. It now lay open on her lap, for she had just read it through again. This letter was quite short, and simply contained the news that Bill Chester, her good friend, sometime lover, and trustee, was going to Switzerland after all, and that he would stop a couple of days in Paris in order to see her.

It was really very nice of Bill to do this, and a month ago Sylvia would have looked forward to seeing him. But now everything was changed, and Sylvia could well have dispensed with Bill Chester's presence.

The thought of Chester at Lacville filled her with unease. When she had left her English home two months ago — it seemed more like two years than two months — she had felt well disposed to the young lawyer, and deep in her inmost heart she had almost brought herself to acknowledge that she might very probably in time become his wife.

She suspected that Chester had been fond of her when she was a girl, at a time when his means would not have justified him in proposing to her, for he was one of those unusual men who think it dishonorable to ask girls to marry them unless they are in a position to keep a wife. She remembered how he had looked — how set and stern his face had become when someone had suddenly told him in her presence of her engagement to George Bailey, the middle-aged man who had been so kind to her, and yet who had counted for so little in her life, though she had given him all she could of love and duty.

Since her widowhood, so she now reminded herself remorsefully, Chester had been extraordinarily good to her, and his devotion had touched her because it was expressed in actions rather than in words, for he was also the unusual type of man, seldom a romantic type, who scorns, however much in love, to take advantage of a fiduciary position to strengthen his own.

The fact that he was her trustee brought them into frequent conflict. Too often Bill was the candid friend instead of the devoted lover. Their only real quarrel — if quarrel it could be called — had been, as we know, over the purchase of her string of pearls. But time, or so Sylvia confidently believed, had proved her to have been right, for her "investment," as she always called it to Bill Chester, had improved in value.

But though she had been right in that comparatively trifling matter, she knew that Chester would certainly disapprove of the kind of life — the idle, purposeless, frivolous life — she was now leading.

Looking out over the lake, which, as it was an exceedingly hot, fine day, was already crowded with boats, Sylvia almost made up her mind to go back into Paris for two or three days.

Bill would think it a very strange thing that she was staying here in Lacville all by herself. But the thought of leaving Lacville just now was very disagreeable to Sylvia. . . . She wondered uncomfortably what her trustee would think of her friendship with Count Paul de Virieu — with this Frenchman who, when he was not gambling at the Casino, spent every moment of his time with her.

But deep in her heart Sylvia knew well that when Bill Chester was there Paul de Virieu would draw back; only when they were really alone together did he talk eagerly, naturally.

In the dining room of the Villa he hardly ever spoke to her, and when they were both in the Baccarat-room of the Club he seldom came and stood by her side, though when she looked up she often found his eyes fixed on her with that ardent, absorbed gaze which made her heart beat, and her cheeks flush with mingled joy and pain.

Suddenly, as if her thoughts had brought him there, she saw Count Paul's straight, slim figure turn in from the road through the gates of the Villa.

He glanced up at her window and took off his hat. He looked cool, unruffled, and self-possessed, but her eager eyes saw a change in his face. He looked very grave, and yet oddly happy. Was it possible that he had news at last of Anna Wolsky?

He mounted the stone-steps and disappeared into the house; and Sylvia, getting up, began moving restlessly about her room. She longed to go downstairs, and yet a feminine feeling of delicacy restrained her from doing so.

A great stillness brooded over everything. The heat had sent everyone indoors. M. Polperro, perhaps because of his Southern up-bringing, always took an early afternoon siesta. It looked as if his servants followed his example. The Villa du Lac seemed asleep.

Sylvia went across to the other window, the window overlooking the large, shady garden, and there, glancing down, she saw Count Paul.

"Come into the garden —," he said softly in English; and Sylvia, leaning over the bar of her window, thought he added the word "Maud" — but of course that could not have been so, for her name, as the Count knew well, was Sylvia! And equally of course he always addressed her as "Madame."

"It's so nice and cool up here," she whispered back. "I don't believe it is half so cool in the garden!"

She gazed down into his upturned face with innocent coquetry, pretending — only pretending — to hesitate as to what she would do in answer to his invitation.

But Sylvia Bailey was but an amateur at the Great Game, the game at which only two — only a man and a woman — can play, and yet which is capable of such infinite, such bewilderingly protean variations. So her next move, one which Paul de Virieu, smiling behind his moustache, foresaw — was to turn away from the window.

She ran down the broad shallow staircase very quickly, for it had occurred to her that the Count, taking her at her word, might leave the garden, and, sauntering off to the Casino, lose his money — for whatever he might be in love, Count Paul was exceedingly unlucky at cards! And lately she had begun to think that she was gradually weaning her friend from what she knew to be in his case, whatever it was in hers, and in that of many of the people about them, the terrible vice of gambling.

When, a little breathless, she joined him in the garden, she found that he had already taken two rocking-chairs into a shady corner which was out of sight of the white villa and of its inquisitive windows.

"Something very serious has happened," said Count Paul slowly.

He took both her hands in his and looked down into her face. With surprise and concern she saw that his eyelids were red. Was it possible that Count Paul had been crying? He almost looked as if he had.

The idea of a grown-up man allowing himself to give way to emotion of that sort would have seemed absurd to Sylvia a short time ago, but somehow the thought that Paul de Virieu had shed tears made her feel extraordinarily moved.

"What is the matter?" she asked anxiously. "Has anything happened to your sister?"

"Thank God — no!" he answered hastily. "But something else, something which was to be expected, but which I did not expect, has happened —"

And then, very gravely, and at last releasing her hands, he added, "My kind godmother, the little Marquise you met last week, died last night."

Sylvia felt the sudden sense of surprise, almost of discomfiture, the young always feel in the neighborhood of death.

"How dreadful! She seemed quite well when we saw her that day —"

She could still hear echoing in her ears the old lady's half-mocking but kindly compliments.

"Ah! but she was very, very old — over ninety! Why, she was supposed to be aged when she became my godmother thirty odd years ago!"

He waited a moment, and then added, quietly, "She has left me in her will two hundred thousand francs."

"Oh, I *am* glad!"

Sylvia stretched out both hands impulsively, and the Comte de Virieu took first one and then the other and raised them to his lips.

"Eight thousand pounds? Does it seem a fortune to you, Madame?"

"Of course it does!" exclaimed Sylvia.

"It frees me from the necessity of being a pensioner on my brother-in-law," he said slowly, and Sylvia felt a little chill of disappointment. Was that his only pleasure in his legacy?

"You will not play with *this* money?" she said, in a low voice.

"It is no use my making a promise, especially to you, that I might not be able to keep —"

He got up, and stood looking down at her.

"But I promise that I will not waste or risk this money if I can resist the temptation to do so."

Sylvia smiled, though she felt more inclined to cry.

He seemed stung by her look.

"Do you wish me to give you my word of honor that I will not risk any of this money at the tables?" he asked, almost in a whisper.

Sylvia's heart began to beat. Count Paul had become very pale. There was a curious expression on his face — an expression of revolt, almost of anger.

"Do you exact it?" he repeated, almost violently.

And Sylvia faltered out, "Could you keep your word if I did exact it?"

"Ah, you have learnt to know me too well!"

He walked away, leaving her full of perplexity and pain.

A few moments passed. They seemed very long moments to Sylvia Bailey. Then Count Paul turned and came back.

He sat down, and made a great effort to behave as if nothing unusual or memorable had passed between them.

"And has anything happened here?" he asked. "Is there any news of your vanished friend?"

Sylvia shook her head gravely. The Polish woman's odd, and, to her, inexplicable, conduct still hurt her almost as much as it had done at first.

The Count leant forward, and speaking this time very seriously indeed, he said, in a low voice: —

"I wish to say something to you, and I am now going to speak as frankly as if you were — my sister. You are wrong to waste a moment of your time in regretting Madame Wolsky. She is an unhappy woman, held tightly in the paws of the tiger — Play. That is the truth, my friend! It is a pity you ever met her, and I am glad she went away without doing you any further mischief. It was bad enough of her to have brought you to Lacville, and taught you to gamble. Had she stayed on, she would have tried in time to make you go on with her to Monte Carlo."

He shook his head expressively

Sylvia looked at him with surprise. He had never spoken to her of Anna in this way before. She hesitated, then said a little nervously,

"Tell me, did you ask Madame Wolsky to go away? Please don't mind my asking you this?"

"*I* ask Madame Wolsky to go away?" he repeated, genuinely surprised. "Such a thought never even crossed my mind. It would have been very impertinent — what English people would call 'cheeky' — of me to do such a thing! You must indeed think me a hypocrite! Have I not shared your surprise and concern at her extraordinary disappearance? And her luggage? If I had wished her to go away, I should not have encouraged her to leave all her luggage behind her!" he spoke with the sarcastic emphasis of which the French are masters.

Sylvia grew very red.

As a matter of fact, it had been Madame Wachner who had suggested that idea to her. Only the day before, when Sylvia had been wondering for the thousandth time where Anna could be, the older woman had exclaimed meaningly, "I should not be surprised if that Count de Virieu persuaded your friend to go away. He wants the field clear for himself."

And then she had seemed to regret her imprudent words, and she had begged Sylvia not to give the Count any hint of her suspicion. Even now Sylvia did not mention Madame Wachner.

"Of course, I don't think you a hypocrite," she said awkwardly, "but you never did like poor Anna, and you were always telling me that Lacville isn't a place where a nice woman ought to stay long. I thought you might have said something of the same kind to Madame Wolsky."

"And do you really suppose," Count Paul spoke with a touch of sharp irony in his voice, "that your friend would have taken my advice? Do you think that Madame Wolsky would look either to the right or the left when the Goddess of Chance beckoned?" — and he waved his hand in the direction where the white Casino lay.

"But the Goddess of Chance did not beckon to her to leave Lacville!" Sylvia exclaimed. "Why, she meant to stay on here till the middle of September —"

"You asked me a very indiscreet question just now" — the Count leant forward, and looked straight into Mrs. Bailey's eyes.

His manner had again altered. He spoke far more authoritatively than he had ever spoken before, and Sylvia, far from resenting this new, possessive attitude, felt thrilled and glad. When Bill Chester spoke as if he had authority over her, it always made her indignant, even angry.

"Did I?" she said nervously.

"Yes! You asked me if I had persuaded Madame Wolsky to leave Lacville. Well, now I ask you, in my turn, whether it has ever occurred to you that the Wachners know more of your Polish friend's departure than they admit? I gathered that impression the only time I talked to your Madame Wachner about the matter. I felt sure she knew more than she would say! Of course, it was only an impression."

Sylvia hesitated.

"At first Madame Wachner seemed annoyed that I made a fuss about it," she said thoughtfully. "But later she seemed as surprised and sorry as I am myself. Oh, no, Count, I am sure you are wrong — why you forget that Madame Wachner walked up to the Pension Malfait that same evening — I mean the evening of the day Anna left Lacville. In fact, it was Madame Wachner who first found out that Anna had not come home. She went up to her bedroom to look for her."

"Then it was Madame Wachner who found the letter?" observed the Count interrogatively.

"Oh, no, it was not Madame Wachner who found it. Anna's letter was discovered the next morning by the chambermaid in a blotting-book on the writing table. No one had thought of looking there. You see they were all expecting her back that night. Madame Malfait still thinks that poor Anna went to the Casino in the afternoon, and after having lost her money came back to the pension, wrote the letter, and then went out and left for Paris without saying anything about it to anyone!"

"I suppose something of that sort did happen," observed the Comte de Virieu thoughtfully.

"And now," he said, getting up from his chair, "I think I will take a turn at the Casino after all!"

Sylvia's lip quivered, but she was too proud to appeal to him to stay. Still, she felt horribly hurt.

"You see what I am like," he said, in a low, shamed voice. "I wish you had made me give you my word of honor."

She got up. It was cruel, very cruel, of him to say that to her. How amazingly their relation to one another had altered in the last half-hour!

For the moment they were enemies, and it was the enemy in Sylvia that next spoke. "I think I shall go and have tea with the Wachners. They never go to the Casino on Saturday afternoons."

A heavy cloud came over Count Paul's face.

"I can't think what you see to like in that vulgar old couple," he exclaimed irritably. "To me there is something" — he hesitated, seeking for an English word which should exactly express the French word "louche" — "sinister — that is the word I am looking for — there is to me something sinister about the Wachners."

"Sinister?" echoed Sylvia, really surprised. "Why, they seem to me to be the most good-natured, commonplace people in the world, and then they're so fond of one another!"

"I grant you that," he said. "I quite agree that that ugly old woman is very fond of her 'Ami Fritz' — but I do not know if he returns the compliment!"

Sylvia looked pained, nay more, shocked.

"I suppose French husbands only like their wives when they are young and pretty," she said slowly.

"Another of the many injustices you are always heaping on my poor country," the Count protested lightly. "But I confess I deserved it this time! Joking apart, I think 'L'Ami Fritz' is very fond of his" — he hesitated, then ended his sentence with "Old Dutch!"

Sylvia could not help smiling.

"It is too bad of you," she exclaimed, "to talk like that! The Wachners are very nice people, and I won't allow you to say anything against them!"

Somehow they were friends again. His next words proved it.

"I will not say anything against the Wachners this afternoon. In fact, if you will allow me to do so, I will escort you part of the way."

And he was even better than his word, for he went on with Sylvia till they were actually within sight of the little, isolated villa where the Wachners lived.

There, womanlike, she made an effort to persuade him to go in with her.

"Do come," she said urgently. "Madame Wachner would be so pleased! She was saying the other day that you had never been to their house."

But Count Paul smilingly shook his head.

"I have no intention of ever going there," he said deliberately. "You see I do not like them! I suppose — I hope" — he looked again straight into Sylvia Bailey's ingenuous blue eyes — "that the Wachners have never tried to borrow money of you?"

"Never!" she cried, blushing violently. "Never, Count Paul! Your dislike of my poor friends makes you unjust — it really does."

"It does! It does! I beg their pardon and yours. I was foolish, nay, far worse, indiscreet, to ask you this question. I regret I did so. Accept my apology."

She looked at him to see if he was sincere. His face was very grave; and she looked at him with perplexed, unhappy eyes.

"Oh, don't say that!" she said. "Why should you mind saying anything to me?"

But the Comte de Virieu was both vexed and angry with himself.

"It is always folly to interfere in anyone else's affairs," he muttered. "But I have this excuse — I happen to know that last week, or rather ten days ago, the Wachners were in considerable difficulty about money. Then suddenly they seemed to have found plenty, in fact, to be as we say here, 'à flot'; I confess that I foolishly imagined, nay, I almost hoped, that they owed this temporary prosperity to you! But of course I had no business to think about it at all — still less any business to speak to you about the matter. Forgive me, I will not so err again."

And then, with one of his sudden, stiff bows, the Comte de Virieu turned on his heel, leaving Sylvia to make her way alone to the little wooden gate on which were painted the words "Châlet des Muguets."

Chapter XVIII

Sylvia pushed open the little white gate of the Châlet des Muguets and began walking up the path which lay through the neglected, untidy garden.

To eyes accustomed to the exquisitely-kept gardens of an English country town, there was something almost offensive in the sight presented by the high, coarse grass and luxuriant unkemptness of the place, and once more Sylvia wondered how the Wachners could bear to leave the land surrounding their temporary home in such a state.

But the quaint, fantastic-looking, one-storeyed châlet amused and rather interested her, for it was so entirely unlike any other dwelling with which she was acquainted.

Today a deep, hot calm brooded over the silent house and deserted-looking garden; the chocolate-colored shutters of the dining room and the drawing room were closed, and Sylvia told herself that it would be delightful to pass from the steamy heat outside into the dimly-lighted, sparsely-furnished little "salon," there to have a cup of tea and a pleasant chat with her friends before accompanying them in the cool of the early evening to the Casino.

Sylvia always enjoyed talking to Madame Wachner. She was a little bit ashamed that this was so, for this cosmopolitan woman's conversation was not always quite refined, but she was good-natured and lively, and her talk was invariably amusing. Above all, she knew how to flatter, and after a chat with Madame Wachner Sylvia Bailey always felt pleased both with herself and with the world about her.

There was very little concerning the young Englishwoman's simple, uneventful life with which Madame Wachner was not by now acquainted. She was aware for instance, that Sylvia had no close relations of her own, and that, like Anna Wolsky, Mrs. Bailey knew nobody — she had not even an acquaintance — living in Paris.

This fact had enlisted to a special degree Madame Wachner's interest and liking for the two young widows.

Sylvia rang the primitive bell which hung by the door which alone gave access, apart from the windows, to the Châlet des Muguets.

After some moments the day-servant employed by Madame Wachner opened the door with the curt words, "Monsieur and Madame are in Paris." The woman added, in a rather insolent tone, "They have gone to fetch some money," and her manner said plainly enough, "Yes, my master and mistress — silly fools — have lost their money at the Casino, and now they are gone to get fresh supplies!"

Sylvia felt vexed and disappointed. After what had been to her a very exciting, agitating conversation with Count Paul, she had unconsciously longed for the cheerful, commonplace talk of Madame Wachner.

As she stood there in the bright sunlight the thought of the long, lonely, hot walk back to the Villa du Lac became odious to her.

Why should she not go into the house and rest awhile? The more so that the Wachners would almost certainly return home very soon. They disliked Paris, and never stayed more than a couple of hours on their occasional visits there.

In her careful, rather precise French, she told the servant she would come in and wait.

"I am sure that Madame Wachner would wish me to do so," she said, smiling; and after a rather ungracious pause the woman admitted her into the house, leading the way into the darkened dining room.

"Do you think it will be long before Madame Wachner comes back?" asked Sylvia.

The woman hesitated — "I cannot tell you that," she mumbled. "They never say when they are going, or when they will be back. They are very odd people!"

She bustled out of the room for a few moments and then came back, holding a big cotton parasol in her hand.

"I do not know if Madame wishes to stay on here by herself? As for me, I must go now, for my work is done. Perhaps when Madame leaves the house she will put the key under the mat."

"Yes, if I leave the house before my friends return home I will certainly do so. But I expect Madame Wachner will be here before long."

Sylvia spoke shortly. She did not like the day-servant's independent, almost rude way of speaking.

"Should the master and mistress come back before Madame has left, will Madame kindly explain that she *insisted* on coming into the house? I am absolutely forbidden to admit visitors unless Madame Wachner is here to entertain them."

The woman spoke quickly, her eyes fixed expectantly on the lady sitting before her.

Mrs. Bailey suddenly realized, or thought she realized, what that look meant. She took her purse out of her pocket and held out a two-franc piece.

"Certainly," she answered coldly, "I will explain to Madame Wachner that I insisted on coming in to rest."

The woman's manner altered; it became at once familiar and servile. After profusely thanking Sylvia for her "tip," she laid the cotton parasol on the dining-table, put her arms akimbo, and suddenly asked, "Has Madame heard any news of her friend? I mean of the Polish lady?"

"No," Sylvia looked up surprised. "I'm sorry to say that there is still no news of her, but, of course, there will be soon."

She was astonished that the Wachners should have mentioned the matter to this disagreeable, inquisitive person.

"The lady stopped here on her way to the station. She seemed in very high spirits."

"Oh, no, you are quite mistaken," said Sylvia quickly. "Madame Wolsky did not come here at all the day she left Lacville. She was expected, both to tea and to supper, but she did not arrive —"

"Indeed, yes, Madame! I had to come back that afternoon, for I had forgotten to bring in some sugar. The lady was here then, and she was still here when I left the house."

"I assure you that this cannot have been on the day my friend left Lacville," said Mrs. Bailey quickly. "Madame Wolsky left on a Saturday afternoon. As I told you just now, Madame Wachner expected her to supper, but she never came. She went to Paris instead."

The servant looked at her fixedly, and Sylvia's face became what it seldom was — very forbidding in expression. She wished this meddling, familiar woman would go away and leave her alone.

"No doubt Madame knows best! One day is like another to me. I beg Madame's pardon."

The Frenchwoman took up her parasol and laid the house key on the table, then, with a *"Bon jour, Madame, et encore merci bien!"* she noisily closed the door behind her.

A moment later, Sylvia, with a sense of relief, found herself in sole possession of the Châlet des Muguets.

*E*ven the quietest, the most commonplace house has, as it were, an individuality that sets it apart from other houses. And even those who would deny that proposition must admit that every inhabited dwelling has its own special nationality.

The Châlet des Muguets was typically French and typically suburban;
but where it differed from thousands of houses of the same type, dotted
round in the countrysides within easy reach of Paris, was that it was let
each year to a different set of tenants.

In Sylvia Bailey's eyes the queer little place lacked all the elements
which go to make a home; and, sitting there, in that airless, darkened
dining room, she wondered, not for the first time, why the Wachners
chose to live in such a comfortless way.

She glanced round her with distaste. Everything was not only cheap,
but common and tawdry. Still, the dining room, like all the other rooms
in the châlet, was singularly clean, and almost oppressively neat.

There was the round table at which she and Anna Wolsky had been
so kindly entertained, the ugly buffet or sideboard, and in place of the
dull parquet floor she remembered on her first visit lay an ugly piece
of linoleum, of which the pattern printed on the surface simulated a
red and blue marble pavement.

Once more the change puzzled her, perhaps unreasonably.

At last Sylvia got up from the hard cane chair on which she had been
sitting.

There had come over her, in the half-darkness, a very peculiar sensation — an odd feeling that there was something alive in the room. She
looked down, half expecting to see some small animal crouching under
the table, or hiding by the walnut-wood buffet behind her.

But, no; nothing but the round table, and the six chairs stiffly placed
against the wall, met her eyes. And yet, still that feeling that there was
in the room some sentient creature besides herself persisted.

She opened the door giving into the hall, and walked through the
short passage which divided the house into two portions, into the tiny
"salon."

Here also the closed shutters gave the room a curious, eerie look of
desolate greyness. But Sylvia's eyes, already accustomed to the half-darkness next door, saw everything perfectly.

The little sitting room looked mean and shabby. There was not a
flower, not even a book or a paper, to relieve its prim ugliness. The only
ornaments were a gilt clock on the mantelpiece, flanked with two sham
Empire candelabra. The shutters were fastened closely, and the room
was dreadfully hot and airless.

Once more Sylvia wondered why the Wachners preferred to live in
this cheerless way, with a servant who only came for a few hours each
day, rather than at an hotel or boarding-house.

And then she reminded herself that, after all, the silent, gaunt man,
and his talkative, voluble wife, seemed to be on exceptionally good terms

the one with the other. Perhaps they really preferred being alone together than in a more peopled atmosphere.

While moving aimlessly about the room, Sylvia began to feel unaccountably nervous and oppressed. She longed to be away from this still, empty house, and yet it seemed absurd to leave just as the Wachners would be returning home.

After a few more minutes, however, the quietude, and the having absolutely nothing to do with which to wile away the time, affected Sylvia's nerves.

It was, after all, quite possible that the Wachners intended to wait in Paris till the heat of the day was over. In that case they would not be back till seven o'clock.

The best thing she could do would be to leave a note inviting Madame Wachner and L'Ami Fritz to dinner at the Villa du Lac. Count Paul was to be in Paris this evening, so his eyes would not be offended by the sight of the people of whom he so disapproved. Madame Wachner would probably be glad to dine out, the more so that no proper meal seemed to have been prepared by that unpleasant day-servant. Why, the woman had not even laid the cloth for her employers' supper!

Sylvia looked instinctively round for paper and envelopes, but there was no writing-table, not even a pencil and paper, in the little drawing room. How absurd and annoying!

But, stay — somewhere in the house there must be writing materials.

Treading softly, and yet hearing her footsteps echoing with unpleasant loudness through the empty house, Sylvia Bailey walked past the open door of the little kitchen, and so to the end of the passage.

Then something extraordinary happened.

While in the act of opening the door of Madame Wachner's bedroom, the young Englishwoman stopped and caught her breath. Again she had suddenly experienced that unpleasant, eerie sensation — the sensation that *she was not alone.* But this time the feeling was far more vivid than it had been in the dining room.

So strong, so definite was Sylvia's perception of another presence, and this time of a human presence, in the still house, that she turned sharply round —

But all she saw was the empty passage, cut by a shaft of light thrown from the open door of the kitchen, stretching its short length down to the entrance hall.

Making a determined effort over what she could but suppose to be her nerves, she walked through into the Wachners' bedroom.

It was very bare and singularly poorly furnished, at least to English eyes, but it was pleasantly cool after the drawing room.

She walked across to the window, and, drawing aside the muslin curtains, looked out.

Beyond the patch of shade thrown by the house the sun beat down on a ragged, unkempt lawn, but across the lawn she noticed, much more particularly than she had done on the two former occasions when she had been in the house, that there lay a thick grove of chestnut trees just beyond the grounds of the Châlet des Muguets.

A hedge separated the lawn from the wood, but like everything else in the little property it had been neglected, and there were large gaps in it.

She turned away from the window —

Yes, there, at last, was what she had come into this room to seek! Close to the broad, low bed was a writing-table, or, rather, a deal table, covered with a turkey red cloth, on which lay a large sheet of ink-stained, white blotting-paper.

Flanking the blotting-paper was a pile of Monsieur Wachner's little red books — the books in which he so carefully noted the turns of the game at the Casino, and which served him as the basis of his elaborate gambling "systems."

Sylvia went up to the writing-table, and, bending over it, began looking for some notepaper. But there was nothing of the sort to be seen; neither paper nor envelopes lay on the table.

This was the more absurd, as there were several pens, and an inkpot filled to the brim.

She told herself that the only thing to do was to tear a blank leaf out of one of L'Ami Fritz's notebooks, and on it write her message of invitation. If she left the little sheet of paper propped up on the dining-table, the Wachners would be sure to see it.

She took up the newest-looking of the red notebooks, and as she opened it she suddenly felt, and for the third time, that there was a living presence close to her — and this time that it was that of Anna Wolsky!

It was an extraordinary sensation — vivid, uncanny, terrifying — the more so that Sylvia Bailey not only believed herself to be alone in the house, but supposed Anna to be far from Lacville. . . .

Fortunately, this unnerving and terrifying impression of an unseen and yet real presence did not endure; and, as she focused her eyes on the open book she held in her hand, it became fainter and fainter, while she realized, with a keen sense of relief, what it was that had brought the presence of her absent friend so very near to her.

There, actually lying open before her, between two leaves of the little notebook, was a letter signed by Anna Wolsky! It was a short note, in

French, apparently an answer to one Madame Wachner had sent reminding her of her engagement. It was odd that the Wachners had said nothing of this note, for it made Anna's conduct seem stranger than ever.

Opposite the page on which lay the little letter, Monsieur Wachner had amused himself by trying to imitate Anna's angular handwriting.

Sylvia tore out one of the blank pages, and then she put the notebook and its enclosure back on the table. She felt vaguely touched by the fact that the Wachners had kept her friend's last letter; they alone, so she reminded herself, had been really sorry and concerned at Anna's sudden departure from the place. They also, like Sylvia herself, had been pained that Madame Wolsky had not cared to say good-bye to them.

She scribbled a few lines on the scrap of paper, and then, quickly making her way to the dining room, she placed her unconventional invitation on the round table, and went out into the hall.

As she opened the front door of the Châlet des Muguets Sylvia was met by a blast of hot air. She looked out dubiously. She was thoroughly unnerved — as she expressed it to herself, "upset." Feeling as she now felt, walking back through the heat would be intolerable.

For the first time Lacville became utterly distasteful to Sylvia Bailey. She asked herself, with a kind of surprise, of self-rebuke, why she was there — away from her own country and her own people? With a choking sensation in her throat she told herself that it would be very comfortable to see once more the tall, broad figure of Bill Chester, and to hear his good, gruff English voice again.

She stepped out of the house, and put up her white parasol.

It was still dreadfully hot, but to the left, across the lawn, lay the cool depths of the chestnut wood. Why not go over there and rest in the shade?

Hurrying across the scorched grass to the place where there was an opening in the rough hedge, she found herself, a moment later, plunged in the grateful green twilight created by high trees.

It was delightfully quiet and still in the wood, and Sylvia wondered vaguely why the Wachners never took their tea out there. But foreigners are very law-abiding, or so she supposed, and the wood, if a piece of no-man's land, was for sale. Up a path she could see the back of a large board.

It was clear that this pretty bit of woodland would have been turned into villa plots long ago had it been nearer to a road. But it was still a stretch of primeval forest. Here and there, amid the tufts of grass, lay the husks of last autumn's chestnuts.

Sylvia slowly followed the little zigzag way which cut across the wood, and then, desiring to sit down for awhile, she struck off to the right, towards a spot where she saw that the brambles and the undergrowth had been cleared away.

Even here, where in summer the sun never penetrated, the tufts of coarse grass were dried up by the heat. She glanced down; no, there was no fear that the hard, dry ground would stain her pretty cotton frock.

And then, as she sat there, Sylvia gradually became aware that close to her, where the undergrowth began again, the earth had recently been disturbed. Over an irregular patch of about a yard square the sods had been dug up, and then planted again.

The thought passed through her mind that children must have been playing there, and that they had made a rude attempt to destroy their handiwork, or rather to prevent its being noticed, by placing the branch of a tree across the little plot of ground where the earth had been disturbed. It was this broken branch, of which the leaves had shriveled up, that had first drawn her attention to the fact that someone must have been there, and recently.

Her thoughts wandered off to Bill Chester. He was now actually journeying towards her as fast as boat and train could bring him; in a couple of hours he would be in Paris, and then, perhaps, he would come out to Lacville in time for dinner.

Sylvia had not been able to get a room for him in the Villa du Lac, but she had engaged one in the Pension Malfait — where she had been able to secure the apartment which had been occupied by Anna Wolsky, whose things had only just been moved out of it.

She could not help being sorry that Bill would see Lacville for the first time on a Sunday. She feared that, to his English eyes, the place, especially on that day, would present a peculiarly — well, disreputable appearance!

Sylvia felt jealous for the good fame of Lacville. Out in the open air her spirits had recovered their balance; she told herself that she had been very happy here — singularly, extraordinarily happy. . . .

Of course it was a pity when people lost more money than they could afford at the Casino; but even in England people betted — the poor, so she had been told, risked all their spare pence on horse racing, and the others, those who could afford it, went to Monte Carlo, or stayed at home and played bridge!

After all, where was the difference? But, of course, Bill Chester, with his tiresome, old-fashioned views of life, would think there was a great difference; he would certainly disapprove of the way she was now spending her money. . . .

Something told her, and the thought was not wholly unpleasing to her, that Bill Chester and the Comte de Virieu would not get on well together. She wondered if Count Paul had ever been jealous — if he were capable of jealousy? It would be rather interesting to see if anything or anyone could make him so!

And then her mind traveled on, far, far away, to a picture with which she had been familiar from her girlhood, for it hung in the drawing room of one of her father's friends at Market Dalling. It was called "The Gambler's Wife." She had always thought it a very pretty and pathetic picture; but she no longer thought it so; in fact, it now appeared to her to be a ridiculous travesty of life. Gamblers were just like other people, neither better nor worse — and often infinitely more lovable than were some other people. . . .

At last Sylvia got up, and slowly made her way out of the wood. She did not go back through the Wachners' garden; instead, she struck off to the left, on to a field path, which finally brought her to the main road.

As she was passing the Pension Malfait the landlady came out to the gate.

"Madame!" she cried out loudly, "I have had news of Madame Wolsky at last! Early this afternoon I had a telegram from her asking me to send her luggage to the cloak-room of the Gare du Nord."

Sylvia felt very glad — glad, and yet once more, perhaps unreasonably, hurt. Then Anna had been in Paris all the time? How odd, how really unkind of her not to have written and relieved the anxiety which she must have known her English friend would be feeling about her!

"I have had Madame Wolsky's room beautifully prepared for the English gentleman," went on Madame Malfait amiably. She was pleased that Mrs. Bailey was giving her a new guest, and it also amused her to observe what prudes Englishwomen could be.

Fancy putting a man who had come all the way from England to see one, in a pension situated at the other end of the town to where one was living oneself!

Chapter XIX

*W*illiam Chester, solicitor, and respected citizen of Market Dalling, felt rather taken aback and bewildered as he joined the great stream of people who were pouring out of the large suburban station of Lacville.

He had only arrived in Paris two hours before, and after a hasty dinner at the Gare du Nord he had made inquiries as to his best way of reaching Lacville. And then he was told, to his surprise, that from the very station in which he found himself trains started every few minutes to the spot for which he was bound.

"Tonight," added the man of whom he had inquired, "there is a fine fête at Lacville, including fireworks on the lake!"

Chester had imagined Sylvia to be staying in a quiet village or little country town. That was the impression her brief letters to him had conveyed, and he was astonished to hear that Lacville maintained so large and constant a train service.

Sylvia had written that she would engage a room for him at the boarding-house where she was staying; and Chester, who was very tired after his long, hot journey, looked forward to a pleasant little chat with her, followed by a good night's rest.

It was nine o'clock when he got into the Lacville train, and again he was vaguely surprised to see what a large number of people were bound for the place. It was clear that something special must be going on there tonight, and that "the fireworks on the lake" must be on a very splendid scale.

When he arrived at Lacville, he joined the great throng of people, who were laughing and talking, each and all in holiday mood, and hailed an open carriage outside the station. "To the Villa du Lac!" he cried.

The cab could only move slowly through the crowd of walkers, and when it finally emerged out of the narrow streets of the town it stopped a moment, as if the driver wished his English fare to gaze at the beautiful panorama spread out before his eyes.

Dotted over the lake, large and mysterious in the starlit night, floated innumerable tiny crafts, each gaily hung with a string of colored lanterns. Now and again a red and blue rocket streamed up with a hiss, dissolving in a shower of stars reflected in the still water.

Down to the right a huge building, with towers and minarets flung up against the sky, was outlined in twinkling lights.

The cab moved on, only for a few yards however, and then drove quickly through high gates, and stopped with a jerk in front of a stone staircase.

"It cannot be here," said Chester incredulously to himself. "This looks more like a fine private house than a small country hotel."

"Villa du Lac?" he asked interrogatively, and the cabman said, *"Oui, M'sieur."*

The Englishman got out of the cab, and ascending the stone steps, rang the bell. The door opened, and a neat young woman stood before him.

"I am come to see Mrs. Bailey," he said in his slow, hesitating French.

There came a torrent of words, of smiles and nods — it seemed to Chester of excuses — in which "Madame Bailey" frequently occurred.

He shook his head, helplessly.

"I will call my uncle!"

The maid turned away; and Chester, with an agreeable feeling of relief that at last his journey was ended, took his bag off the cab, and dismissed the man.

What a delightful, spacious house! Sylvia had not been so very foolish after all.

M. Polperro came forward, bowing and smiling.

"M'sieur is the gentleman Madame Bailey has been expecting?" he said, rubbing his hands. "Oh, how sad she will be that she has already gone to the Casino! But Madame did wait for M'sieur till half-past nine; then she concluded that he must mean to spend the night in Paris."

"Do you mean that Mrs. Bailey has gone out?" asked Chester, surprised and disappointed.

"Yes, M'sieur. Madame has gone out, as she always does in the evening, to the Casino. It is, as M'sieur doubtless knows, the great attraction of our delightful and salubrious Lacville."

Chester had not much sense of humor, but he could not help smiling to himself at the other's pompous words.

"Perhaps you will kindly show me to the room which Mrs. Bailey has engaged for me," he said, "and then I will go out and try and find her."

M. Polperro burst into a torrent of agitated apologies. There was alas! no room for Madame Bailey's friend — in fact the Villa du Lac was so extraordinarily prosperous that there never was a room there from May till October, unless one of the guests left unexpectedly!

But Mr. Chester — was not that his name? — must not be cast down, for Mrs. Bailey had secured a beautiful room for him in another pension, a very inferior pension to the Villa du Lac, but still one in which he would be comfortable.

Chester now felt annoyed, and showed it. The thought of turning out again was not a pleasant one.

But what was this funny little Frenchman saying?

"Oh, if M'sieur had only arrived an hour ago! Madame Bailey was so terribly disappointed not to see M'sieur at dinner! A very nice special dinner was prepared, cooked by myself, in honor of Madame Bailey's little party."

And he went on to tell Chester, who was getting bewildered with the quick, eager talk, that this special dinner had been served at eight o'clock, and that Madame Bailey had entertained two friends that evening.

"You say that Mrs. Bailey is at the Casino?"

"Mais oui, M'sieur!"

It had never occurred to Chester that there would be a Casino in the place where Sylvia was spending the summer. But then everything at Lacville, including the Villa du Lac, was utterly unlike what the English lawyer had expected it to be.

M. Polperro spread out his hands with an eloquent gesture. "I beg of M'sieur," he said, "to allow me to conduct him to the Casino! Madame Bailey will not be here for some time, not perhaps for one hour, perhaps for two hours. I will have the luggage sent on to the Pension Malfait."

Strange — very strange! At home in Market Dalling Sylvia had always been fond of going to bed quite early; yet now, according to the hotel-keeper, she was perhaps going to stay out till one o'clock — till one o'clock on Sunday morning!

M. Polperro led Chester into the stately, long drawing room; but in a very few moments he reappeared, having taken off his white apron and his chef's cap, and put on a light grey alpaca coat and a soft hat.

As they hurried along the path which skirts the lake, Chester began to feel the charm of the place. It was very gay and delightful — "very French," so the English lawyer told himself. The lake, too, looked beautiful — mysteriously beautiful and fairylike, in the moonlight.

Soon they turned into a narrow dark lane.

"This is not a grand entrance to our beautiful Casino," said M. Polperro, ruefully, "but no matter, it is lovely once you get inside!" and he chuckled happily.

When in front of the great glass doors, he touched Chester on the arm.

"I wonder whether M'sieur would care to become a member of the Club," he said in a low voice. "I do not press M'sieur to do so! But you see, both Madame Bailey and her friends are members of the Club, and it is almost certain that it is there we shall find them. I fear it is no use our going to the Playing Rooms downstairs."

The Playing Rooms? Sylvia a member of a club? And — for Chester's quick, legal mind had leapt on the fact — of a gambling club?

No, that was incredible.

"I think there must be some mistake," he said distantly. "I do not think that Mrs. Bailey is a member of a club."

M. Polperro looked very much surprised.

"Oh, yes, indeed she is," he answered confidently. "It is only the quite common people who content themselves, M'sieur, with risking a franc and playing the little games. But just as M'sieur likes —" he shrugged his shoulders. "I do not press M'sieur to become a member of the Club."

Without answering, Chester paid the couple of francs admission for himself and his companion, and they walked slowly through the lower rooms, threading their way through the crowd.

"You see, M'sieur, I was right! Madame Bailey is in the Club!"

"Very well. Let us go to the Club," said Chester, impatiently.

He was beginning, or so he thought, to understand. The Club was evidently a quiet, select part of the Casino, with a reading room and so on. Sylvia had probably made friends with some French people in her hotel, and they had persuaded her to join the Club.

He was beginning to throw off his tiredness; the unaccustomed atmosphere in which he found himself amused and interested, even if it rather shocked him.

Ten minutes later he also, thanks to the kind offices of M. Polperro, and by the payment of twenty francs, found himself a member of the Club; free of that inner sanctuary where the devotees of the fickle goddess play with gold instead of silver; and where, as even Chester could see, the people who stood round the table, risking with quiet, calculating eyes their twenty-franc pieces and bank-notes, were of a very different social standing from the merry, careless crowd downstairs.

In the Baccarat Room most of the men were in evening clothes, and the women with them, if to Chester's eyes by no means desirable or reputable-looking companions, were young, pretty, and beautifully dressed.

Still, the English lawyer felt a thrill of disgust at the thought that Sylvia Bailey could possibly be part of such a company.

Baccarat was being played at both tables, but the crowd of players centered rather round one than the other, as is almost always the way.

M. Polperro touched his companion on the arm. "And now, M'sieur," he said briefly, "I will with your permission depart home. I think you will find Madame Bailey at that further table."

Chester shook the owner of the Villa du Lac cordially by the hand. The little man had been really kind and helpful. It was a pity there was no vacant room in his hotel.

He made his way to the further table, and gradually reached a point of vantage where he could see those of the players who were seated round the green cloth.

As is generally the case when really high play is going on, the people who were playing, as also those watching them, were curiously quiet.

And then, with a shock of surprise which sent the blood to his cheeks, Chester suddenly saw that Sylvia Bailey was sitting nearly opposite to where he himself was standing.

There are certain scenes, certain human groupings of individuals, which remain fixed forever against the screen of memory. Bill Chester will never forget the sight which was presented to him in the Lacville Casino by the particular group on which his tired eyes became focused with growing amazement and attention.

Sylvia was sitting at the baccarat table next to the man who was acting as Banker. She was evidently absorbed in the fortunes of the game, and she followed the slow falling of the fateful cards with rather feverish intentness.

Her small gloved hands rested on the table, one of them loosely holding a tiny ivory rake; and on a bank-note spread open on the green cloth before her were two neat piles of gold, the one composed of twenty-franc, the other of ten-franc pieces.

Chester, with a strange feeling of fear and anger clutching at his heart, told himself that he had never seen Sylvia look as she looked tonight. She was more than pretty – she was lovely, and above all, alive – vividly alive. There was a bright color on her cheek, and a soft light shining in her eyes.

The row of pearls which had occasioned the only serious difference which had ever arisen between them, rose and fell softly on the bosom of her black lace dress.

Chester also gradually became aware that his beautiful friend and client formed a center of attraction to those standing round the gambling-table. Both the men and the women stared at her, some enviously, but more with kindly admiration, for beauty is sure of its tribute in any French audience, and Sylvia Bailey tonight looked radiantly lovely – lovely and yet surely unhappy and ill-at-ease.

Well might she look both in such a place and among such a crew! So the English lawyer angrily told himself.

Now and again she turned and spoke in an eager, intimate fashion to a man sitting next her on her left. This man, oddly enough, was not playing.

Sylvia Bailey's companion was obviously a Frenchman, or so Chester felt sure, for now he found himself concentrating his attention on Mrs. Bailey's neighbor rather than on her. This man, to whom she kept turning and speaking in a low, earnest tone, was slim and fair, and what could be seen of his evening clothes fitted scrupulously well. The Englishman, looking at him with alien, jealous eyes, decided within himself that the Frenchman with whom Sylvia seemed to be on such friendly terms, was a foppish-looking fellow, not at all the sort of man she ought to have "picked up" on her travels.

Suddenly Sylvia raised her head, throwing it back with a graceful gesture, and Chester's eyes traveled on to the person who was standing just behind her, and to whom she had now begun speaking with smiling animation.

This was a woman – short, stout, and swarthy – dressed in a bright purple gown, and wearing a pale blue bonnet which was singularly unbecoming to her red, massive face. Chester rather wondered that such an odd, and yes – such a respectable-looking person could be a member of this gambling club. She reminded him of the stout old housekeeper in a big English country house near Market Dalling.

Sylvia seemed also to include in her talk a man who was standing next the fat woman. He was tall and lanky, absurdly and unsuitably dressed, to the English onlooker, in a white alpaca suit and a shabby Panama hat. In his hand he held a little book, in which he noted down every turn of the game, and it was clear to Chester that, though he listened to Mrs. Bailey with civility, he was quite uninterested in what she was saying.

Very different was the attitude of the woman; she seemed absorbed in Sylvia's remarks, and she leant forward familiarly, throwing all her weight on the back of the chair on which Mrs. Bailey was sitting. Sometimes as she spoke she smiled in a way that showed her large, strong teeth.

Chester thought them both odd, common-looking people. He was surprised that Sylvia knew them – nay more, that she seemed on such friendly terms with them; and he noticed that the Frenchman sitting next to her – the dandyish-looking fellow to whom she had been talking just now – took no part at all in her present conversation. Once, indeed, he looked up and frowned, as if the chatter going on between Mrs. Bailey and her fat friend fretted and disturbed him.

Play had again begun in earnest, and Sylvia turned her attention to the table. Her neighbor whispered something which at once caused her to take up two napoleons and a ten-franc piece from the pile of gold in front of her. Very deliberately she placed the coins within the ruled-off space reserved for the stakes.

Bill Chester, staring across at her, felt as if he were in a nightmare — gazing at something which was not real, and which would vanish if looked at long enough.

Could that lovely young woman, who sat there, looking so much at home, with the little rake in her hand be Sylvia Bailey, the quiet young widow whose perfect propriety of conduct had always earned the praise of those matrons of Market Dalling, whom Chester's own giddier sisters called by the irreverent name of "old cats?" It was fortunate that none of these respectable ladies could see Sylvia now!

To those who regard gambling as justifiable, provided the gambler's means allow of it, even to those who habitually see women indulging in games of chance, there will, of course, be something absurd in the point of view of the solicitor. But to such a man as Bill Chester, the sight of the woman for whom he had always felt a very sincere respect, as well as a far more enduring and jealous affection than he quite realized, sitting there at a public gaming table, was a staggering — nay, a disgusting — spectacle.

He reminded himself angrily that Sylvia had a good income — so good an income that she very seldom spent it all in the course of any one year. Why, therefore, should she wish to increase it?

Above all, how could she bear to mingle with this queer, horrid crowd? Why should she allow herself to be contaminated by breathing the same air as some of the women who were there round her? She and the stout, middle-aged person standing behind her were probably the only "respectable" women in the Club.

And then, it was all so deliberate! Chester had once seen a man whom he greatly respected drunk, and the sight had ever remained with him. But, after all, a man may get drunk by accident — nay, it may almost be said that a man always gets drunk by accident. But, in this matter of risking her money at the baccarat table, Sylvia Bailey knew very well what she was about.

With a thrill of genuine distress the lawyer asked himself whether she had not, in very truth, already become a confirmed gambler. It was with an assured, familiar gesture that Sylvia placed her money on the green cloth, and then with what intelligent knowledge she followed the operations of the Banker!

He watched her when her fifty francs were swept away, and noted the calm manner with which she immediately took five louis from her pile, and pushed them, with her little rake, well on to the table.

But before the dealer of the cards had spoken the fateful words: *"Le jeu est fait. Rien ne va plus!"* Mrs. Bailey uttered an exclamation under her breath, and hurriedly rose from her chair.

She had suddenly seen Chester — seen his eyes fixed on her with a perplexed, angry look in them, and the look had made her wince.

Forgetting that she still had a stake on the green cloth, she turned away from the table and began making her way round the edge of the circle.

For a moment Chester lost sight of her — there were so many people round the table. He went on staring, hardly knowing what he was doing, at the four pounds she had left on the green cloth.

The cards were quickly dealt, and the fateful, to Chester the incomprehensible, words were quickly uttered. Chester saw that Sylvia, unknowing of the fact, had won — that five louis were added to her original stake. The fair-haired Frenchman in evening dress by whom Mrs. Bailey had been sitting looked round; not seeing her, he himself swept up the stake and slipped the ten louis into his pocket.

"Bill! You here? I had quite given you up! I thought you had missed the train — at any rate, I never thought you would come out to Lacville as late as this."

The bright color, which was one of Sylvia's chief physical attributes, had faded from her cheeks. She looked pale, and her heart was beating uncomfortably. She would have given almost anything in the world for Bill Chester not to have come down to the Club and caught her like this — "caught" was the expression poor Sylvia used to herself.

"I am so sorry," she went on, breathlessly, "so very sorry! What a wretch you must have thought me! But I have got you such a nice room in a pension where a friend of mine was for a time. I couldn't get you anything at the Villa du Lac. But you can have all your meals with me there. It's such good cooking, and there's a lovely garden, Bill —"

Chester said nothing. He was still looking at her, trying to readjust his old ideas and ideals of Sylvia Bailey to her present environment.

Sylvia suddenly grew very red. After all, Bill Chester was not her keeper! He had no right to look as angry, as — as disgusted as he was now doing.

Then there came to both a welcome diversion.

"Ma jolie Sylvie! Will you not introduce me to your friend?"

Madame Wachner had elbowed her way through the crowd to where Chester and Mrs. Bailey were standing. Her husband lagged a little way behind, his eyes still following the play. Indeed, even as his wife spoke L'Ami Fritz made a note in the little book he held in his hand. When in the Baccarat Room he was absolutely absorbed in the play going on. Nothing could really distract him from it.

Sylvia felt and looked relieved.

"Oh, Bill," she exclaimed, "let me introduce you to Madame Wachner? She has been very kind to me since I came to Lacville."

"I am enchanted to meet you, sir. We 'oped to see you at dinner."

Chester bowed. She had a pleasant voice, this friend of Sylvia's, and she spoke English well, even if she did drop her aitches!

"It is getting rather late" — Chester turned to Sylvia, but he spoke quite pleasantly.

"Yes, we must be going; are you staying on?" Sylvia was addressing the woman she had just introduced to Chester, but her eyes were wandering towards the gambling table. Perhaps she had suddenly remembered her five louis.

Chester smiled a little grimly to himself. He wondered if Sylvia would be surprised to hear that her neighbor, the fair Frenchman to whom she had been talking so familiarly, had "collared" her stakes and her winnings.

"No, indeed! We, too, must be going 'ome. Come, Fritz, it is getting late." The devoted wife spoke rather crossly. They all four turned, and slowly walked down the room.

Sylvia instinctively fell behind, keeping step with Monsieur Wachner, while Chester and Madame Wachner walked in front.

The latter had already taken the measure of the quiet, stolid-looking Englishman. She had seen him long before Sylvia had done so, and had watched him with some attention, guessing almost at once that he must be the man for whom Mrs. Bailey had waited dinner.

"I suppose that this is your first visit to Lacville?" she observed smiling. "Very few of your countrymen come 'ere, sir, but it is an interesting and curious place — more really curious than is Monte Carlo."

She lowered her voice a little, but Chester heard her next words very clearly.

"It is not a proper place for our pretty friend, but — ah! she loves play now! The Polish lady, Madame Wolsky, was also a great lover of baccarat; but now she 'as gone away. And so, when Mrs. Bailey come 'ere, like this, at night, my 'usband and I — we are what you English people call old-fashioned folk — we come, too. Not to play — oh, no, but, *you* understand, just to look after 'er. She is so innocent, so young, so beautiful!"

Chester looked kindly at Madame Wachner. It was very decent of her — really good-natured and motherly — to take such an interest in poor Sylvia and her delinquencies. Yes, that was the way to take this — this matter which so shocked him. Sylvia Bailey — lovely, willful, spoilt Sylvia — was a very young woman, and ridiculously innocent, as this old lady truly said.

He, Chester, knew that a great many nice people went to Monte Carlo, and spent sometimes a good deal more money than they could afford at the tables. It was absurd to be angry with Sylvia for doing here what very many other people did in another place. He felt sincerely grateful to this fat, vulgar looking woman for having put the case so clearly.

"It's very good of you to do that," he answered awkwardly; "I mean it's very good of you to accompany Mrs. Bailey to this place," he looked round him with distaste.

They were now downstairs, part of a merry, jostling crowd, which contained, as all such crowds naturally contain, a rather rowdy element. "It certainly is no place for Mrs. Bailey to come to by herself —"

He was going to add something, when Sylvia walked forward.

"Where's Count Paul?" she asked, anxiously, of Madame Wachner. "Surely he did not stay on at the table after we left?"

Madame Wachner shook her head slightly.

"I don't know at all," she said, and then cast a meaning glance at Chester. It was an odd look, and somehow it inspired him with a prejudice against the person, this "Count Paul," of whom Sylvia had just spoken.

"Ah, here he is!" There was relief, nay gladness, ringing in Mrs. Bailey's frank voice.

The Comte de Virieu was pushing his way through the slowly moving crowd. Without looking at the Wachners, he placed ten louis in Sylvia's hand.

"Your last stake was doubled," he said, briefly. "Then that means, does it not, Madame, that you have made thirty-two louis this evening? I congratulate you."

Chester's prejudice grew, unreasonably. "Damn the fellow; then he was honest, after all! But why should he congratulate Mrs. Bailey on having won thirty-two louis?"

He acknowledged Sylvia's introduction of the Count very stiffly, and he was relieved when the other turned on his heel — relieved, and yet puzzled to see how surprised Sylvia seemed to be by his departure. She actually tried to keep the Count from going back to the Club.

"Aren't you coming to the Villa du Lac? It's getting very late," she said, in a tone of deep disappointment.

But he, bowing, answered, "No, Madame; it is impossible." He waited a moment, then muttered, "I have promised to take the Bank in a quarter of an hour."

Sylvia turned away. Tears had sprung to her eyes. But Chester saw nothing of her agitation, and a moment later they were all four out in the kindly darkness.

Chapter XX

*E*ven to Chester there was something grateful in the sudden stillness in which he and the three others found themselves on leaving the Casino.

"Not a very safe issue out of a place where people carry about such a lot of money!" he exclaimed, as they made their way up the rough little lane. "One could half-throttle anyone here, and have a very good chance of getting off!"

"Oh, Lacville is a very safe place!" answered Madame Wachner, laughing her jovial laugh. "Still, considering all the money made by the Casino, it is too bad they 'aven't made a more splendid — what do you call it — ?"

"— Approach," said L'Ami Fritz, in his deep voice, and Chester turned, rather surprised. It was the first word he had heard Monsieur Wachner utter.

Sylvia was trying hard to forget Count Paul and his broken promise, and to be her natural self.

As they emerged into the better-lighted thoroughfare, where stood a row of carriages, she said, "I will drive with you to the Pension Malfait, Bill."

Madame Wachner officiously struck in, "Do not think of driving your friend to the Pension Malfait, dear friend! We will gladly leave Mr.

Chester there. But if 'e does not mind we will walk there; it is too fine a night for driving."

"But how about your luggage?" said Sylvia, anxiously. "Has your luggage gone on to the Pension?"

"Yes," said Chester, shortly. "Your landlord very kindly said he would see to its being sent on."

They were now close to the Villa du Lac. "Of course, I shall expect you to lunch tomorrow," said Sylvia. "Twelve o'clock is the time. You'll want a good rest after your long day."

And then Chester started off with his two strange companions. How very unlike this evening had been to what he had pictured it would be! Years before, as a boy, he had spent a week at a primitive seaside hotel near Dieppe. He had thought Lacville would be like that. He had imagined himself arriving at a quiet, rural, little country inn, and had seen himself kindly, if a little shyly, welcomed by Sylvia. He could almost have laughed at the contrast between the place his fancy had painted and the place he had found, at what he had thought would happen, and at what had happened!

As they trudged along, Chester, glancing to his right, saw that there were still a great many boats floating on the lake. Did Lacville folk never go to bed?

"Yes," said Madame Wachner, quickly divining his thoughts, "some of the people 'ere — why, they stay out on the water all night! Then they catch the early train back to Paris in the morning, and go and work all day. Ah, yes, it is indeed a splendid thing to be young!"

She sighed, a long, sentimental sigh, and looked across, affectionately, at L'Ami Fritz.

"I do not feel my youth to be so very far away," she said. "But then, the people in my dear country are not cynical as are the French!"

Her husband strode forward in gloomy silence, probably thinking over the money he might have made or lost had he played that evening, instead of only noting down the turns of the game.

Madame Wachner babbled on, making conversation for Chester.

She was trying to find out something more about this quiet Englishman. Why had he come to Lacville? How long was he going to stay here? What was his real relation to Sylvia Bailey?

Those were the questions that the pretty English widow's new friend was asking herself, finding answers thereto which were unsatisfactory, because vague and mysterious.

At last she ventured a direct query.

"Are you going to stay long in this beautiful place, Monsieur?"

"I don't know," said Chester shortly. "I don't suppose I shall stay very long. I'm going on to Switzerland. How long I stay will a little bit depend on Mrs. Bailey's plans. I haven't had time to ask her anything yet. What sort of a place is the Villa du Lac?"

He asked the question abruptly; he was already full of dislike and suspicion of everything, though not of everybody, at Lacville. These Wachners were certainly nice, simple people.

"Oh, the Villa du Lac is a very respectable 'ouse," said Madame Wachner cautiously. "It is full of respectable — what do you call them? — dowagers. Oh, you need have no fear for your friend, sir; she is quite safe there. And you know she does not often go to the Casino" — she told the lie with bold deliberation. Some instinct told her that while Chester was at Lacville Sylvia would not go to the Casino as often as she had been in the habit of doing.

There was a pause — and then again Madame Wachner asked the Englishman a question:

"Perhaps you will go on to Switzerland, leaving Mrs. Bailey here, and then come back for her?"

"Perhaps I shall," he said heavily, without really thinking of what he was saying.

They were now walking along broad, shady roads which reminded him of those in a well-kept London suburb. Not a sound issued from any of the houses which stood in gardens on either side, and in the moonlight he saw that they were all closely shuttered. It might almost have been a little township of empty houses.

Again the thought crossed his mind what a dangerous place these lonely roads might be to a man carrying a lot of gold and notes on his person. They had not met a single policeman, or, indeed, anyone, after they had left the side of the lake.

At last Madame Wachner stopped short before a large wooden door.

"'Ere we are!" she said briskly. "I presume they are expecting you, sir? If they are not expecting you, they will probably 'ave all gone to bed. So we will wait, will we not, Ami Fritz, and see this gentleman safe in? If the worst came to the worst, you could come with us to our villa and sleep there the night."

"You are awfully kind!" said Chester heartily — and, indeed, he did feel this entire stranger's kindness exceptional.

How fortunate that Sylvia had come across such a nice, simple, kindly woman in such a queer place as Lacville!

But Madame Wachner's good-natured proposal had never to be seriously considered, for when her vigorous hand found and pulled the bell there came sounds in the courtyard beyond, and a moment later the door swung open.

"Who's there?" cried M. Malfait in a loud voice.

"It is the English gentleman, Mrs. Bailey's friend," said Madame Wachner quickly; and at once the Frenchman's voice softened.

"Ah! we had quite given up M'sieur," he said amiably. "Come in, come in! Yes, the bag has arrived; but people often send their luggage before they come themselves. Just as they sometimes leave their luggage after they themselves have departed!"

Chester was shaking hands cordially with the Wachners.

"Thank you for all your kindness," he said heartily. "I hope we shall meet again soon! I shall certainly be here for some days. Perhaps you will allow me to call on you?"

Once the good-natured couple had walked off arm in arm into the night, the door of the Pension Malfait was locked and barred, and Chester followed his landlord into the long, dark house.

"One has to be careful. There are so many queer characters about," said M. Malfait; and then, "Will M'sieur have something to eat? A little refreshment, a bottle of lemonade, or of pale ale? We have splendid Bass's ale," he said, solicitously.

But the Englishman shook his head, smiling. "Oh, no," he said slowly, in his bad French, "I dined in Paris. All I need now is a good night's rest."

"And that M'sieur will certainly have," said the landlord civilly. "Lacville is famous for its sleep-producing qualities. That is why so many Parisians content themselves with coming here instead of going further afield."

They were walking through the lower part of the house, and then suddenly M. Malfait exclaimed, "I was forgetting the bathroom! I know how important to English gentlemen the bathroom is!"

The pleasant vista of a good hot bath floated before Chester's weary brain and body. Really the house was not as primitive as he had thought it when he had seen the landlord come forward with a candle.

M. Malfait turned round and flung open a door.

"It was an idea of my wife's," he said proudly. "You see, M'sieur, the apartment serves a double purpose —"

And it did! For the odd little room into which Chester was shown by his host served as store cupboard as well as bathroom. It was lined with shelves on which stood serried rows of pots of home-made jam, jars of oil and vinegar, and huge tins of rice, vermicelli, and tapioca, in a corner a round zinc basin — but a basin of Brobdignagian size — stood under a cold water tap.

"The bath is for those of our visitors who do not follow the regular hydropathic treatment for which Lacville is still famous," said the landlord pompously. "But I must ask M'sieur not to fill the bath too full, for it is a great affair to empty it!"

He shut the door carefully, and led the way upstairs.

"Here we are," he whispered at last. "I hope M'sieur will be satisfied. This is a room which was occupied by a charming Polish lady, Madame Wolsky, who was a friend of M'sieur's friend, Madame Bailey. But she left suddenly a week ago, and so we have the room at M'sieur's disposal."

He put the candle down, and bowed himself out of the room.

Chester looked round the large, bare sleeping chamber in which he found himself with the agreeable feeling that his long, hot, exciting day was now at an end.

Yes, it was a pleasant room — bare, and yet furnished with everything essential to comfort. Thus there was a good big, roomy armchair, a writing-table, and a clock, of which the hands now pointed to a quarter to one o'clock.

The broad, low bed, pushed back into an alcove as is the French fashion, looked delightfully cool and inviting by the light of his one candle.

When M. Malfait had shown him into the room the window was wide open to the hot, starless night, but the landlord, though he had left the window open, had drawn the thick curtains across it. That was all right; Chester had no wish to be wakened at five in the morning by the sunlight streaming into the room. He meant to have a really long rest. He was too tired to think — too tired to do anything but turn in.

And then an odd thing happened. Chester's brain was so thoroughly awake, he had become so overexcited, that he could not, try as he might, fall asleep.

He lay awake tossing about hour after hour. And then, when at last he did fall into a heavy, troubled slumber, he was disturbed by extraordinary and unpleasant dreams — nightmares in which Sylvia Bailey seemed to play a part.

At last he roused himself and pulled back the curtains from across the window. It was already dawn, but he thought the cool morning air might induce sleep, and for a while, lying on his side away from the light, he did doze lightly.

Quite suddenly he was awakened by the sensation, nay, the knowledge, that there was someone in the room! So vivid was this feeling of unwished-for companionship that he got up and looked in the shadowed recess of the alcove in which stood his bed; but, of course, there was no one there. In fact there would not have been space there for any grown-up person to squeeze into.

He told himself that what he had heard — if he had heard anything — was someone bringing him his coffee and rolls, and that the servant had probably been trying to attract his attention, for, following his prudent custom, he had locked his door the night before.

He unlocked the door and looked out, staring this way and that along the empty passage. But no, in spite of the now-risen sun, it was still early morning; the Pension Malfait was sunk in sleep.

Chester went back to bed. He felt tired, disturbed, uneasy; sleep was out of the question; so he lay back, and with widely-open eyes, began to think of Sylvia Bailey and of the strange events of the night before.

He lived again the long hour he had spent at the Casino. He could almost smell the odd, sweet, stuffy smell of the Baccarat Room, and there rose before him its queer, varied inmates. He visioned distinctly Sylvia Bailey as he had suddenly seen her, sitting before the green cloth, with her money piled up before her, and a look of eager interest and absorption on her face.

There had always been in Sylvia something a little rebellious, a touch of individuality which made her unlike the other women he knew, and which fascinated and attracted him. She was a woman who generally knew her own mind, and who had her own ideas of right and wrong. Lying there, he remembered how determined she had been about those pearls. . . .

Chester's thoughts took a softer turn. How very, very pretty she had looked last evening — more than pretty — lovelier than he had ever seen her. There seemed to be new depths in her blue eyes.

But Chester was shrewd enough to know that Sylvia had felt ashamed to be caught by him gambling — gambling, too, in such very mixed company. Well, she would soon be leaving Lacville! What a pity those friends of hers had given up their Swiss holiday! It would have been so jolly if they could have gone on there together.

He got tired of lying in bed. What a long night, as well as a very short night, it had been! He rose and made his way down to the primitive bathroom. It would be delightful to have any sort of bath, and the huge zinc basin had its points —

As Chester went quickly back to his room, instead of feeling refreshed after his bath, he again experienced the disagreeable sensation that he was not alone. This time he felt as if he were being accompanied by an invisible presence. It was a very extraordinary and a most unpleasant feeling, one which Chester had never experienced before, and it made him afraid — afraid he knew not of what.

Being the manner of man he was, he began to think that he must be ill — that there must be something the matter with his nerves. Had he been at home, in Market Dalling, he would have gone to a doctor without loss of time.

Long afterwards, when people used to speak before him of haunted houses, Bill Chester would remember the Pension Malfait and the extraordinary sensations he had experienced there — sensations the more extraordinary that there was nothing to account for them.

But Chester never told anyone of his experiences, and indeed there was nothing to tell. He never saw anything, he never even heard anything, but now and again, especially when he was lying awake at night and in the early morning, the lawyer felt as if some other entity was struggling to communicate with him and could not do so. . . .

The whole time he was there — and he stayed on at Lacville, as we shall see, rather longer than he at first intended — Chester never felt, when in his room at the Pension Malfait really alone, and sometimes the impression became almost intolerably vivid.

Chapter XXI

*B*ut the longest night, the most haunted night, and Chester's night had indeed been haunted, comes to an end at last. After he had had another bath and a good breakfast he felt a very different man to what he had done three of four hours ago, lying awake in the sinister, companioned atmosphere of his bedroom at the Pension Malfait.

Telling his courteous landlord that he would not be in to luncheon, Chester left the house, and as it was still far too early to seek out Sylvia, he struck out, with the aid of the little pocket-map of the environs of Paris with which he had been careful to provide himself, towards the open country.

And as he swung quickly along, feeling once more tired and depressed, the Englishman wondered more and more why Sylvia Bailey cared to stay in such a place as Lacville. It struck him as neither town nor country — more like an unfinished suburb than anything else, with almost every piece of spare land up for sale.

He walked on and on till at last he came to the edge of a great stretch of what looked like primeval woodland. This surely must be part of the famous Forest of Montmorency, which his guide-book mentioned as being the great attraction of Lacville? He wondered cynically whether Sylvia had ever been so far, and then he plunged into the wood, along one of the ordered alleys which to his English eyes looked so little forestlike, and yet which made walking there very pleasant.

Suddenly there fell on his ear the sound of horses trotting quickly. He looked round, and some hundred yards or so to his right, at a place where four roads met under high arching trees, he saw two riders, a man and a woman, pass by. They had checked their horses to a walk, and as their voices floated over to him, the woman's voice seemed extraordinarily, almost absurdly, familiar — in fact, he could have sworn it was Sylvia Bailey's voice.

Chester stopped in his walk and shrugged his shoulders impatiently. She must indeed be dwelling in his thoughts if he thus involuntarily evoked her presence where she could by no stretch of possibility be.

But that wandering echo brought Sylvia Bailey very near to Chester, and once more he recalled her as he had seen her sitting at the gambling table the night before.

In grotesque juxtaposition he remembered, together with that picture of Sylvia as he had seen her last night, the case of a respectable old lady, named Mrs. Meeks, the widow of a clergyman who had had a living in the vicinity of Market Dalling.

Not long after her husband's death this old lady — she had about three hundred a year, and Chester had charge of her money matters — went abroad for a few weeks to Mentone. Those few weeks had turned Mrs. Meeks into a confirmed gambler. She now lived entirely at Monte Carlo in one small room.

He could not help remembering now the kind of remarks that were made by the more prosperous inhabitants of Market Dalling, his fellow citizens, when they went off for a short holiday to the South, in January or February. They would see this poor lady, this Mrs. Meeks, wandering round the gaming tables, and the sight would amuse and shock them. Chester knew that one of the first things said to him after the return of such people would be, "Who d'you think I saw at Monte Carlo? Why, Mrs. Meeks, of course! It's enough to make her husband turn in his grave."

And now he told himself ruefully that it would be enough to make honest George Bailey turn in his grave could he see his pretty, sheltered Sylvia sitting in the Casino at Lacville, surrounded by the riffraff collected there last night, and actually taking an active part in the game as well as risking her money with businesslike intentness.

He wondered if he could persuade Sylvia to leave Lacville soon. In any case he would himself stay on here three or four days — he had meant only to stay twenty-four hours, for he was on his way to join a friend whose Swiss holiday was limited. The sensible thing for Sylvia to do would be to go back to England.

Chester reached the Villa du Lac at half-past eleven and as he went out into the charming garden where he was told he would find Mrs. Bailey he told himself that Lacville was not without some innocent attractions. But Mrs. Bailey was not alone in this lovely garden. Sitting on the lawn by her was the Frenchman who had been with her when Chester had first caught sight of her at the Casino the night before.

The two were talking so earnestly that they only became aware of his approach when he was close to them, and though Chester was not a particularly observant man, he had an instant and most unpleasant impression that he had come too soon; that Sylvia was not glad to see him; and that the Frenchman was actually annoyed, even angered, by his sudden appearance.

"We might begin lunch a little earlier than twelve o'clock," said Sylvia, getting up. "They serve lunch from half-past eleven, do they not?" she turned to the Comte de Virieu.

"Yes, Madame, that is so," he said; and then he added, bowing, "And now perhaps I should say good-bye. I am going into Paris, as you know, early this afternoon, and then to Brittany. I shall be away two nights."

"You will remember me to your sister, to — to the Duchesse," faltered Sylvia.

Chester looked at her sharply. This Frenchman's sister? The Duchesse? — how very intimate Sylvia seemed to be with the fellow!

As the Count turned and sauntered back to the house she said rather breathlessly,

"The Comte de Virieu has been very kind to me, Bill. He took me into Paris to see his sister; she is the Duchesse d'Eglemont. You will remember that the Duc d'Eglemont won the Derby two years ago?"

And as he made no answer she went on, as if on the defensive.

"The Comte de Virieu has to go away to the funeral of his godmother. I am sorry, for I should have liked you to have become friends with him. He was at school in England — that is why he speaks English so well."

While they were enjoying the excellent luncheon prepared for them by M. Polperro, Chester was uncomfortably aware that the Count, sitting at his solitary meal at another table, could, should he care to do so, overhear every word the other two were saying.

But Paul de Virieu did not look across or talk as an Englishman would probably have done had he been on familiar terms with a fellow-guest in an hotel. Instead he devoted himself, in the intervals of the meal, to reading a paper. But now and again Chester, glancing across, could see the other man's eyes fixed on himself with a penetrating, thoughtful look. What did this Frenchman mean by staring at him like that?

As for Sylvia, she was obviously ill at ease. She talked quickly, rather disconnectedly, of the many things appertaining to her life at home, in Market Dalling, which she had in common with the English lawyer. She only touched on the delightful time she had had in Paris, and she said nothing of Lacville.

Long before the others had finished, Count Paul got up; before leaving the dining room, he turned and bowed ceremoniously to Sylvia and her companion. With his disappearance it seemed to Chester that Sylvia at once became her natural, simple, eager, happy self. She talked less, she listened more, and at last Chester began to enjoy his holiday.

They went out again into the garden, and the wide lawn, with its shaded spaces of deep green, was a delicious place in which to spend a quiet, idle hour. They sat down and drank their coffee under one of the cedars of Lebanon.

"This is a very delightful, curious kind of hotel," he said at last. "And I confess that now I understand why you like Lacville. But I do wonder a little, Sylvia" — he looked at her gravely — "that you enjoy going to that Casino."

"You see, there's so very little else to do here!" she exclaimed, deprecatingly. "And then, after all, Bill, I don't see what harm there is in risking one's money if one can afford to do so!"

He shook his head at her — playfully, but seriously too. "Don't you?" he asked dryly.

"Why, there's Madame Wachner," said Sylvia suddenly, and Chester thought there was a little touch of relief in her voice.

"Madame Wachner?" And then the Englishman, gazing at the stout, squat figure which was waddling along the grass towards them, remembered.

This was the good lady who had been so kind to him the night before; nay, who had actually offered to give him a bed if the Pension Malfait had been closed.

"We 'ave lunched in the town," she said, partly addressing Chester, "and so I thought I would come and ask you, Madame Sylvia, whether you and your friend will come to tea at the Villa des Muguets today?" She fixed her bright little eyes on Sylvia's face.

Sylvia looked at Chester; she was smiling; he thought she would like him to accept.

"That is very kind of you," he said cordially.

Sylvia nodded her head gaily: "You are more than kind, dear Madame Wachner," she exclaimed. "We shall be delighted to come! I thought of taking Mr. Chester a drive through the Forest of Montmorency. Will it do if we are with you about five?"

"Yes," said Madame Wachner.

And then, to Chester's satisfaction, she turned and went away. "I cannot stay now," she said, "for l'Ami Fritz is waiting for me. 'E does not like to be kept waiting."

"What a nice woman!" said Chester heartily, "and how lucky you are, Sylvia, to have made her acquaintance in such a queer place as this. But I suppose you have got to know quite a number of people in the hotel?"

"Well, no —," she stopped abruptly. She certainly had come to know the Comte de Virieu, but he was the exception, not the rule.

"You see, Bill, Lacville is the sort of place where everyone thinks everyone else rather queer! I fancy some of the ladies here — they are mostly foreigners, Russians, and Germans — think it very odd that I should be by myself in such a place."

She spoke without thinking — in fact she uttered her thoughts aloud.

"Then you admit that it *is* rather a queer place for you to be staying in by yourself," he said slowly.

"No, I don't!" she protested eagerly. "But don't let's talk of disagreeable things — I'm going to take you such a splendid drive!"

C hester never forgot that first day of his at Lacville. It was by far the pleasantest day he spent there, and Sylvia Bailey, womanlike, managed entirely to conceal from him that she was not as pleased with their expedition as was her companion.

Thanks to M. Polperro's good offices, they managed to hire a really good motor; and once clear of the fantastic little houses and the waste ground which was all up for sale, how old-world and beautiful were the little hamlets, the remote stretches of woodland and the quiet country towns through which they sped!

On their way back, something said by Sylvia surprised and disturbed Chester very much. She had meant to conceal the fact that she was riding with Paul de Virieu each morning, but it is very difficult for one accustomed always to tell the truth to use deceit. And suddenly a careless word revealed to Chester that the horsewoman whose voice had sounded so oddly familiar to him in the Forest that morning had really been Sylvia herself!

He turned on her quickly: "Then do you ride every morning with this Frenchman?" he asked quietly.

"Almost every morning," she answered. "His sister lent me a horse and a riding habit. It was very kind of her," she raised her voice, and blushed deeply in the rushing wind.

Chester felt his mind suddenly fill with angry suspicion. Was it possible that this Comte de Virieu, this man of whom that nice Madame Wachner had spoken with such scorn as a confirmed gambler, was "making up" to Sylvia? It was a monstrous idea – but Chester, being a solicitor, knew only too well that in the matter of marriage the most monstrous and disastrous things are not only always possible but sometimes probable. Chester believed that all Frenchmen regard marriage as a matter of business. To such a man as this Count, Mrs. Bailey's fortune would be a godsend.

"Sylvia!" he exclaimed, in a low, stern voice.

He turned round and looked at her. She was staring straight before her; the color had faded from her cheek; she looked pale and tired.

"Sylvia!" he repeated. "Listen to me, and – and don't be offended."

She glanced quickly at the man sitting by her side. His voice was charged with emotion, with anger.

"Don't be angry with me," he repeated. "If my suspicion, my fear, is unfounded, I beg your pardon with all my heart."

Sylvia got up and touched the driver on the shoulder. "Please slow down," she said in French, "we are going faster than I like."

Then she sank back in her seat. "Yes, Bill! What is it you wish to ask me? I couldn't hear you properly. We were going too fast."

"Is it possible, is it conceivable, that you are thinking of marrying this Frenchman?"

"No," said Sylvia, very quietly, "I am not thinking of marrying the Comte de Virieu. But he is my friend. I – I like and respect him. No, Bill, you need not fear that the Comte de Virieu will ever ask me to become his wife."

"But if he did?" asked Chester, hoarsely.

"You have no right to ask me such a question," she answered, passionately; and then, after a pause, she added, in a low voice: "But if he did, I should say no, Bill."

Her eyes were full of tears. As for Chester, he felt a variety of conflicting emotions, of which perhaps the strongest was a determination that if he could not get her no one else should do so. This — this damned French gambler had touched Sylvia's kind heart. Surely she couldn't care for a man she had only known a month, and such an affected, dandified fellow, too?

It was with relief that they both became aware a few moments later that they were on the outskirts of Lacville.

"Here is the Châlet des Muguets!" exclaimed Sylvia. "Isn't it a funny little place?"

The English lawyer stared at the bright pink building; with curiosity and amusement. It was indeed a funny little place, this brick-built bungalow, so fantastically and, to his British eyes, so ridiculously decorated with blue china lozenges, on which were painted giant lilies of the valley.

But he had not long to look, for as the car drew up before the white gate Madame Wachner's short, broad figure came hurrying down the path.

She opened the gate, and with boisterous heartiness welcomed Chester and Sylvia into the neglected garden.

Chester looked round him with an involuntary surprise. The Wachners' home was entirely unlike what he had expected to find it. He had thought to see one of those trim, neat little villas surrounded by gay, exquisitely tended little gardens which are the pride of the Parisian suburban dweller.

Madame Wachner caught his glance, and the thought crossed her mind uncomfortably that she had perhaps made a mistake, a serious mistake, in asking this priggish-looking Englishman to come to the Châlet des Muguets. He evidently did not like the look of the place.

"You wonder to see our garden so untidy," she exclaimed, regretfully. "Well, it is the owner's fault, not ours! You would not believe such a thing of a Frenchman, but 'e actually made us promise that we would do nothing — no, nothing at all, to 'is garden. 'E spoke of sending a man once a week to see after it, but no, 'e never did so."

"I have often wondered," broke in Sylvia frankly, "why you allowed your garden to get into such a state, but now, of course, I understand. What a very odd person your landlord must be, Madame Wachner! It might be such a delightful place if kept in good order. But I'm glad you have had the grass cut. I remember the first time I came here the grass was tremendously high, both in front and behind the house. Yesterday I saw that you have had it cut."

"Yes," said Madame Wachner, glancing at her, "yes, we had the grass cut a few days ago. Fritz insisted on it."

"If it had been as high as it was the first time I came here, I could never have made my way through it to the delightful little wood that lies over there, behind the châlet," went on Sylvia. "I don't think I told you that I went over there yesterday and waited a while, hoping that you would come back."

"You went into the wood!" echoed Madame Wachner in a startled tone. "You should not have done that," she shook her head gravely. "We are forbidden to go into the wood. We 'ave never gone into the wood."

L'Ami Fritz stood waiting for his visitors in the narrow doorway. He looked more good-tempered than usual, and as they walked in he chatted pleasantly to Chester.

"This way," he said, importantly. "Do not trouble to go into the salon, Madame! We shall have tea here, of course."

And Sylvia Bailey was amused, as well as rather touched, to see the preparations which had been made in the little dining room for the entertainment of Bill Chester and of herself.

In the middle of the round table which had looked so bare yesterday was a bowl of white roses — roses that had never grown in the untidy garden outside. Two dessert dishes were heaped up with delicious cakes — the cakes for which French pastry cooks are justly famed. There was also a basin full of the Alpine strawberries which Sylvia loved, and of which she always ordered a goodly supply at the Villa du Lac. Madame Wachner had even remembered to provide the thick cream, which, to a foreign taste, spoils the delicate flavor of strawberries.

They were really very kind people, these Wachners!

Looking round the funny little dining room, Sylvia could not help remembering how uncomfortable she had felt when sitting there alone the day before. It was hard now to believe that she should have had that queer, eerie feeling of discomfort and disquietude in such a commonplace, cheerful room. She told herself that there probably had been some little creature hidden there — some shy, wild thing, which maybe had crept in out of the wood.

"And now I will go and make the tea," said Madame Wachner pleasantly, and Sylvia gaily insisted on accompanying her hostess into the kitchen.

"We shall 'ave a nicer tea than that first time we made tea 'ere together," said Madame Wachner jovially.

The young Englishwoman shook her head, smiling.

"I had a very good time that afternoon!" she cried. "And I shall always feel grateful for your kindness to me and to poor Anna, Madame Wachner. I do so often wonder what Anna is doing with herself, and where she is staying in Paris." She looked wistfully at her companion.

Madame Wachner was in the act of pouring the boiling water into her china teapot.

"Ah, well," she said, bending over it, "we shall never know that. Your friend was a strange person, what I call a *solitaire*. She did not like gambling when there were people whom she knew in the Baccarat Room with her. As to what she is doing now —" she shrugged her shoulders, expressively.

"You know she telegraphed for her luggage yesterday?" said Sylvia slowly.

"In that case — if it has had time to arrive — Madame Wolsky is probably on her way to Aix, perhaps even to Monte Carlo. She did not seem to mind whether it was hot or cold if she could get what she wanted — that is, Play —"

Madame Wachner had now made the tea. She turned and stood with arms akimbo, staring out of the little window which gave on the sun-baked lawn bounded by the chestnut wood.

"No," she said slowly, "I do not for a moment suppose that you will ever see Madame Wolsky again. It would surprise me very much if you were to do so. For one thing, she must be — well, rather ashamed of the way she treated you — you who were so kind to her, Sylvie!"

"She was far kinder to me than I was to her," said Sylvia in a low voice.

"Ah, my dear" — Madame Wachner put her fat hand on Sylvia's shoulder — "you have such a kind, warm, generous heart — that is the truth! No, no, Anna Wolsky was not able to appreciate such a friend as you are! But now the tea is made, made strong to the English taste, we must not leave L'Ami Fritz and Mr. Chester alone together. Gentleman are dull without ladies."

Carrying the teapot she led the way into the dining room, and they sat down round the table.

The little tea-party went off fairly well, but Chester could not forget his strange conversation with Sylvia in the motor. Somehow, he and she had never come so really near to one another as they had done that afternoon. And yet, on the other hand, he felt that she was quite unlike what he had thought her to be. It was as if he had come across a new Sylvia.

Madame Wachner, looking at his grave, absorbed face, felt uneasy. Was it possible that this Englishman intended to take pretty Mrs. Bailey away from Lacville? That would be a pity — a very great pity!

She glanced apprehensively at her husband. L'Ami Fritz would make himself very unpleasant if Sylvia left Lacville just now. He would certainly taunt his wife with all the money they had spent on her entertainment — it was money which they both intended should bear a very high rate of interest.

Chapter XXII

The two following days dragged themselves uneventfully away. Sylvia did her best to be kind to Bill Chester, but she felt ill at ease, and could not help showing it.

And then she missed the excitement and interest of the Casino. Bill had not suggested that they should go there, and she would not be the one to do so.

The long motoring expeditions they took each afternoon gave her no pleasure. Her heart was far away, in Brittany; in imagination she was standing by a grave surrounded by a shadowy group of men and women, mourning the old Marquise who had left Count Paul the means to become once more a self-respecting and respected member of the world to which he belonged by right of birth. . . .

Had it not been for the Wachners, these two days of dual solitude with Chester would have been dreary indeed, but Madame Wachner was their companion on more than one long excursion and wherever Madame Wachner went there reigned a kind of jollity and sense of cheer.

Sylvia wondered if the Comte de Virieu was indeed coming back as he had said he would do. And yet she knew that were he to return now, at once, to his old ways, his family, those who loved him, would have the right to think him incorrigible.

As is the way with a woman when she loves, Sylvia did not consider herself as a factor affecting his return to Lacville. Nay, she was bitterly hurt that he had not written her a line since he had left.

And now had come the evening of the day when Count Paul had meant to come back. But M. Polperro said no word of his return. Still, it was quite possible that he would arrive late, and Sylvia did not wish to see him when in the company, not only of Bill Chester, but also of the Wachners.

Somehow or other, she had fallen into the habit each evening of asking the Wachners to dinner. She did so today, but suggested dining at a restaurant.

"Yes, if this time, dear Sylvia, the host is L'Ami Fritz!" said Madame Wachner decidedly. And after a slight demur Sylvia consented.

They dined at the hotel which is just opposite the Casino. After the pleasant meal was over, for it had been pleasant, and the cheerful hostess had taken special pains over the menu, Sylvia weary at the thought of another long, dull evening in the drawing room of the Villa du Lac, was secretly pleased to hear Madame Wachner exclaim coaxingly:

"And now, I do 'ope, Mr. Chester, that you will come over and spend this evening at the Casino! I know you do not approve of the play that goes on there, but still, believe me, it is the only thing to do at Lacville. Lacville would be a very dull place were it not for the Casino!"

Chester smiled.

"You think me far more particular than I am really," he said, lightly. "I don't in the least mind going to the Casino." Why should he be a spoil-sport? "But I confess I cannot understand the kind of attraction play has for some minds. For instance, I cannot understand the extraordinary fascination it seems to exercise over such an intelligent man as is that Comte de Virieu."

Madame Wachner looked at the speaker significantly.

"Ah!" she said. "The poor Count! 'E is what you call 'confirmed' — a confirmed gambler. And 'e will now be able to play more than ever, for I 'ear a fortune 'as been left to 'im!"

Sylvia was startled. She wondered how the Wachners could have come to know of the Count's legacy. She got up, with a nervous, impatient gesture.

How dull, how long, how intolerable had been the last two days spent by her in the company of Bill Chester, varied by that of talkative Madame Wachner and the silent, dour Ami Fritz!

Her heart felt very sore. During that last hour she and Count Paul had spent together in the garden, she had begged him to stay away — to spend the rest of the summer with his sister. Supposing he took her at her word — supposing he never came back to Lacville at all? Sylvia tried to tell herself that in that case she would be glad, and that she only wanted her friend to do the best, the wisest thing for himself.

Such were her thoughts — her painful thoughts — as she walked across from the restaurant to the entrance of the Casino. Two whole days had gone by since she had been there last, and oh! how long each hour of those days had seemed!

The two oddly-assorted couples passed through into the hall, and so up to the closely-guarded doors of the Club.

The Baccarat Room was very full, fuller than usual, for several parties of merry, rather boisterous young men had come out from Paris to spend the evening.

She heard the words that were now so familiar, solemnly shouted out at the further table: *"La Banque est aux enchères. Qui prend la Banque?"*

There was a pause, and there fell on Sylvia's ears the murmur of two voices — the voice of the official who represented the Casino authorities, and the deep, low voice which had become so dear to her — which thrilled her heart each time she heard it.

Then Count Paul had come back? He had not followed her advice? And instead of being sorry, as she ought to have been, she was glad — glad! Not glad to know that he was here in the Casino — Sylvia was sorry for that — but glad that he was once more close to her. Till this moment she had scarcely realized how much his mere presence meant to her.

She could not see Paul de Virieu, for there was a crowd — a noisy, chattering crowd of overdressed men, each with a gaudily-dressed feminine companion — encompassing her on every side.

"Vingt mille francs en Banque! Une fois, deux fois, messieurs?" A pause — then the words repeated. *"Vingt mille francs en Banque!"*

Monsieur Wachner leant his tall, lean form over Sylvia. She looked up surprised, L'Ami Fritz very seldom spoke to her, or for the matter of that to anyone.

"You must play tonight, Madame!" he said imperiously. "I have a feeling that tonight you will bring us luck, as you did that first time you played."

She looked at him hesitatingly. His words made her remember the friend to whom she so seldom gave a thought nowadays.

"Do you remember how pleased poor Anna was that night?" she whispered.

Monsieur Wachner stared at her, and a look of fear, almost of terror, came over his drawn, hatchet face.

"Do not speak of her," he exclaimed harshly. "It might bring us ill-luck!"

And then Chester broke in, "Sylvia, do play if you want to play!" he cried rather impatiently. It angered him to feel that she would not do in his presence what she would most certainly have done were he not there.

And then Sylvia suddenly made up her mind that she would play. Count Paul was holding the Bank. He was risking — how much was it? — twenty thousand francs. Eight hundred pounds of his legacy? That was madness, absolute madness on his part! Well, she would gamble too! There came across her a curious feeling — one that gave her a certain painful joy — the feeling that they two were one. While he was risking his money, she would try to win his money. Were he in luck tonight, she would be glad to know that it would be her money he would win.

M. Wachner officiously made room for her at the table; and, as she sat down, the Comte de Virieu, looking round, saw who had come there, and he flushed and looked away, straight in front of him.

"*A Madame la main,*" said Monsieur Wachner eagerly indicating Sylvia. And the croupier, with a smile, pushed the two fateful cards towards the fair young Englishwoman.

Sylvia took up the two cards. She glanced down at them. Yes, L'Ami Fritz had been right. She was in luck tonight! In a low voice she uttered the welcome words — in French, of course — the words "Nine" and "The King," as she put the cards, face upwards, on the green cloth.

And then there came for her and for those who backed her, just as there had done on that first fateful evening at the Casino, an extraordinary run of good fortune.

Again and again the cards were dealt to Sylvia, and again and again she turned up a Nine, a Queen, a King, an Eight —. Once more the crowd excitedly followed her luck, staring at her with grateful pleasure, with fascinated interest, as she brought them temporary wealth.

The more she won, the more she made other people win, the more miserable Sylvia felt, and as she saw Count Paul's heap of notes and gold diminishing, she grew unutterably wretched. Eight hundred pounds? What an enormous lot of money to risk in an evening!

Then there came a change. For a few turns of the game luck deserted her, and Sylvia breathed more freely. She glanced up into Count Paul's impassive face. He looked worn and tired, as well he might be after his long journey from Brittany.

Then once more magic fortune came back. It seemed as if only good cards — variations on the fateful eights and nines — could be dealt her.

Suddenly she pushed her chair back and got up. Protesting murmurs rose on every side.

"If Madame leaves, the luck will go with her!" she heard one or two people murmur discontentedly.

Chester was looking at her with amused, sarcastic, disapproving eyes. "Well!" he exclaimed. "I don't wonder you enjoy gambling, Sylvia! Are you often taken this way? How much of that poor fellow's money have you won?"

"Ninety pounds," she answered mechanically.

"Ninety pounds! And have you ever lost as much as that, may I ask, in an evening?" he was still speaking with a good deal of sarcasm in his voice. But still, "money talks," and even against his will Chester was impressed. Ninety pounds represents a very heavy bill of costs in a country solicitor's practice.

Sylvia looked dully into his face.

"No," she said slowly. "No, the most I ever lost in one evening was ten pounds. I always left off playing when I had lost ten pounds. That is the one advantage the player has over the banker — he can stop playing when he has lost a small sum."

"Oh! I see!" exclaimed Chester dryly.

And then they became silent, for close by where they now stood, a little apart from the table, an angry altercation was going on between Monsieur and Madame Wachner. It was the first time Sylvia had ever heard the worthy couple quarreling in public the one with the other.

"I tell you I will *not* go away!" L'Ami Fritz was saying between his teeth. "I feel that tonight I am in luck, in great luck! What I ask you to do, Sophie, is to go away yourself, and leave me alone. I have made a thousand francs this evening, and at last I have an opportunity of trying my new system. I am determined to try it now, tonight! No — it is no use your speaking to me, no use reminding me of any promise I made to you. If I made such a promise, I mean to break it!"

Sylvia looked round, a good deal concerned. Madame Wachner's face was red, and she was plainly very angry and put out. But when she saw that she and her husband had attracted the attention of their English friends, she made a great effort to regain her self-control and good humor.

"Very well," she said, "Very well, Fritz! Do not speak to me as if I were an ogress or a dragon. I am your wife; it is my duty to obey you. But I will not stay to see you lose the good money you have made with the help of our kind friend, Madame Sylvia. Yes, I will go away and leave you, my poor Fritz."

And suiting her action to her words, she put her arm familiarly through Sylvia's and together they walked out of the Baccarat Room, followed by Chester.

When they were in the vestibule Madame Wachner turned to him with a rueful smile:

"It is a pity," she said, "that Fritz did not come away with us! 'E 'as made a thousand francs. It is a great deal of money for us to make — or to lose. I do not believe 'e will keep it, for, though you bring 'im luck, my dear" — she turned to Sylvia — "that Count always brings 'im bad luck. It 'as been proved to me again and again. Just before you arrived at Lacville with poor Madame Wolsky, Fritz 'ad a 'eavy loss! — a very 'eavy loss, and all because the Comte de Virieu 'eld the Bank!"

"Perhaps the Count will not hold the Bank again tonight," said Sylvia slowly.

"Of course, 'e will do so!" the other spoke quite crossly, "Did I not tell you, Sylvia, that our day servant heard from M. Polperro's wife, whose sister is cook to the Duchesse d'Eglemont, that the Comte de Virieu 'as been left an immense fortune by 'is godmother? Well, it is a fortune that will soon melt" — she chuckled, as if the thought was very pleasant to her. "But I do not think that any of it is likely to melt into Fritz's pocket — though, to be sure, we 'ave been very lucky, all of us, tonight," she looked affectionately at Sylvia.

"Even you, Sir" — Madame Wachner turned to Chester with a broad smile — "even you must be pleased that we came to the Casino tonight. What a pity it is you did not risk something! Even one pound! You might 'ave made quite a nice lot of money to take back to England with you —"

"— Or to spend in Switzerland!" said Chester, laughing. "It is to Switzerland I am going, Madame! I shall leave here the day after tomorrow."

"And will you not come back again?" asked Madame Wachner inquisitively.

"I may come back again if Mrs. Bailey is still here; but I do not suppose she will be, for I intend to spend at least a fortnight in Switzerland."

The three were now approaching the gates of the Villa du Lac.

"Well, Sylvia," cried Chester. "I suppose I must now say good-night? I do not envy you your ill-gotten gains!" He spoke lightly, but there was an undercurrent of reproach in his voice, or so Sylvia fancied.

"Good-night!" she said, and her voice was tremulous.

As she held out her hand the little fancy bag which held all her winnings, the bundle of notes and loose pieces of gold, fell to the ground.

Madame Wachner stooped down and picked it up. "How 'eavy it is!" she exclaimed, enviously. "Good gracious, Sylvia! What a lot you must 'ave made tonight?"

"And the notes don't weigh much," said Sylvia. "It's only the gold that is heavy!"

But she was not thinking of what she was saying. Her heart was full of anguish. How could Paul de Virieu have been so mad as to risk such an immense sum, a tenth part of the fortune — for fortune it was — which had just been left to him?

Sylvia hated herself for having contributed to his losses. She knew that it was absurd that she should feel this, for the same cards would certainly have been dealt to whoever had happened to take them from the *croupier*. But still, superstition is part of the virus which fills the gambler's blood, and she had certainly won a considerable part of the money Count Paul had lost tonight.

"May I see you back to your house?" asked Chester of Madame Wachner.

"Oh no, Monsieur, I must go hack to the Casino and look after Fritz! 'E is a child — quite a child as regards money." Madame Wachner sighed heavily. "No, no, you go 'ome to bed in the Pension Malfait."

"I shouldn't think of doing such a thing!" he said kindly. "I will come back with you to the Casino, and together we will persuade Monsieur Wachner to go home. He has had time to make or lose a good deal of money in the last few minutes."

"Yes, indeed he 'as —" again Madame Wachner sighed, and Chester's heart went out to her. She was a really nice old woman — clever and intelligent, as well as cheerful and brave. It seemed a great pity that she should be cursed with a gambler for a husband.

As they went back into the Casino they could hear the people round them talking of the Comte de Virieu, and of the high play that had gone on at the club that evening.

"No, he is winning now," they heard someone say. And Madame Wachner looked anxious. If Count Paul were winning, then her Fritz must be losing.

And alas! her fears were justified. When they got up into the Baccarat Room they found L'Ami Fritz standing apart from the tables, his hands in his pockets, staring abstractedly out of a dark window on to the lake.

"Well?" cried Madame Wachner sharply, "Well, Fritz?"

"I have had no luck!" he shook his head angrily. "It is all the fault of that cursed system! If I had only begun at the right, the propitious moment — as I should have done if you had not worried me and asked me to go away — I should probably have made a great deal of money," he looked at her disconsolately, deprecatingly.

Chester also looked at Madame Wachner. He admired the wife's self-restraint. Her red face got a little redder. That was all.

"It cannot be helped," she said a trifle coldly, and in French. "I knew how it would be, so I am not disappointed. Have you anything left? Have you got the five louis I gave you at the beginning of the evening?"

Monsieur Wachner shook his head gloomily.

"Well then, it is about time we went home." She turned and led the way out.

Chapter XXIII

*A*s Sylvia went slowly and wearily up to her room a sudden horror of Lacville swept over her excited brain.

For the first time since she had been in the Villa du Lac, she locked the door of her bedroom and sat down in the darkness.

She was overwhelmed with feelings of humiliation and pain. She told herself with bitter self-scorn that Paul de Virieu cared nothing for her. If he had cared ever so little he surely would never have done what he had done tonight?

But such thoughts were futile, and soon she rose and turned on the electric light. Then she sat down at a little writing-table which had been thoughtfully provided for her by M. Polperro, and hurriedly, with feverish eagerness, wrote a note.

DEAR COUNT DE VIRIEU —
    I am very tired tonight, and I do not feel as if I should be well enough to ride tomorrow. — Yours sincerely,
                                        SYLVIA BAILEY

That was all, but it was enough. Hitherto she had evidently been — hateful thought — what the matrons of Market Dalling called "coming on" in her manner to Count Paul; henceforth she would be cold and distant to him.

She put her note into an envelope, addressed it, and went downstairs again. It was very late, but M. Polperro was still up. The landlord never went to bed till each one of his clients was safe indoors.

"Will you kindly see that the Comte de Virieu gets this tonight?" she said briefly. And then, as the little man looked at her with some surprise, "It is to tell the Count that I cannot ride tomorrow morning. It is late, and I am very tired; sleepy, too, after the long motoring expedition I took this afternoon!" She tried to smile.

M. Polperro bowed.

"Certainly, Madame. The Count shall have this note the moment he returns from the Casino. He will not be long now."

But the promises of Southerners are pie-crust. Doubtless M. Polperro meant the Count to have the note that night, but he put it aside and forgot all about it.

Sylvia had a broken night, and she was still sleeping heavily when she was wakened by the now familiar sound of the horses being brought into the courtyard. She jumped out of bed and peeped through an opening in the closed curtains.

It was a beautiful morning. The waters of the lake dimpled in the sun. A door opened, and Sylvia heard voices. Then Count Paul was going riding after all, and by himself? Sylvia felt a pang of unreasoning anger and regret.

Paul de Virieu and M. Polperro were standing side by side; suddenly she saw the hotel-keeper hand the Count, with a gesture of excuse, the note she had written the night before. Count Paul read it through, then he put it back in its envelope, and placed it in the breast pocket of his coat.

He did not send the horses away, as Sylvia in her heart had rather hoped he would do, but he said a word to M. Polperro, who ran into the Villa and returned a moment later with something which he handed, with a deferential bow to the Count.

It was a card case, and Paul de Virieu scribbled something on a card and gave it to M. Polperro. A minute later he had ridden out of the gates.

Sylvia moved away from the window, but she was in no mood to go back to bed. She felt restless, excited, sorry that she had given up her ride.

When at last her tea was brought in, she saw the Count's card lying on the tray:

Madame —
 I regret very much to hear that you are not well — so ran his penciled words — but I trust you will be able to come down this morning, for I have a message to give you from my sister.
 Believe me, Madame, of all your servants the most devoted.
                                                Paul de Virieu

They met in the garden — the garden which they had so often had to themselves during their short happy mornings; and, guided by an instinctive longing for solitude, and for being out of sight and out of mind of those about them, they made their way towards the arch in the wall which led to the *potager.*

It was just ten o'clock, and the gardeners were leaving off work for an hour; they had earned their rest, for their work begins each summer day at sunrise. It was therefore through a sweet-smelling, solitary wilderness that Count Paul guided his companion.

They walked along the narrow paths edged with fragrant herbs till they came to the extreme end of the kitchen-garden, and then —

"Shall we go into the orangery?" he asked abruptly.

Sylvia nodded. These were the first words he had uttered since his short "Good morning. I hope, Madame, you are feeling better?"

He stepped aside to allow her to go first into the large, finely-proportioned building, which was so charming a survival of eighteenth-century taste. The orangery was cool, fragrant, deserted; remote indeed from all that Lacville stands for in this ugly, utilitarian world.

"Won't you sit down?" he said slowly. And then, as if echoing his companion's thoughts, "It seems a long, long time since we were first in the orangery, Madame —"

"— When you asked me so earnestly to leave Lacville," said Sylvia, trying to speak lightly. She sat down on the circular stone seat, and, as he had done on that remembered morning when they were still strangers, he took his place at the other end of it.

"Well?" he said, looking at her fixedly. "Well, you see I came back after all!"

Sylvia made no answer.

"I ought not to have done so. It was weak of me." He did not look at her as he spoke; he was tracing imaginary patterns on the stone floor.

"I came back," he concluded, in a low, bitter tone, "because I could not stay any longer away from you."

And still Sylvia remained silent.

"Do you not believe that?" he asked, rather roughly.

And then at last she looked up and spoke.

"I think you imagine that to be the case," she said, "but I am sure that it is not I, alone, who brought you back to Lacville."

"And yet it is you — you alone!" he exclaimed and he jumped up and came and stood before her.

"God knows I do not wish to deceive you. Perhaps, if I had not come back here, I should in time — not at once, Madame, — have gone somewhere else, where I could enjoy the only thing in life which had come to be worth while living for. But it was you — you alone — that brought me back here, to Lacville!"

"Why did you go straight to the Casino?" she faltered. "And why? — oh, why did you risk all that money?"

He shrugged his shoulders.

"Because I am a fool!" he answered, bitterly — "a fool, and what the English rightly call 'a dog in the manger!' I ought to rejoice when I see you with that excellent fellow, Mr. Chester — and as your friend," he stopped short and then ended his sentence with the words, "I ought to be happy to know that you will have so excellent a husband!"

Sylvia also got up.

"You are quite mistaken," she said, coldly. "I shall never marry Mr. Chester."

"I regret to hear you say that," said Count Paul, seriously. "A woman should not live alone, especially a woman who is young and beautiful, and — and who has money."

Sylvia shook her head. She was angry — more hurt and angry than she had ever felt before in her life. She told herself passionately that the Comte de Virieu was refusing that which had not been offered to him.

"You are very kind," she answered, lightly. "But I have managed very well up to now, and I think I shall go on managing very well. You need not trouble yourself about the matter, Count Paul. Mr. Chester and I thoroughly understand one another —" She waited, and gently she added, "I wish I could understand you —"

"I wish I understood myself," he said somberly. "But there is one thing that I believe myself incapable of doing. Whatever my feeling, nay, whatever my love, for a woman, I would never do so infamous a thing as to try and persuade her to join her life to mine. I know too well to what I should be exposing her — to what possible misery, nay, to what probable degradation! After all, a man is free to go to the devil alone — but he has no right to drag a woman there with him!"

His voice had sunk to a hoarse whisper, and he was gazing into Sylvia's pale face with an anguished look of questioning and of pleading pain.

"I think that is true, Count Paul." Sylvia heard herself uttering gently, composedly, the words which meant at once so much and so little to them both. "It is a pity that all men do not feel about this as you do," she concluded mechanically.

"I felt sure you would agree with me," he answered slowly.

"Ought we not to be going back to the villa? I am expecting Mr. Chester to lunch, and though I know it is quite early, he has got into the way, these last few days, of coming early."

Her words stung him in his turn.

"Stop!" he said roughly. "Do not go yet, Mrs. Bailey." He muttered between his teeth, "Mr. Chester's turn will come!" And then aloud, "Is this to be the end of everything – the end of our – our friendship? I shall leave Lacville tonight for I do not care to stay on here after you have taunted me with having come back to see you!"

Sylvia gave a little cry of protest.

"How unkind you are, Count Paul!" She still tried to speak lightly, but the tears were now rolling down her cheeks – and then in a moment she found herself in Paul de Virieu's arms. She felt his heart beating against her breast.

"Oh, my darling!" he whispered brokenly, in French, "my darling, how I love you!"

"But if you love me," she said piteously, "what does anything else matter?"

Her hand had sought his hand. He grasped it for a moment and then let it go.

"It is because I love you – because I love you more than I love myself that I give you up," he said, but, being human, he did not give her up there and then. Instead, he drew her closer to him, and his lips sought and found her sweet, tremulous mouth.

*A*nd Chester? Chester that morning for the first time in his well-balanced life felt not only ill but horribly depressed. He had come back to the Pension Malfait the night before feeling quite well, and as cheerful as his disapproval of Sylvia Bailey's proceedings at the Casino allowed him to be. And while thoroughly disapproving, he had yet – such being human nature – been glad that Sylvia had won and not lost!

The Wachners had offered to drive him back to his pension, and he had accepted, for it was very late, and Madame Wachner, in spite of her Fritz's losses, had insisted on taking a carriage home.

And then, though he had begun by going to sleep, Chester had waked at the end of an hour to feel himself encompassed, environed, oppressed by the *perception* — it was far more than a sensation — that he was no longer alone.

He sat up in bed and struck a match, at once longing and fearing to see a form, — the semblance of a human being — rise out of the darkness.

But all he saw, when he had lighted the candle which stood on the table by his bed, was the barely furnished room which, even in this poor and wavering light, had so cheerful and commonplace an appearance.

Owing no doubt to his excellent physical condition, as well as to his good conscience, Chester was a fearless man. A week ago he would have laughed to scorn the notion that the dead ever revisit the earth, as so many of us believe they do, but the four nights he had spent at the Pension Malfait, had shaken his conviction that "dead men rise up never."

Most reluctantly he had come to the conclusion that the Pension Malfait was haunted.

And the feeling of unease did not vanish even after he had taken his bath in the queer bathroom, of which the Malfaits were so proud, or later, when he had eaten the excellent breakfast provided for him. On the contrary, the thought of going up to his bedroom, even in broad daylight, filled him with a kind of shrinking fear.

He told himself angrily that this kind of thing could not go on. The sleepless nights made him ill — he who never was ill; also he was losing precious days of his short holiday, while doing no good to himself and no good to Sylvia.

Sending for the hotel-keeper, he curtly told him that he meant to leave Lacville that evening.

M. Malfait expressed much sorrow and regret. Was M'sieur not comfortable? Was there anything he could do to prolong his English guest's stay?

No, M'sieur had every reason to be satisfied, but — but had M. Malfait ever had any complaints of noises in the bedroom occupied by his English guest?

The Frenchman's surprise and discomfiture seemed quite sincere; but Chester, looking into his face, suspected that the wondering protests, the assertion that this particular bedroom was the quietest in the house, were not sincere. In this, however he wronged poor M. Malfait.

Chester went upstairs and packed. There seemed to be a kind of finality in the act. If she knew he was ready to start that night, Sylvia would not be able to persuade him to stay on, as she probably would try to do.

At the Villa du Lac he was greeted with, "Madame Bailey is in the garden with the Comte de Virieu" — and he thought he saw a twinkle in merry little M. Polperro's eyes.

Poor Sylvia! Poor, foolish, willful Sylvia! Was it conceivable that after what she had seen the night before she still liked, she still respected, that mad French gambler?

He looked over the wide lawn; no, there was no sign of Sylvia and the Count. Then, all at once, coming through a door which gave access, as he knew, to the big kitchen-garden of the villa, he saw Mrs. Bailey's graceful figure; a few steps behind her walked Count Paul.

Chester hurried towards them. How odd they both looked — and how ill at ease! The Comte de Virieu looked wretched, preoccupied, and gloomy — as well he might do, considering the large sum of money he had lost last night. As for Sylvia — yes, there could be no doubt about it — she had been crying! When she saw Chester coming towards her, she instinctively tilted her garden hat over her face to hide her reddened eyelids. He felt at once sorry for, and angry with, her.

"I came early in order to tell you," he said abruptly, "that I find I must leave Lacville today! The man whom I am expecting to join me in Switzerland is getting impatient, so I've given notice to the Pension Malfait — in fact, I've already packed."

Sylvia gave him a listless glance, and made no comment on his news.

Chester felt rather nettled. "You, I suppose, will be staying on here for some time?" he said.

"I don't know," she answered in a low voice. "I haven't made up my mind how long I shall stay here."

"I also am leaving Lacville," said the Comte de Virieu.

And then, as he saw, or fancied he saw, a satirical expression pass over the Englishman's face, he added rather haughtily:

"Strange to say, my luck turned last night — I admit I did not deserve it — and I left off with a good deal to the good. However, I feel I have played enough for a while, and, as I have been telling Mrs. Bailey, I think it would do me good to go away. In fact" — and then Count Paul gave an odd little laugh — "I also am going to Switzerland! In old days I was a member of our Alpine Club."

Chester made a sudden resolve, and, what was rare in one so constitutionally prudent, acted on it at once.

"If you are really going to Switzerland," he said quietly, "then why should we not travel together? I meant to go tonight, but if you prefer to wait till tomorrow, Count, I can alter my arrangements."

The Comte de Virieu remained silent for what seemed to the two waiting for his answer a very long time.

"This evening will suit me just as well as tomorrow," he said at last.

He did not look at Sylvia. He had not looked her way since Chester had joined them. With a hand that shook a little he took his cigarette-case out of his pocket, and held it out to the other man.

The die was cast. So be it. Chester, prig though he might be, was right in his wish to remove Sylvia from his, Paul de Virieu's, company. The Englishman was more right than he would ever know.

How amazed Chester would have been had he been able to see straight into Paul de Virieu's heart! Had he divined the other's almost unendurable temptation to take Sylvia Bailey at her word, to impose on her pathetic ignorance of life, to allow her to become a gambler's wife.

Had the woman he loved been penniless, the Comte de Virieu would probably have yielded to the temptation which now came in the subtle garb of jealousy — keen, poisoned-fanged jealousy of this fine looking young Englishman who stood before them both.

Would Sylvia ever cling to this man as she had clung to him — would she ever allow Chester to kiss her as she had allowed Paul to kiss her, and that after he had released the hand she had laid in his?

But alas! there are kisses and kisses — clingings and clingings. Chester, so the Frenchman with his wide disillusioned knowledge of life felt only too sure, would win Sylvia in time.

"Shall we go in and find out the time of the Swiss express?" he asked the other man, "or perhaps you have already decided on a train?"

"No, I haven't looked one out yet."

They strolled off together towards the house, and Sylvia walked blindly on to the grass and sat down on one of the rocking-chairs of which M. Polperro was so proud.

She looked after the two men with a sense of oppressed bewilderment. Then they were both going away — both going to leave her?

After today — how strange, how utterly unnatural the parting seemed — she would probably never see Paul de Virieu again.

*T*he day went like a dream — a fantastic, unreal dream.

Sylvia did not see Count Paul again alone. She and Chester went a drive in the afternoon — the expedition had been arranged the day before with the Wachners, and there seemed no valid reason why it should be put off.

And then Madame Wachner with her usual impulsive good nature, on hearing that both Chester and the Comte de Virieu were going away, warmly invited Sylvia to supper at the Châlet des Muguets for that same night, and Sylvia listlessly accepted. She did not care what she did or where she went.

At last came the moment of parting.

"I'll go and see you off at the station," she said, and Chester, rather surprised, raised one or two objections. "I'm determined to come," she cried angrily. "What a pity it is, Bill, that you always try and manage other people's business for them!"

And she did go to the station — only to be sorry for it afterwards.

Paul de Virieu, holding her hand tightly clasped in his for the last time, had become frightfully pale, and as she made her way back to the Casino, where the Wachners were actually waiting for her, Sylvia was haunted by his reproachful, despairing eyes.

Chapter XXIV

*I*t was nearly nine o'clock, and for the moment the Casino was very empty, for the afternoon players had left, and the evening *serie*, as M. Polperro contemptuously called them — the casual crowd of night visitors to Lacville — had not yet arrived from Paris.

"And now," said Madame Wachner, suddenly, "is it not time for us to go and 'ave our little supper?"

The "citizeness of the world" had been watching her husband and Sylvia playing at Baccarat; both of them had won, and Sylvia had welcomed, eagerly, the excitement of the tables.

Count Paul's muttered farewell echoed in her ears, and the ornately decorated gambling room seemed full of his presence.

She made a great effort to put any intimate thought of him away. The next day, so she told herself, she would go back to England, to Market Dalling. There she must forget that such a place as Lacville existed; there she must banish Paul de Virieu from her heart and memory. Yes, there was nothing now to keep her here, in this curious place, where she had eaten, in more than one sense, of the bitter fruit of the tree of knowledge.

With a deep, involuntary sigh, she rose from the table.

She looked at the green cloth, at the people standing round it, with an odd feeling that neither the table nor the people round her were quite real. Her heart and thoughts were far away, with the two men both of whom loved her in their very different ways.

Then she turned with an unmirthful smile to her companions. It would not be fair to let her private griefs sadden the kindly Wachners. It was really good of them to have asked her to come back to supper at the Châlet des Muguets. She would have found it terribly lonely this evening at the Villa du Lac. . . .

"I am quite ready," she said, addressing herself more particularly to Madame Wachner; and the three walked out of the Club rooms.

"Shall we take a carriage?" Sylvia asked diffidently; she knew her stout friend disliked walking.

"No, no," said Monsieur Wachner shortly. "There is no need to take a carriage tonight; it is so fine, and, besides, it is not very far."

He so seldom interfered or negatived any suggestion that Sylvia felt a little surprised, the more so that it was really a long walk from the Casino to the lonely Châlet des Muguets. But as Madame Wachner had nodded assent to her husband's words, their English guest said no more.

They started out into the moonlit night, Sylvia with her light, springing step keeping pace with L'Ami Fritz, while his wife lagged a step behind. But, as was usual with him, M. Wachner remained silent, while his companions talked.

Tonight, however, Madame Wachner did not show her usual tact; she began discussing the two travelers who were now well started, no doubt, on their way to Switzerland, and she expressed contemptuous surprise that the Comte de Virieu had left Lacville.

"I am glad 'e 'as gone away," she said cheerfully, "for the Count is what English people call so supercilious — so different to that excellent Mr. Chester! I wonder Mr. Chester was willing for the Count's company. But you 'ave not lost 'im, my pretty Sylvia! 'E will soon be back!"

As she spoke she laughed coarsely, and Sylvia made no answer. She thought it probable that she would never see the Comte de Virieu again, and the conviction hurt intolerably. It was painful to be reminded of him now, in this way, and by a woman who she knew disliked and despised him.

She suddenly felt sorry that she had accepted the Wachner's invitation.

Tonight the way to the Châlet des Muguets seemed longer than usual — far longer than it had seemed the last time Sylvia had walked there, when Count Paul had been her companion. It seemed as if an immense time had gone by since then. . . .

Sylvia was glad when at last the three of them came within sight of the familiar white gate. How strangely lonely the little house looked, standing back in the twilit darkness of a summer night.

"I wonder" — Sylvia Bailey looked up at her silent companion, L'Ami Fritz had not opened his lips once during the walk from the Casino, "I wonder that you and Madame Wachner are not afraid to leave the châlet alone for so many hours of each day! Your servant always goes away after lunch, doesn't she?"

"There is nothing to steal," he answered shortly. "We always carry all our money about with us — all sensible people do so at Lacville and at Monte Carlo."

Madame Wachner was now on Sylvia's other side.

"Yes," she interposed, rather breathlessly, "that is so; and I 'ope that you, dear friend, followed the advice we gave you about the matter? I mean, I 'ope you do not leave your money in the hotel?"

"Of course I don't," said Sylvia, smiling. "Ever since you gave me those pretty little leather pouches I always carry all my money about with me, strapped round my waist. At first it wasn't very comfortable, but I have got quite used to it now."

"That is right," said Madame Wachner, heartily, "that is quite right! There are rogues everywhere, perhaps even in the Villa du Lac, if we knew everything!" and Sylvia's hostess laughed in the darkness her hearty, jovial laugh.

Suddenly she bent forward and addressed her husband. "By the way, Ami Fritz, have you written that letter to the Villa du Lac?" She nodded, explaining to Sylvia, "We are anxious to get a room in your beautiful pension for a rich friend of ours."

Sylvia had the instant feeling — she could not have told why — that his wife's question had greatly annoyed Monsieur Wachner.

"Of course I have written the letter!" he snapped out. "Do I ever forget anything?"

"But I'm afraid there is no room vacant in the Villa du Lac," said Sylvia. "And yet — well, I suppose they have not yet had time to let the Comte de Virieu's room. They only knew he was going this morning.

But you need not have troubled to write a letter, Monsieur Wachner. I could have given the message when I got back tonight. In any case let me take your letter."

"Ah! but the person in question may arrive before you get back," said Madame Wachner. "No, no, we have arranged to send the letter by a cabman who will call for it."

Monsieur Wachner pushed opened the white gate, and all three began walking up through the garden. The mantle of night now draped every straggling bush, every wilted flower, and the little wilderness was filled with delicious, pungent night scents.

When they reached the front door L'Ami Fritz stooped down, and began looking under the mat.

Sylvia smiled in the darkness; there seemed something so primitive, so simple, in keeping the key of one's front door outside under the mat! And yet foolish, prejudiced people spoke of Lacville as a dangerous spot, as the plague pit of Paris.

Suddenly the door was opened by the day-servant. And both the husband and wife uttered an involuntary exclamation of surprise and displeasure.

"What are you doing here?" asked Madame Wachner harshly. There was a note of dismay, as well as of anger, in her voice.

The woman began to excuse herself volubly. "I thought I might be of some use, Madame. I thought I might help you with all the last details."

"There was no necessity — none at all — for doing anything of the kind," said her mistress, in a low, quick voice. "You had been paid! You had had your present! However, as you are here, you may as well lay a third place in the dining room, for, as you see, we have brought Madame Bailey back to have a little supper. She will only stay a very few moments, as she has to be at the Villa du Lac by ten o'clock."

The woman turned and threw open the door of the dining room. Then she struck a match, and lighted a lamp which stood on the table.

Sylvia, as is often the case with those who have been much thrown with French people, could understand French much better than she could speak it, and what Madame Wachner had just hissed out in rapid, mumbling tones, surprised and puzzled her.

It was quite untrue that she, Sylvia, had to be back at the Villa du Lac by ten o'clock — for the matter of that, she could stay out as long and as late as she liked.

Then, again, although the arrangement that she should come to supper at the Châlet des Muguets tonight had been made that afternoon, the Wachners had been home, but they had evidently forgotten to tell their servant that they were expecting a visitor, for only two places were laid in the little dining room into which they all three walked on entering the house.

Propped up against the now lighted lamp was a letter addressed to Monsieur Polperro in a peculiar, large handwriting. L'Ami Fritz, again uttering that queer guttural exclamation, snatched up the envelope, and hurriedly put it into his breast-pocket.

"I brought that letter out of M'sieur's bedroom," observed the day-servant, cringingly. "I feared M'sieur had forgotten it! Would M'sieur like me to take it to the Villa du Lac on my way home?"

"No," said Monsieur Wachner, shortly. "There is no need for you to do that; Madame Bailey will kindly take it for me."

And again Sylvia felt surprised. Surely he had said — or was it Madame Wachner? — that they had arranged for a man to call for it.

His wife shouted out his name imperiously from the dark passage, "Fritz! Fritz! Come here a moment; I want you."

He hurried out of the room, and Sylvia and the servant were thus left alone together for a few moments in the dining room.

The woman went to the buffet and took up a plate; she came and placed it noisily on the table, and, under cover of the sound she made, "Do not stay here, Madame," she whispered, thrusting her wrinkled, sharp-featured face close to the Englishwoman's. "Come away with me! Say you want me to wait a bit and conduct you back to the Villa du Lac."

Sylvia stared at her distrustfully. This *femme de ménage* had a disagreeable face; there was a cunning, avaricious look in her eyes, or so Mrs. Bailey fancied; no doubt she remembered the couple of francs which had been given to her, or rather extorted by her, on the occasion of the English lady's last visit to the Châlet des Muguets.

"I will not say more," the servant went on, speaking very quickly, and under her breath. "But I am an honest woman, and these people frighten me. Still, I am not one to want embarrassments with the police."

And Sylvia suddenly remembered that those were exactly the words which had been uttered by Anna Wolsky's landlady in connection with Anna's disappearance. How frightened French people seemed to be of the police!

There came the sound of steps in the passage, and the Frenchwoman moved away quickly from Sylvia's side. She took up the plate she had just placed on the table, and to Sylvia's mingled disgust and amusement began rubbing it vigorously with her elbow.

Monsieur Wachner entered the room.

"That will do, that will do, Annette," he said patronizingly. "Come here, my good woman! Your mistress and I desire to give you a further little gift as you have shown so much zeal today, so here is twenty francs."

"*Merci, M'sieur.*"

Without looking again at Sylvia the woman went out of the room, and a moment later the front door slammed behind her.

"My wife discovered that it is Annette's fête day tomorrow, and gave her a trifle. But she was evidently not satisfied, and no doubt that was why she stayed on tonight," observed Monsieur Wachner solemnly.

Madame Wachner now came in. She had taken off her bonnet and changed her elastic-sided boots for easy slippers.

"Oh, those French people!" she exclaimed. "How greedy they are for money! But — well, Annette has earned her present very fairly —" She shrugged her shoulders.

"May I go and take off my hat?" asked Sylvia; she left the room before Madame Wachner could answer her, and hurried down the short, dark passage.

The door of the moonlit kitchen was ajar, and to her surprise she saw that a large trunk, corded and even labeled, stood in the middle of the floor. Close to the trunk was a large piece of sacking — and by it another coil of thick rope.

Was it possible that the Wachners, too, were leaving Lacville? If so, how very odd of them not to have told her!

As she opened the door of the bedroom Madame Wachner waddled up behind her.

"Wait a moment!" she cried. "Or perhaps, dear friend, you do not want a light? You see, we have been rather upset today, for L'Ami Fritz has to go away for two or three days, and that is a great affair! We are so very seldom separated. 'Darby and Joan,' is not that what English people would call us?"

"The moon is so bright I can see quite well," Sylvia was taking off her hat; she put it, together with a little fancy bag in which she kept the loose gold she played with at the gambling tables, on Madame Wachner's bed. She felt vaguely uncomfortable, for even as Madame Wachner had spoken she had become aware that the bedroom was almost entirely cleared of everything belonging to its occupants. However, the Wachners, like Anna Wolsky, had the right to go away without telling anyone of their intention.

As they came back into the dining room together, Mrs. Bailey's host, who was already sitting down at table, looked up.

"Words! Words! Words!" he exclaimed harshly. "Instead of talking so much why do you not both come here and eat your suppers? I am very hungry."

Sylvia had never heard the odd, silent man speak in such a tone before, but his wife answered quite good-humoredly,

"You forget, Fritz, that the cabman is coming. Till he has come and gone we shall not have peace."

And sure enough, within a moment of her saying those words there came a sound of shuffling footsteps on the garden path.

Monsieur Wachner got up and went out of the room. He opened the front door, and Sylvia overheard a few words of the colloquy between her host and his messenger.

"Yes, you are to take it now, at once. Just leave it at the Villa du Lac. You will come for us — you will come, that is, for *me*" — Monsieur Wachner raised his voice — "tomorrow morning at half-past six. I desire to catch the 7.10 train to Paris."

There was a jingle of silver, and then Sylvia caught the man's answering, *"Merci, c'est entendu, M'sieur."*

But L'Ami Fritz did not come back at once to the dining room. He went out into the garden and accompanied the man down to the gate.

When he came back again he put a large key on the dining-table.

"There!" he said, with a grunt of satisfaction. "Now there will be nothing to disturb us anymore."

They all three sat down at the round dining-table. To Sylvia's surprise a very simple meal was set out before them. There was only one small dish of galantine. When Sylvia Bailey had been to supper with the Wachners before, there had always been two or three tempting cold dishes, and some dainty friandizes as well, the whole evidently procured from the excellent confectioner who drives such a roaring trade at Lacville. Tonight, in addition to the few slices of galantine, there was only a little fruit.

Then a very odd thing happened.

L'Ami Fritz helped first his wife and himself largely, then Sylvia more frugally. It was perhaps a slight matter, the more so that Monsieur Wachner was notoriously forgetful, being ever, according to his wife, absorbed in his calculations and "systems." But all the same, this extraordinary lack of good manners on her host's part added to Sylvia's feeling of strangeness and discomfort.

Indeed, the Wachners were both very unlike their usual selves this evening. Madame Wachner had suddenly become very serious, her stout red face was set in rather grim, grave lines; and twice, as Sylvia was eating the little piece of galantine which had been placed on her plate by L'Ami

Fritz, she looked up and caught her hostess's eyes fixed on her with a curious, alien scrutiny.

When they had almost finished the meat, Madame Wachner suddenly exclaimed in French.

"Fritz! You have forgotten to mix the salad! Whatever made you forget such an important thing? You will find what is necessary in the drawer behind you."

Monsieur Wachner made no answer. He got up and pulled the drawer of the buffet open. Taking out of it a wooden spoon and fork, he came back to the table and began silently mixing the salad.

The two last times Sylvia had been at the Châlet des Muguets, her host, in deference to her English taste, had put a large admixture of vinegar in the salad dressing, but this time she saw that he soused the lettuce-leaves with oil.

At last, "Will you have some salad, Mrs. Bailey?" he said brusquely, and in English. He spoke English far better than did his wife.

"No," she said. "Not tonight, thank you!"

And Sylvia, smiling, looked across at Madame Wachner, expecting to see in the older woman's face a humorous appreciation of the fact that L'Ami Fritz had forgotten her well-known horror of oil.

Mrs. Bailey's dislike of the favorite French salad-dressing ingredient had long been a joke among the three, nay, among the four, for Anna Wolsky had been there the last time Sylvia had had supper with the Wachners. It had been such a merry meal!

Tonight no meaning smile met hers; instead she only saw that odd, grave, considering look on her hostess's face.

Suddenly Madame Wachner held out her plate across the table, and L'Ami Fritz heaped it up with the oily salad.

Sylvia Bailey's plate was empty, but Monsieur Wachner did not seem to notice that his guest lacked anything. And at last, to her extreme astonishment, she suddenly saw him take up one of the two pieces of meat remaining on the dish, and, leaning across, drop it on his wife's plate. Then he helped himself to the last remaining morsel.

It was such a trifling thing really, and due of course to her host's singular absent-mindedness; yet, even so, taken in connection with both the Wachners' silence and odd manner, this lack of the commonest courtesy struck Sylvia with a kind of fear — with fear and with pain. She felt so hurt that the tears came into her eyes.

There was a long moment's pause — then,

"Do you not feel well," asked Madame Wachner harshly, "or are you grieving for the Comte de Virieu?"

Her voice had become guttural, full of coarse and cruel malice, and even as she spoke she went on eating voraciously.

Sylvia Bailey pushed her chair back, and rose to her feet.

"I should like to go home now," she said quietly, "for it is getting late," – her voice shook a little. She was desperately afraid of disgracing herself by a childish outburst of tears. "I can make my way back quite well without Monsieur Wachner's escort."

She saw her host shrug his shoulders. He made a grimace at his wife; it expressed annoyance, nay, more, extreme disapproval.

Madame Wachner also got up. She wiped her mouth with her napkin, and then laid her hand on Sylvia's shoulder.

"Come, come," she exclaimed, and this time she spoke quite kindly, "you must not be cross with me, dear friend! I was only laughing, I was only what you call in England 'teasing.' The truth is I am very vexed and upset that our supper is not better. I told that fool Frenchwoman to get in something really nice, and she disobeyed me! I was 'ungry, too, for I 'ad no déjeuner today, and that makes one 'ollow, does it not? But now L'Ami Fritz is going to make us some good coffee! After we 'ave 'ad it you shall go away if so is your wish, but my 'usband will certainly accompany you –"

"Most certainly I will do so; you will not move – no, not a single step – without me," said Monsieur Wachner solemnly.

And then Madame Wachner burst out into a sudden peal of laughter – laughter which was infectious.

Sylvia smiled too, and sat down again. After all, as Paul de Virieu had truly said, not once, but many times, the Wachners were not refined people – but they were kind and very good-natured. And then she, Sylvia, was tired and low-spirited tonight – no doubt she had imagined the change in their manner, which had so surprised and hurt her.

Madame Wachner was quite her old self again; just now she was engaged in heaping all the cherries which were in the dessert dish on her guest's plate, in spite of Sylvia's eager protest.

L'Ami Fritz got up and left the room. He was going into the kitchen to make the coffee.

"Mr. Chester was telling me of your valuable pearls," said Madame Wachner pleasantly. "I *was* surprised! What a lot of money to 'ang round one's neck! But it is worth it if one 'as so lovely a neck as 'as the beautiful Sylvia! May I look at your pearls, dear friend? Or do you never take them off?"

Sylvia unclasped the string of pearls and laid it on the table.

"Yes, they are rather nice," she said modestly. "I always wear them, even at night. Many people have a knot made between each pearl, for that, of course, makes the danger of losing them much less should the string break. But mine are not knotted, for a lady once told me that it made the pearls hang much less prettily; she said it would be quite safe if I had them restrung every six months. So that is what I do. I had them restrung just before coming to France."

Madame Wachner reverentially took up the pearls in her large hand; she seemed to be weighing them.

"How heavy they are," she said at length, and now she spoke French.

"Yes," said Sylvia, "you can always tell a real pearl by its weight."

"And to think," went on her hostess musingly, "that each of these tiny balls is worth — how much is it worth? — at least five or six hundred francs, I suppose?"

"Yes," said Sylvia again, "I'm glad to say they have increased in value during the last few years. You see, pearls are the only really fashionable gems just now."

"And they cannot be identified like other fine jewels," observed Madame Wachner, "but I suppose they are worth more together than separately?" she was still speaking in that thoughtful, considering tone.

"Oh, I don't know that," said Sylvia, smiling. "Each separate pearl is worth a good deal, but still I daresay you are right, for these are beautifully matched. I got them, by a piece of great luck, without having to pay — well, what I suppose one would call the middle-man's profit! I just paid what I should have done at a good London sale."

"And you paid? — seven — eight 'undred pounds?" asked Madame Wachner, this time in English, and fixing her small, dark eyes on the fair Englishwoman's face.

"Oh, rather more than that." Sylvia grew a little red. "But as I said just now, they are always increasing in value. Even Mr. Chester, who did not approve of my getting these pearls, admits that I made a good bargain."

Through the open door she thought she heard Monsieur Wachner coming back down the passage. So she suddenly took the pearls out of the other woman's hand and clasped the string about her neck again.

L'Ami Fritz came into the room. He was holding rather awkwardly a little tray on which were two cups — one a small cup, the other a large cup, both filled to the brim with black coffee. He put the small cup before his guest, the large cup before his wife.

"I hope you do not mind having a small cup," he said solemnly. "I remember that you do not care to take a great deal of coffee, so I have given you the small cup."

Sylvia looked up.

"Oh dear!" she exclaimed, "I ought to have told you before you made it, Monsieur Wachner — but I won't have any coffee tonight. The last time I took some I lay awake all night."

"Oh, but you must take coffee!" Madame Wachner spoke good-humoredly, but with great determination. "The small amount you have in that little cup will not hurt you; and besides it is a special coffee, L'Ami Fritz's own mixture" — she laughed heartily.

And again? Sylvia noticed that Monsieur Wachner looked at his wife with a fixed, rather angry look, as much as to say, "Why are you always laughing? Why cannot you be serious sometimes?"

"But tonight, honestly, I would really rather not have any coffee!"

Sylvia had suddenly seen a vision of herself lying wide awake during long dark hours — hours which, as she knew by experience, generally bring to the sleepless, worrying thoughts.

"No, no, I will not have any coffee tonight," she repeated.

"Yes, yes, dear friend, you really must," Madame Wachner spoke very persuasively. "I should be truly sorry if you did not take this coffee. Indeed, it would make me think you were angry with us because of the very bad supper we had given you! L'Ami Fritz would not have taken the trouble to make coffee for his old wife. He has made it for you, only for you; he will be hurt if you do not take it!"

The coffee did look very tempting and fragrant.

Sylvia had always disliked coffee in England, but somehow French coffee was quite different; it had quite another taste from that of the mixture which the ladies of Market Dalling pressed on their guests at their dinner-parties.

She lifted the pretty little cup to her lips — but the coffee, this coffee of L'Ami Fritz, his special mixture, as his wife had termed it, had a rather curious taste, it was slightly bitter — decidedly not so nice as that which she was accustomed to drink each day after déjeuner at the Villa du Lac. Surely it would be very foolish to risk a bad night for a small cup of indifferent coffee?

She put the cup down, and pushed it away.

"Please do not ask me to take it," she said firmly. "It really is very bad for me!"

Madame Wachner shrugged her shoulders with an angry gesture.

"So be it," she said, and then imperiously, "Fritz, will you please come with me for a moment into the next room? I have something to ask you."

He got up and silently obeyed his wife. Before leaving the room he slipped the key of the garden gate into his trousers pocket.

A moment later Sylvia, left alone, could hear them talking eagerly to one another in that strange, unknown tongue in which they sometimes — not often — addressed one another.

She got up from her chair, seized with a sudden, eager desire to slip away before they came back. For a moment she even thought of leaving the house without waiting for her hat and little fancy bag; and then, with a strange sinking of the heart she remembered that the white gate was locked, and that L'Ami Fritz had now the key of it in his pocket.

But in no case would Sylvia have had time to do what she had thought of doing, for a moment later her host and hostess were back in the room.

Madame Wachner sat down again at the dining-table,

"One moment!" she exclaimed, rather breathlessly. "Just wait till I 'ave finished my coffee, Sylvia dear, and then L'Ami Fritz will escort you 'ome."

Rather unwillingly, Sylvia again sat down.

Monsieur Wachner was paying no attention either to his guest or to his wife. He took up the chair on which he had been sitting, and placed it out of the way near the door. Then he lifted the lighted lamp off the table and put it on the buffet.

As he did so, Sylvia, looking up, saw the shadow of his tall, lank figure thrown grotesquely, hugely, against the opposite wall of the room.

"Now take the cloth off the table," he said curtly. And his wife, gulping down the last drops of her coffee, got up and obeyed him.

Sylvia suddenly realized that they were getting ready for something — that they wanted the room cleared.

As with quick, deft fingers she folded up the cloth, Madame Wachner exclaimed, "As you are not taking any coffee, Sylvia, perhaps it is time for you now to get up and go away."

Sylvia Bailey looked across at the speaker, and reddened deeply. She felt very angry. Never in the course of her pleasant, easy, prosperous life had anyone ventured to dismiss her in this fashion from their house.

She rose, for the second time during the course of her short meal, to her feet —

And then, in a flash, there occurred that which transformed her anger into agonized fear — fear and terror.

The back of her neck had been grazed by something sharp and cold, and as she gave a smothered cry she saw that her string of pearls had parted in two. The pearls were now falling quickly one by one, and rolling all over the floor.

Instinctively she bent down, but as she did so she heard the man behind her make a quick movement.

She straightened herself and looked sharply round.

L'Ami Fritz was still holding in his hand the small pair of nail scissors with which he had snipped asunder her necklace; with the other he was in the act of taking out something from the drawer of the buffet.

She suddenly saw what that something was.

Sylvia Bailey's nerves steadied; her mind became curiously collected and clear. There had leapt on her the knowledge that this man and woman meant to kill her — to kill her for the sake of the pearls which were still bounding about the floor, and for the comparatively small sum of money which she carried slung in the leather bag below her waist.

L'Ami Fritz now stood staring at her. He had put his right hand — the hand holding the thing he had taken out of the drawer — behind his back. He was very pale; the sweat had broken out on his sallow, thin face.

For a horrible moment there floated across Sylvia's sub-conscious mind the thought of Anna Wolsky, and of what she now knew to have been Anna Wolsky's fate.

But she put that thought, that awful knowledge, determinedly away from her. The instinct of self-preservation possessed her wholly.

Already, in far less time than it would have taken to formulate the words, she had made up her mind to speak, and she knew exactly what she meant to say.

"It does not matter about my pearls," Sylvia said, quietly. Her voice shook a little, but otherwise she spoke in her usual tone. "If you are going into Paris tomorrow morning, perhaps you would take them to be restrung?"

The man looked questioningly across at his wife.

"Yes, that sounds a good plan," he said, in his guttural voice.

"No," exclaimed Madame Wachner, decidedly, "that will not do at all! We must not run that risk. The pearls must be found, now, at once! Stoop!" she said imperiously. "Stoop, Sylvia! Help me to find your pearls!"

She made a gesture as if she also meant to bend down. . . .

But Sylvia Bailey made no attempt to obey the sinister order. Slowly, warily she edged herself towards the closed window. At last she stood with her back to it — at bay.

"No," she said quietly, "I will not stoop to pick up my pearls now, Madame Wachner. It will be easier to find them in the daylight. I am sure that Monsieur Wachner could pick them all up for me tomorrow morning. Is not that so, Ami Fritz?" and there was a tone of pleading, for the first time of pitiful fear, in her soft voice.

She looked at him piteously, her large blue eyes wide open, dilated —

"It is not my husband's business to pick up your pearls!" exclaimed Madame Wachner harshly.

She stepped forward and gripped Sylvia by the arm, pulling her violently forward. As she did so she made a sign to her husband, and he pushed a chair quickly between Mrs. Bailey and the window.

Sylvia had lost her point of vantage, but she was young and lithe; she kept her feet.

Nevertheless, she knew with a cold, reasoned knowledge that she was very near to death – that it was only a question of minutes, – unless – unless she could make the man and woman before her understand that they would gain far more money by allowing her to live than by killing her now, tonight, for the value of the pearls that lay scattered on the floor, and the small, the pitiably small sum on her person.

"If you will let me go," she said, desperately, "I swear I will give you everything I have in the world!"

Madame Wachner suddenly laid her hand on Sylvia's arm, and tried to force her down on to her knees.

"What do you take us for?" she cried, furiously. "We want nothing from you – nothing at all!"

She looked across at her husband, and there burst from her lips a torrent of words, uttered in the uncouth tongue which the Wachners used for secrecy.

Sylvia tried desperately to understand, but she could make nothing of the strange, rapid-spoken syllables – until there fell on her ear, twice repeated, the name *Wolsky*. . . .

Madame Wachner stepped suddenly back, and as she did so L'Ami Fritz moved a step forward.

Sylvia looked at him, an agonized appeal in her eyes. He was smiling hideously, a nervous grin zigzagging across his large, thin-lipped mouth.

"You should have taken the coffee," he muttered in English. "It would have saved us all so much trouble!"

He put out his left hand, and the long, strong fingers closed, tentacle-wise, on her slender shoulder.

His right hand he kept still hidden behind his back –

Chapter XXV

The great open-air restaurant in the Champs Élysées was full of foreigners, and Paul de Virieu and Bill Chester were sitting opposite to one another on the broad terrace dotted with little tables embowered in flowering shrubs.

They were both smoking, — the Englishman a cigar, the Frenchman a cigarette. It was now half-past seven, and instead of taking the first express to Switzerland they had decided to have dinner comfortably in Paris and to go on by a later train.

Neither man felt that he had very much to say to the other, and Chester started a little in his seat when Paul de Virieu suddenly took his cigarette out of his mouth, put it down on the table, and leant forward. He looked at the man sitting opposite to him straight in the eyes.

"I do not feel at all happy at our having left Mrs. Bailey alone at Lacville," he said, deliberately.

Chester stared back at him, telling himself angrily as he did so that he did not in the least know what the Frenchman was driving at!

What did Paul de Virieu mean by saying this stupid, obvious thing, and why should he drag in the question of his being happy or unhappy?

"You know that I did my best to persuade her to leave the place," said Chester shortly. Then, very deliberately he added, "I am afraid, Count, that you've got quite a wrong notion in your mind concerning myself and Mrs. Bailey. It is true I am her trustee, but I have no power of making her do what I think sensible, or even what I think right. She is absolutely her own mistress."

He stopped abruptly, for he had no wish to discuss Sylvia and Sylvia's affairs with this foreigner, however oddly intimate Mrs. Bailey had allowed herself to get with the Comte de Virieu.

"Lacville is such a very queer place," observed the Count, meditatively. "It is perhaps even queerer than you know or guess it to be, Mr. Chester."

The English lawyer thought the remark too obvious to answer. Of course Lacville was a queer place – to put it plainly, little better than a gambling hell. He knew that well enough! But it was rather strange to hear the Comte de Virieu saying so – a real case, if ever there was one, of Satan rebuking sin.

So at last he answered, irritably, "Of course it is! I can't think what made Mrs. Bailey go there in the first instance." His mind was full of Sylvia. He seemed to go on speaking of her against his will.

"Her going to Lacville was a mere accident," explained Paul de Virieu, quickly. "She was brought there by the Polish lady, Madame Wolsky, of whom you must have heard her speak, whom she met in an hotel in Paris, and who disappeared so mysteriously. It is not a place for a young lady to be at by herself."

Bill Chester tilted back the chair on which he was sitting. Once more he asked himself what on earth the fellow was driving at? Were these remarks a preliminary to the Count's saying that he was not going to Switzerland after all – that he was going back to Lacville in order to take care of Sylvia.

Quite suddenly the young Englishman felt shaken by a very primitive and, till these last few days, a very unfamiliar feeling – that of jealousy.

Damn it – he wouldn't have that. Of course he was no longer in love with Sylvia Bailey, but he was her trustee and lifelong friend. It was his duty to prevent her making a fool of herself, either by gambling away her money – the good money the late George Bailey had toiled so hard to acquire – or, what would be ever so much worse, by making some wretched marriage to a foreign adventurer.

He stared suspiciously at his companion. Was it likely that a real count – the French equivalent to an English earl – would lead the sort of life this man, Paul de Virieu, was leading, and in a place like Lacville?

"If you really feel like that, I think I'd better give up my trip to Switzerland, and go back to Lacville tomorrow morning."

He stared hard at the Count, and noted with sarcastic amusement the other's appearance – so foppish, so effeminate to English eyes; particularly did he gaze with scorn at the Count's yellow silk socks, which matched his lemon-colored tie and silk pocket-handkerchief. Fancy starting for a long night journey in such a "get-up." Well! Perhaps women liked that sort of thing, but he would never have thought Sylvia Bailey to be that sort of woman.

A change came over Paul de Virieu's face. There was unmistakable relief – nay, more – even joy in the voice with which the Frenchman answered,

"That is excellent! That is quite right! That is first-rate! Yes, yes, Mr. Chester, you go back to Lacville and bring her away. It is not right that Mrs. Bailey should be by herself there. It may seem absurd to you, but, believe me, Lacville is not a safe spot in which to leave an unprotected woman. She has not one single friend, not a person to whom she could turn to for advice, – excepting, of course, the excellent Polperro himself, and he naturally desires to keep his profitable client."

"There's that funny old couple – I mean the man called Fritz Something-or-other and his wife. Surely they're all right?" observed Chester.

Paul de Virieu shook his head decidedly.

"The Wachners are not nice people," he said slowly. "They appear to be very fond of Mrs. Bailey, I know, but they are only fond of themselves. They are adventurers; 'out for the stuff,' as Americans say. Old Fritz is the worst type of gambler – the type that believes he is going to get rich, rich beyond dreams of avarice, by a 'system.' Such a man will do anything for money. I believe they knew far more of the disappearance of Madame Wolsky than anyone else did."

The Count lowered his voice, and leant over the table.

"I have suspected," he went on – "nay, I have felt sure from the very first, Mr. Chester, that the Wachners are *blackmailers*. I am convinced that they discovered something to that poor lady's discredit, and – after making her pay – drove her away! Just before she left Lacville they were trying to raise money at the Casino money-changer's on some worthless shares. But after Madame Wolsky's disappearance they had plenty of gold and notes."

Chester looked across at his companion. At last he was really impressed. Blackmailing is a word which has a very ugly sound in an English lawyer's ears.

"If that is really true," he said suddenly, "I almost feel as if I ought to go back to Lacville tonight. I suppose there are heaps of trains?"

"You might, at all events, wait till tomorrow morning," said Paul de Virieu, dryly.

He also had suddenly experienced a thrill of that primitive passion, jealousy, which had surprised Chester but a few moments before. But the Count was a Frenchman. He was familiar with the sensation – nay, he welcomed it. It showed that he was still young – still worthy to be one of the great company of lovers.

Sylvia, his "petite amie Anglaise," seemed to have come very near to him in the last few moments. He saw her blue eyes brim with tears at his harsh words – he thrilled as he had thrilled with the overmastering impulse which had made him take her into his arms – her hand lay once more in his hand, as it had lain, for a moment this morning.

Had he grasped and retained that kind, firm little hand in his, an entirely new life had been within his reach.

A vision rose before Paul de Virieu – a vision of Sylvia and himself living heart to heart in one of those small, stately manor-houses which are scattered throughout Brittany. And it was no vague house of dreams. He knew the little château very well. Had not his sister driven him there only the other day? And had she not conveyed to him in delicate, generous words how gladly she would see his sweet English friend established there as châtelaine?

A sense of immeasurable loss came over Paul de Virieu – But, no, he had been right! Quite right! He loved Sylvia far too well to risk making her as unhappy as he would almost certainly be tempted to make her, if she became his wife.

He took off his hat and remained silent for what seemed to his companion quite a long time.

"By the way, what is Mrs. Bailey doing tonight?" he asked at last.

"Tonight?" replied Chester. "Let me see? Why, tonight she is spending the evening with those very people – the Wachners, of whom you were speaking just now. I heard her arranging it with them this afternoon." He added, stiffly, "But I doubt if your impression as to these people is a right one. They seem to me a very respectable couple."

Paul de Virieu shrugged his shoulders. He felt suddenly uneasy – afraid he hardly knew of what.

There was no risk that Sylvia Bailey would fall a victim to blackmailers – she had nothing to be ashamed of, nothing to conceal. But still he hated to think that she was, even now, alone with a man and woman of whom he had formed such a bad impression.

He took his watch out of his pocket. "There's a train for Lacville at a quarter to ten," he said slowly. "That would be an excellent train for – for *us* – to take –"

"Then are you thinking of going back to Lacville too?" There was that sarcastic inflection in the Englishman's voice which the Count had learned to look for and to resent.

"Yes."

Count Paul looked at Bill Chester significantly, and his look said, "Take care, my friend! We do not allow a man to sneer at another man in this country unless he is willing to stand certain unpleasant consequences. Our duels are not always *pour rire!*"

During the short train journey back to Lacville they hardly spoke. Each thought that the other was doing a strange and unreasonable thing

— a thing which the thinker could have done much better if left to himself.

At Lacville station they jumped into a victoria.

"I suppose we had better drive straight to the Villa du Lac," said Chester, hesitatingly.

"Yes, we had better go first to the Villa du Lac, for Mrs. Bailey should be home by now. By the way, Mr. Chester, you had better ask to have my room tonight; we know that it is disengaged. As for me, I will go on somewhere else as soon as I know you have seen our friend. Please do not tell Mrs. Bailey that I came with you. Where would be the use? I may go back to Paris tonight." Paul de Virieu spoke in a constrained, preoccupied voice.

"But aren't you coming in? Won't you stay at Lacville at least till tomorrow?"

Chester's voice unwittingly became far more cordial; if the Frenchman did not wish to see Sylvia, why had he insisted on coming back, too, to Lacville.

The hall of the Villa du Lac was brightly lit up, and as the victoria swept up the short drive to the stone horseshoe stairway, the Comte de Virieu suddenly grasped the other's hand.

"Good luck!" he exclaimed, "Good luck, fortunate man! As the Abbot at my English school used to say to me when he met me, as a little boy, running about the cloisters, 'God bless you!'"

Chester was rather touched, as well as surprised. But what queer, emotional fellows Frenchmen are to be sure! Although Count Paul, as Sylvia used to call him, had evidently been a little bit in love with her himself, he was quite willing to think of her as married to another man!

But — but there was the rub! Chester was no longer so sure that he wanted to marry Sylvia. She had become a different woman — she seemed to be another Sylvia to the one he had always known.

"I'll just come out and tell you that it's all right," he said a little awkwardly. "But I wish you'd come in — if only for a minute. Mrs. Bailey would be so pleased to see you."

"No, no," muttered the other. "Believe me, she would not!"

Chester jumped out of the carriage and ran quickly up the stone steps, and rang the bell.

The door was opened by M. Polperro himself. Even busier than usual was the merry, capable little chef, for as it happened Madame Polperro had had to go away for two or three days.

"I want to know," said Chester abruptly, "if you can let me have a room for tonight? The room the Comte de Virieu occupied is, I suppose, disengaged?"

"I will see, M'sieur — I will inquire!"

M. Polperro did not know what to make of this big Englishman who had come in out of the night, bringing no luggage with him but one little bag.

Then he suddenly remembered! Why, of course, this was the friend of the pretty, charming, wealthy Madame Bailey; the English gentleman who had been staying during the past few days at the Pension Malfait! A gentleman who was called after a well-known cheese — yes, Chester was his name.

Then this Mr. Chester's departure from Lacville had been a *fausse sortie* — a *ruse* to get rid of the Comte de Virieu, who was also in love with the lovely young English widow?

Ah! Ah! M. Polperro felt very much amused. Never had he heard of anything so droll! But the Englishman's tale of love was not to run smooth after all, for now another complication had arisen, and the very last one any sensible man would have expected!

"Yes, M'sieur," said M. Polperro demurely, "it is all right! I had forgotten! As you say, the Comte de Virieu's room is now empty, but" — he hesitated, and with a sly look added, "indeed we have another room empty tonight — a far finer room, with a view over the lake — the room Madame Bailey occupied."

"The room Mrs. Bailey occupied?" echoed Chester. "Has Mrs. Bailey changed her room today?"

"Oh, no, M'sieur! She left Lacville this very evening. I have but just now received a letter from her."

The little man could hardly keep serious. Oh! those Englishmen, who are said to be so cold! When in love they behave just like other people.

For Chester was staring at him with puzzled, wrathful eyes.

"Ah! what a charming lady, M'sieur; Madame Polperro and I shall miss her greatly. We hoped to keep Madame Bailey all the summer. But perhaps she will come back — now that M'sieur has returned." He really could not resist that last thrust.

"Left Lacville!" repeated Chester incredulously. "But that's impossible! It isn't more than three hours since we said good-bye to her at the station. She had no intention of leaving Lacville *then*. Do you say you've received a letter from her?"

"Yes, M'sieur."

"Will you please show it me?"

"Certainly, M'sieur."

M. Polperro, followed closely by the Englishman, trotted off into his office, a funny little hole of a place which had been contrived under

the staircase. It was here that Madame Polperro was supposed to spend
her busy days.

M. Polperro felt quite lost without his wife. Slowly, methodically, he
began to turn over the papers on the writing-table, which, with one chair,
filled up all the place.

There had evidently been a lovers' quarrel between these two peculiar
English people. What a pity that the gentleman, who had very properly
returned to beg the lady's pardon, had found his little bird flown — in
such poetic terms did the landlord in his own mind refer to Sylvia Bailey.

The pretty Englishwoman's presence in the Villa du Lac had delighted
M. Polperro's southern, sentimental mind; he felt her to be so decora-
tive, as well as so lucrative, a guest for his beloved hotel. Mrs. Bailey
had never questioned any of the extras Madame Polperro put in her
weekly bills, and she had never become haggard and cross as other ladies
did who lost money at the Casino.

As he turned over the papers — bills, catalogues, and letters with which
the table was covered, these thoughts flitted regretfully through M.
Polperro's mind.

But he had an optimistic nature, and though he was very sorry
Madame Bailey had left the Villa du Lac so abruptly, he was gratified
by the fact that she had lived up to the ideal he had formed of his
English guest. Though Madame Bailey had paid her weekly bill only
two days before — she was en pension by the day — she had actually sent
him a hundred francs to pay for the two days' board; the balance to be
distributed among the servants. . . .

There could surely be no harm in giving this big Englishman the
lady's letter? Still, M. Polperro was sorry that he had not Madame
Polperro at his elbow to make the decision for him.

"Here it is," he said at last, taking a piece of paper out of the drawer.
"I must have put it there for my wife to read on her return. It is a very
gratifying letter — M'sieur will see that for himself!"

Chester took the folded-up piece of notepaper out of the little
Frenchman's hand with a strange feeling of misgiving.

He came out into the hall and stood under the cut-glass chandelier —

"You have made a mistake," he exclaimed quickly; "this is not Mrs.
Bailey's handwriting!"

"Oh, yes, M'sieur, it is certainly Mrs. Bailey's letter. You see there is
the lady's signature written as plainly as possible!"

Chester looked down to where the man's fat finger pointed.

In the strange, the alien handwriting, were written two words which
for a moment conveyed nothing to Chester, "Silvea" and "Baylee"; as
for the writing, stiff, angular, large, it resembled Sylvia's sloping English

calligraphy as little as did the two words purporting to be her signature resemble the right spelling of her name.

A thrill of fear, of terrifying suspicion, flooded Bill Chester's shrewd but commonplace mind.

Slowly he read the strange letter through:

"MONSIEUR POLPERRO (so ran the missive in French) —

"I am leaving Lacville this evening in order to join my friend Madame Wolsky. I request you therefore to send on my luggage to the cloak room at the Gare du Nord. I enclose a hundred-franc note to pay you what I owe. Please distribute the rest of the money among the servants. I beg to inform you that I have been exceedingly comfortable at the Villa du Lac, and I will recommend your hotel to all my friends.

"Yours very cordially,
"SYLVEA BAYLEE"

Turning on his heel, and without even throwing a word of apology to the astonished, and by now indignant, M. Polperro, Chester rushed out of the hall and down the stone steps, below which stood the victoria.

"Well?" cried out Paul de Virieu.

"Come into the house — now, at once!" cried Chester, roughly. "Something extraordinary has happened!" —

The Count jumped out of the carriage, and a moment later the two men stood together in the hall, careless of the fact that M. Polperro was staring at them with affrighted eyes.

"This letter purports to be from Sylvia Bailey," exclaimed Chester hoarsely, "but of course it is nothing of the sort! She never wrote a line of it. It's entirely unlike her handwriting — and then look at the absurd signature! What does it mean, Virieu? Can you give me any clue to what it means?"

The Comte de Virieu raised his head from over the thin sheet of notepaper, and even Chester, frightened and angry as he now was, could not help noticing how the other man's face had changed in the last few moments. From being of a usual healthy sunburn, it had turned so white as to look almost green under the bright electric light.

"Yes, I think I know what it means," said Count Paul between his teeth. "A letter like this purported to come from Madame Wolsky when she disappeared. But do not let us make a scene here. Let us go at once where I believe she is, for if what I fear is true every moment is of value."

He plucked the Englishman by the sleeve, and hurried him out into the grateful darkness.

"Get into the carriage," he said, imperiously. "I will see to everything."

Chester heard him direct the driver to the police station. "We may need two or three gendarmes," muttered Count Paul. "It's worth the three minutes delay."

The carriage drew up before a shabby little house across which was painted in large black letters the word "Gendarmerie."

The Count rushed into the guardroom, hurriedly explained his errand to the superintendent, and came out, but a moment later, with three men.

"We must make room for these good fellows somehow," he said briefly, and room was made. Chester noticed with surprise that each man was armed, not only with a stave, but with a revolver. The French police do not stand on ceremony even with potential criminals.

"And now," said the Count to the coachman, "five louis, my friend, if you can get us to the Châlet des Muguets in seven minutes —"

They began driving at a breakneck pace, the driver whipping up his horse, lashing it in a way that horrified Chester. The light little carriage rocked from side to side.

"If the man doesn't drive more carefully," cried out the Englishman, "we shall be spilt — and that won't do us any good, will it?"

The Count called out, "If there's an accident you get nothing, my friend! Drive as quickly as you like, but drive carefully."

They swept on through the town, and so along the dimly-lighted shady avenues with which even Chester had become so familiar during the last few days.

Paul de Virieu sat with clenched hands, staring in front of him. Remorse filled his soul — remorse and anguish. If Sylvia had been done to death, as he now had very little doubt Anna Wolsky had been done to death, then he would die too. What was the vice which had meant all to him for so many years compared to his love for Sylvia?

The gendarmes murmured together in quick, excited tones. They scented that something really exciting, something that would perhaps lead to promotion, was going to happen.

At last, as the carriage turned into a dark road, Count Paul suddenly began to talk, at the very top of his voice.

"Speak, Mr. Chester, speak as loud as you can! Shout! Say anything that you like! They may as well hear that we are coming —"

But Chester could not do what the other man so urgently asked him to do. Not to save his life could he have opened his mouth and shouted as the other was now doing.

"We are going to pay an evening call — what you in England call an evening call! We are going to fetch our friend — our friend, Mrs. Bailey;

she is so charming, so delightful! We are going to fetch her because she has been spending the evening with her friends, the Wachners. That old she-devil — you remember her, surely? The woman who asked you concerning your plans? It is she I fear —"

"*Je crois que c'est ici, Monsieur?*" the man turned round on his seat. "I have done it in six minutes!"

The horse was suddenly brought up short opposite the white gate. Was this where the Wachners lived? Chester stooped down. The place looked very different now from what it had looked in the daylight.

The windows of the small, low house were closely shuttered, but where the shutters met in one of the rooms glinted a straight line of light.

"We are in time. Thank God we are in time," said the Count, with a queer break in his voice. "If we were not in time, there would be no light. The house of the wicked ones would be in darkness."

And then, in French, he added, turning to the gendarmes:

"You had better all three stay in the garden, while my friend and I go up to the house. If we are gone more than five minutes, then you follow us up to the house and get in somehow!"

In varying accents were returned the composed answers, "*Oui, M'sieur.*"

There came a check, for the little gate was locked. Each man helped another over very quietly, and then the three gendarmes dispersed with swift, noiseless steps, each seeking a point of vantage commanding the house.

Chester and Paul de Virieu walked quickly up the path.

Suddenly a shaft of bright light pierced the moonlit darkness. The shutters of the dining room of the Châlet des Muguets had been unbarred, and the window was thrown wide open.

"*Qui va là?*" the old military watchword, as the Frenchman remembered with a sense of terrible irony, was flung out into the night in the harsh, determined voice of Madame Wachner.

They saw her stout figure, filling up most of the window, outlined against the lighted room. She was leaning out, peering into the garden with angry, fear-filled eyes.

Both men stopped simultaneously, but neither answered her.

"Who goes there?" she repeated; and then, "I fear, Messieurs, that you have made a mistake. You have taken this villa for someone else's house!" But there was alarm as well as anger in her voice.

"It is I, Paul de Virieu, Madame Wachner."

The Count spoke quite courteously, his agreeable voice thickened, made hoarse by the strain to which he had just subjected it.

"I have brought Mr. Chester with me, for we have come to fetch Mrs. Bailey. In Paris Mr. Chester found news making her return home to England tomorrow a matter of imperative necessity."

He waited a moment, then added, raising his voice as he spoke: "We have proof that she is spending the evening with you," and he walked on quickly to where he supposed the front door to be.

"If they deny she is there," he whispered to his companion, "we will shout for the gendarmes and break in. But I doubt if they will dare to deny she is there unless — unless —"

He had hoped to hear Sylvia's voice, but Madame Wachner had shut the window, and a deathly silence reigned in the villa.

The two men stood in front of the closed door for what seemed to them a very long time. It was exactly two minutes; and when at last the door opened, slowly, and revealed the tall, lanky figure of L'Ami Fritz, they both heard the soft, shuffling tread of the gendarmes closing in round the house.

"I pray you to come in," said Monsieur Wachner in English, and then, addressing Bill Chester,

"I am pleased to see you, sir, the more so that your friend, Mrs. Bailey, is indisposed. A moment ago, to our deep concern, she found herself quite faint — no doubt from the heat. I will conduct you, gentlemen, into the drawing room; my wife and Mrs. Bailey will join us there in a minute," and only then did he move back sufficiently to allow the two men to cross the threshold.

Paul de Virieu opened his lips — but no sound came from them. The sudden sense of relief from what had been agonized suspense gripped him by the throat.

He brushed past Wachner, and made straight for the door behind which he felt sure of finding the woman whom some instinct told him he had saved from a terrible fate. . . .

He turned the handle of the dining room door, and then stopped short, for he was amazed at the sight which met his eyes.

Sylvia was sitting at a round table; behind her was the buffet, still laden with the remains of a simple meal. Her face was hidden in her hands, and she was trembling — shaking as though she had the ague.

But what amazed Paul de Virieu was the sight of Sylvia's hostess. Madame Wachner was crawling about on her hands and knees on the floor, and she remained in the same odd position when the dining room door opened.

At last she looked up, and seeing who stood there, staring down at her, she raised herself with some difficulty, looking to the Frenchman's sharpened consciousness, like some monstrous greedy beast, suddenly baulked of its prey.

"Such a misfortune!" she exclaimed in English. "Such a very great misfortune! The necklace of our friend 'as broken, and 'er beautiful pearls are rolling all over the floor! We 'ave been trying, Fritz and myself, to pick them up for 'er. Is not that so, Sylvia? Mrs. Bailey is so distressed! It 'as made 'er feel very faint, what English people call 'queer'. But I tell 'er we shall find them all — it is only a matter of a little time. I asked 'er to take some cognac my 'usband keeps for such bad moments, but no, she would not! Is not that so, Sylvia?"

She stared down anxiously at the bowed head of her guest.

Sylvia looked up. As if hypnotized by the other woman's voice, she rose to her feet — a wan, pitiful little smile came over her white face.

"Yes," she said dully, "the string of my pearls broke. I was taken faint. I felt horribly queer — perhaps it was the heat."

Paul de Virieu took a sudden step forward into the room. He had just become aware of something which had made him also feel what English people call "queer."

That something had no business in the dining room, for it belonged to the kitchen — in fact it was a large wooden mallet of the kind used by French cooks to beat meat tender. Just now the club end of the mallet was sticking out of the drawer of the walnut-wood buffet.

The drawer had evidently been pulled out askew, and had stuck — as is the way with drawers forming part of ill-made furniture.

Chester came to the door of the dining room. M. Wachner had detained him for a moment in the hall, talking volubly, explaining how pleasant had been their little supper party till Mrs. Bailey had suddenly felt faint.

Chester looked anxiously at Sylvia. She was oddly pale, all the color drained from her face, but she seemed on quite good terms with Madame Wachner! As for that stout, good-natured looking woman, she also was unlike her placid smiling self, for her face looked red and puffy. But still she nodded pleasantly to Chester.

It seemed to the lawyer inconceivable that this commonplace couple could have seriously meant to rob their guest. But there was that letter — that strange, sinister letter which purported to be from Sylvia! Who had written that letter, and with what object in view?

Chester began to feel as if he was living through a very disagreeable, bewildering nightmare. But no scintilla of the horrible truth reached his cautious, well-balanced brain. The worst he suspected, and that only because of the inexplicable letter, was that these people meant to extract money from their guest and frighten her into leaving Lacville the same night.

"Sylvia," he said rather shortly, "I suppose we ought to be going now. We have a carriage waiting at the gate, so we shall be able to drive you back to the Villa du Lac. But, of course, we must first pick up all your pearls. That won't take long!"

But Sylvia made no answer. She did not even look round at him. She was still staring straight before her, as if she saw something, which the others could not see, written on the distempered wall.

L'Ami Fritz entered the room quietly. He looked even stranger than usual, for while in one hand he held Mrs. Bailey's pretty black tulle hat and her little bag, in the other was clutched the handle of a broom.

"I did not think you would want to go back into my wife's bedroom," he said, deprecatingly; and Mrs. Bailey, at last turning her head round, actually smiled gratefully at him.

She was reminding herself that there had been a moment when he had been willing to let her escape. Only once — only when he had grinned at her so strangely and deplored her refusal of the drugged coffee, had she felt the sick, agonizing fear of him that she had felt of Madame Wachner.

Laying the hat and bag on the table, L'Ami Fritz began sweeping the floor with long skillful movements.

"This is the best way to find the pearls," he muttered; and three of the four people present stood and looked on at what he was doing. As for the one most concerned, Sylvia had again begun to stare dully before her, as if what was going on did not interest her one whit.

At last Monsieur Wachner took a long spoon off the table; with its help he put all that he had swept up — pearls, dust, and fluff — into the little fancy bag.

"There," he said, with a sigh of relief, "I think they are all there."

But even as he spoke he knew well enough that some of the pearls — perhaps five or six — had found their way up his wife's capacious sleeve.

And then, quite suddenly, Madame Wachner uttered a hoarse exclamation of terror. One of the gendarmes had climbed up on to the windowsill, and was now half into the room. She waddled quickly across to the door, only to find another gendarme in the hall.

Sylvia's eyes glistened, and a sensation which had hitherto been quite unknown to her took possession of her, soul and body. She longed for revenge — revenge, not for herself so much as for her murdered friend. She clutched Paul by the arm. "They killed Anna Wolsky," she whispered. "She is lying buried in the wood, where they meant to put me if you had not come just — only just — in time!"

Paul de Virieu took Sylvia's hat off the dining room table, and placed it in her hand, closing her fingers over the brim. With a mechanical gesture she raised her arms and put it on her head. Then he ceremoniously offered her his arm, and led her out of the dining room into the hall.

While actually within the Châlet des Muguets Count Paul only once broke silence. That was when Madame Wachner, still talking volubly, held out her hand in farewell to the young Englishwoman.

"I forbid you to touch her!" the Count muttered between his teeth, and Sylvia, withdrawing her half-outstretched hand, meekly obeyed him.

Paul de Virieu beckoned to the oldest of the police officials present. "You will remember the disappearance from Lacville of a Polish lady? I have reason to believe these people murdered her. When once I have placed Madame Bailey under medical care, I will return here. Meanwhile you, of course, know what to do."

"But M'sieur, ought I not to detain this English lady?"

"Certainly not. I make myself responsible for her. She is in no state to bear an interrogation. Lock up these people in separate rooms. I will send you reinforcements, and tomorrow morning *dig up the little wood behind the house.*"

Behind them came the gruff and the shrill tones of L'Ami Fritz and his wife raised in indignant expostulation.

"Are you coming, Sylvia?" called out Chester impatiently.

He had gone on into the garden, unwilling to assume any responsibility as to the police. After all, there was no *evidence*, not what English law would recognize as evidence, against these people.

Out in the darkness, with the two men, one on either side of her, Sylvia walked slowly to the gate. Between them they got her over it and into the victoria.

Paul de Virieu pulled out the little back seat, but Chester, taking quick possession of it, motioned him to sit by Mrs. Bailey.

"To Paris, Hôtel du Louvre," the Count called out to the driver. "You can take as long as you like over the journey!"

Then he bent forward to Chester, "The air will do her good," he murmured.

By his side, huddled up in a corner of the carriage, Sylvia lay back inertly; but her eyes were wide open, and she was staring hungrily at the sky, at the stars. She had never thought to see the sky and the stars again.

They were now moving very slowly, almost at a foot's pace.

The driver was accustomed to people who suddenly decided to drive all the way back to Paris from Lacville after an evening's successful or, for the matter of that, unsuccessful play. He had been very much relieved to see his two gentlemen come back from the châlet and to leave the gendarmes behind. He had no wish to get mixed up in a *fracas*, no wish, that is, to have any embarrassments with the police.

They drove on and on, into the open country; through dimly-lit, leafy thoroughfares, through long stretches of market gardens, till they came on to the outskirts of the great city — and still Sylvia remained obstinately silent.

Paul de Virieu leant forward.

"Speak to her," he said in an urgent whisper. "Take her hand and try to rouse her, Mr. Chester. I feel very anxious about her condition."

Chester in the darkness felt himself flushing. With a diffident, awkward gesture he took Sylvia's hand in his — and then he uttered an exclamation of surprise and concern.

The hand he held was quite cold — cold and nerveless to the touch, as if all that constitutes life had gone out of it. "My dear girl!" he exclaimed. "I'm afraid those people frightened you badly? I suppose you began to suspect they meant to steal your pearls?"

But Sylvia still remained obstinately silent. She did not want to speak, she only wanted to live.

It was so strange to feel oneself alive — alive and whole at a time when one had thought to be dead, having been done to death after an awful, disfiguring struggle — for Sylvia had determined to struggle to the end with her murderers.

"My God!" muttered Paul de Virieu. "Do you not understand, Chester, what happened tonight? They meant to kill her!"

"To kill her?" repeated Chester incredulously.

Then there came over him a rush and glow of angry excitement. Good God! If that was the case they ought to have driven back at once to the Lacville police station!

"Sylvia!" he exclaimed. "Rouse yourself, and tell us what took place! If what the Count says is true, something must be done, and at once!"

He turned to Paul de Virieu: "The police ought to take Mrs. Bailey's full statement of all that occurred without any loss of time!" All the lawyer in him spoke angrily, agitatedly.

Sylvia moved slightly. Paul de Virieu could feel her shuddering by his side.

"Oh, Bill, let me try to forget!" she moaned. And then, lifting up her voice, she wailed, "They killed Anna Wolsky —"

Her voice broke, and she began to sob convulsively. "I would not think of her — I forced myself not to think of her — but now I shall never, never think of anyone else anymore!"

Paul de Virieu turned in the kindly darkness, and putting his arm round Sylvia's slender shoulders, he tenderly drew her to him.

A passion of pity, of protective tenderness, filled his heart, and suddenly lifted him to a higher region than that in which he had hitherto been content to dwell.

"You must not say that, *ma chérie*," he whispered, laying his cheek to hers as tenderly as he would have caressed a child, "it would be too cruel to the living, to those who love you — who adore you."

Then he raised his head, and, in a very different tone, he exclaimed,

"Do not be afraid, Mr. Chester, those infamous people shall not be allowed to escape! Poor Madame Wolsky shall surely be avenged. But Mrs. Bailey will not be asked to make any statement, except in writing — in what you in England call an affidavit. You do not realize, although you doubtless know, what our legal procedure is like. Not even in order to secure the guillotine for Madame Wachner and her Fritz would I expose Mrs. Bailey to the ordeal of our French witness-box."

"And how will it be possible to avoid it?" asked Chester, in a low voice.

Paul de Virieu hesitated, then, leaning forward and holding Sylvia still more closely and protectively to him, he said very deliberately the fateful words he had never thought to say,

"I have an announcement to make to you, Mr. Chester. It is one which I trust will bring me your true congratulations. Mrs. Bailey is about to do me the honor of becoming my wife."

He waited a moment, then added very gravely, "I am giving her an undertaking, a solemn promise by all I hold most sacred, to abandon play —"

Chester felt a shock of amazement. How utterly mistaken, how blind he had been! He had felt positively certain that Sylvia had refused Paul de Virieu; and he had been angered by the suspicion, nay, by what he had thought the sure knowledge, that the wise refusal had cost her pain.

But women are extraordinary creatures, and so, for the matter of that, are Frenchmen —

Still, his feelings to the man sitting opposite to him had undergone a complete change. He now liked — nay, he now respected — Paul de Virieu. But for the Count, whom he had thought to be nothing more than an effeminate dandy, a hopeless gambler, where would Sylvia be now? The unspoken answer to this question gave Chester a horrible inward tremor.

He leant forward, and grasped Paul de Virieu's left hand.

"I do congratulate you," he said, simply and heartily; "you deserve your great good fortune." Then, to Sylvia, he added quietly, "My dear, it is to him you owe your life."

Printed in the United States
111062LV00004B/73/P